THE GARDEN CLUB MURDER

A Selection of Titles by Amy Patricia Meade

A Marjorie McClelland Mystery

MILLION DOLLAR BABY
GHOST OF A CHANCE
SHADOW WALTZ
BLACK MOONLIGHT

The Tish Tarragon Series

COOKIN' THE BOOKS *
THE GARDEN CLUB MURDER *

The Vermont Mystery Series

WELL-OFFED IN VERMONT
SHORT-CIRCUITED IN CHARLOTTE

* *available from Severn House*

THE GARDEN CLUB MURDER

Amy Patricia Meade

This first world edition published 2019
in Great Britain and the USA by
SEVERN HOUSE PUBLISHERS LTD of
Eardley House, 4 Uxbridge Street, London W8 7SY.
Trade paperback edition first published
in Great Britain and the USA 2020 by
SEVERN HOUSE PUBLISHERS LTD.

British Library Cataloguing in Publication Data
A CIP catalogue record for this title is available from the British Library.

ISBN-13: 978-0-7278-8944-7 (cased)
ISBN-13: 978-1-78029-612-8 (trade paper)
ISBN-13: 978-1-4483-0229-1 (e-book)

All Severn House titles are printed on acid-free paper.

Severn House Publishers support the Forest Stewardship Council™ [FSC™],
the leading international forest certification organisation.
All our titles that are printed on FSC certified paper carry the FSC logo.

Typeset by Palimpsest Book Production Ltd.,
Falkirk, Stirlingshire, Scotland.
Printed and bound in Great Britain by
TJ International, Padstow, Cornwall.

ONE

'Good Lord!' Julian Jefferson Davis exclaimed as he drew a manicured hand to his impeccably clean-shaven and bronzed face. 'It's like *The Stepford Wives* meets *Cocoon*.'

Letitia 'Tish' Tarragon, owner of Cookin' the Books Café and Catering, steered her fire-engine-red 2015 Toyota Matrix past row upon row of tidy cookie-cutter homes and their impossibly – especially after a long, hot Virginia summer – verdant and well-groomed lawns. 'It's an adult community, Jules. Not a nursing home.'

'Does it matter? There's not a soul out there who doesn't have gray hair.' He gave a reluctant wave out the passenger window as the residents of Coleton Creek Sixty-Plus Community bade Tish and Julian a friendly welcome. 'And look at their clothes. It's like we've driven into my nana's old Montgomery Ward catalogs.'

'Montgomery Ward? Don't know about that one. We only saw Blair and Sears catalogs back up in New York.' Tish ran a hand through her wavy blond bob and adjusted her sunglasses to shield her blue eyes against the brilliant late-morning sunshine.

'And why are they all smiling and waving?' Jules continued. 'It's creepy. Like they're going to drain our blood and drink it to make themselves young again.'

'Young?' Tish challenged. 'Who are you calling young? We're only one generation behind them. Why, just yesterday Amazon Now delivered your nose- and ear-hair trimmer to my café because you didn't want anyone at the station to see it.'

'I'm a television celebrity,' Jules explained, alluding to his job as Channel Ten weatherman and, in recent weeks, occasional desk anchor. 'I have an image to uphold.' He punctuated the sentence by adjusting the collar of his perfectly pressed beige linen shirt.

Jules had risen to prominence at the news station due to a viral video of him being wiped out by a snowplow outside the Edgar Allen Poe Museum while covering Richmond's biggest snowstorm of the year. Thankfully, Jules's reputation as a serious journalist had begun to improve after a tough interview with Hobson Glen's former mayor, Jarrod Whitley, made top story on the eleven o'clock nightly news.

'Well, I certainly appreciate you leaving fame and fortune behind to tend bar this weekend,' Tish acknowledged.

'Honey, I wouldn't miss it for the world. Unless I'm called in to the newsroom, like last weekend.'

'Oh, how I missed you last weekend, Jules. Not only was the event far less fun without you, but the bartender the temp agency sent looked like she'd gone for a Botox injection that afternoon. The drinks she mixed were fine, but it's off-putting to request a simple Cosmopolitan or Vodka Collins and be met with a wide-eyed, startled stare.'

'Have no fear. Jules is back in gear,' he announced ceremoniously.

'I can't tell you how relieved I am. Again, thank you.'

'No worries. Not only do I love helping out a bestie, but I'm looking forward to working this luncheon. I've never served tea in china cups before. It's so posh.'

'Posh?' Tish repeated. In the twenty years since she, Jules, and their other 'bestie,' Mary Jo Okensholt, met at University of Virginia, she had never heard him utter that word, unless it was in reference to one of the Spice Girls.

'Sorry, I've been searching BBC Online and watching tons of British cooking shows in order to perfect my orange squash and "Gin and It" drink recipes. I guess I just picked up the lingo.' Jules gave another wave out the passenger window. 'Look! That little gray poodle has the same hairstyle as the woman walking him.'

Tish laughed as she turned off the main street, aptly named Coleton Creek Way, and into the lifestyle-center parking lot. With its colonnaded façade, ornamental cupola, and lush landscaping, the lifestyle center more closely resembled the entrance to a luxury resort hotel than the centerpiece of everyday life for a senior community in Virginia.

'Swank,' Jules remarked as Tish pulled the Matrix into the visitor's parking area. 'Ooh, is that a pool I see?'

'One of two. There's an indoor pool next to the fitness room,' Tish explained as she shut off the car engine and tossed the keys into an oversized scarlet handbag. 'And a Jacuzzi too.'

'A hot tub?' Jules remarked as he climbed out of the passenger door and followed Tish across the parking lot.

'Don't get too excited,' she warned as she tugged at the hem of her red floral-print sheath dress. 'We're setting up in the patio garden at the back of the lifestyle center. There's no direct access to the hot tub or pools unless you walk through the building.'

Jules frowned.

'What difference does it make? You can't relax in a hot tub while serving drinks. Then again, knowing you . . .'

'Don't be silly. Not only am I a professional, but I have the perfect outfit already picked out for the luncheon and it's not waterproof. I just thought that after work it might have been nice to take a dip or relax poolside in a chaise lounge with a Gin and It.'

'Forget it. In addition to being on the other side of the building, the pool and other facilities are for residents only,' she stated before swinging open the glass door of the lifestyle center and stepping inside. A disappointed Jules trailed closely behind her.

The entrance hall of the lifestyle center was just as lavish as the exterior. Boasting marble tile, a giant crystal chandelier, more columns, oversized artificial floral arrangements, and scads of gold accents, the area looked as if it had been modeled on a trendy, overpriced wedding venue.

'Ms Tarragon,' greeted an auburn-haired woman from behind the reception desk.

'Ms Hilton,' Tish replied.

'Oh, please call me Susannah.'

'Only if you call me Tish. And this is our bartender, Julian Davis. How are things today?'

'After a bumpy start, surprisingly good,' Susannah stated with a sigh, her deep-set brown eyes belying her positive attitude.

'I hope my food delivery didn't cause you any trouble.'

'Not at all,' the forty-something woman assured Tish. 'I had an issue with a problematic resident this morning, but it's all over now. As for the event, I'm happy to report that everything is on track. The landscaping crew tidied the patio area, and the supplies you ordered arrived on schedule. Everything is stacked on the kitchen counter. Perishable items are, of course, in the refrigerator.' She stepped out from behind the desk, revealing a lithe figure swathed in a beautiful soft-brown peasant dress. 'Here's the receipt and bill of lading so you can double-check you have everything you need.'

'Terrific.' Tish took two stapled sheets of printer paper from Susannah's hand. 'Thanks for receiving the delivery. It saved me from having to cart everything here myself.'

'No problem, and it's I who thank you. I'm so glad you're catering our garden awards luncheon. Everyone is super excited to see how you carry out *The Secret Garden* theme in the food and the décor.'

'Well, you shouldn't have to wait too long for either. Jules and I are going to work on the staging and decorations today. Tomorrow, my assistant cook, Celestine, and I will focus on the food. And Sunday afternoon is the event.'

'Hard to believe it's already here,' Susannah noted. 'I'll take you out to the patio to show you the work the gardeners did. Is there anything I can help carry?'

'I have some boxes in the trunk of my car,' Tish indicated. 'But nothing we can't handle on our own. We'll just make a few trips.'

'Nonsense,' Susannah, the soul of professionalism, dismissed. 'Let's get everything in and then I'll introduce you to Mr Ainsley. He's dying to meet you.'

'Mr Ainsley?' Tish's face was a question.

'Jim Ainsley. The president of the garden club. He's the one you'll be working for this weekend.'

'Oh, I thought you were the organizer.'

'Organizer, yes, but it's the garden club that funds the annual award luncheon and the prize trophy. Their garden competition has grown into a major event at Coleton Creek these past ten years. It started off as a friendly rivalry between neighbors, but as the number of homes in the development grew, so did the competition. Now there are so many entrants each year that the members are usually too busy with the judging and garden preparations to plan the luncheon. That's why I, as the activities director and resident liaison, stepped in to facilitate.'

'That's kind of you,' Jules praised.

Susannah shrugged off the compliment. 'It's my job to make sure the residents are happy.'

'I always thought garden competitions were held in the spring and summer,' Tish questioned.

'I thought that too, and perhaps most are, but this competition compares the residents' gardens and lawns at different intervals between spring and early fall to find the property that looks best in all seasons. Mr Ainsley will be able to tell you more. He's the master gardener around here. He's also very excited to have you on board as caterer. When he saw your photo in the papers a few weeks back, he said, "Susannah, I want Ms Tarragon for our event."'

'Seems you're a celebrity, Tish,' Jules observed with glee. 'Don't worry, I'll let you borrow my trimmer.'

Tish wrinkled her nose at her friend before addressing Susannah. 'I'm glad Mr Ainsley thought enough to hire me, but I wish it was for my food.'

'Mr Ainsley isn't much of a foodie; that's why I did the tasting. He's a sweet man, though. He told me he wanted to hire you because you had "gumption" for solving that murder case the way you did,' Susannah smiled. 'I admit, I'm more than a little impressed myself. With your cooking *and* your detective skills.'

'Thanks. Not to disappoint, but I plan on demonstrating only one of those skills this weekend,' Tish teased before the trio walked out to the Matrix to retrieve the decorations for Sunday's luncheon.

TWO

'Ms Tarragon, so good to have you here at Coleton Creek.' Jim Ainsley, six feet tall, slim, with close-cropped light-brown hair that was graying at the temples, and a military bearing, extended a hand to Tish. 'Everyone in the garden club is thrilled with your idea for our luncheon.'

'I'm glad to hear it.' Tish took Mr Ainsley's hand in hers and gave it a sturdy shake. 'I only hope my menu lives up to expectations.'

'I'm sure it will. I'm not an adventurous eater, but the concept of sausage rolls intrigues me. Meat. Pastry. How can you go wrong?'

'It's traditional English picnic and celebratory fare.'

'Consider this country boy sold. I'm also very much sold on the Victoria sponge cake Ms Hilton told me about.' Ainsley went on to shake Jules's hand. 'I admit I had to look up *The Secret Garden* on the internet, but once I did, I thought it was a brilliant choice. You're truly an expert in your field.'

'Thank you.' Tish was gracious. 'However, I'd appreciate it if you reserved the title of expert until you taste the food on Sunday. Besides, I'm sure your knowledge of gardens and plant varieties runs rings around my knowledge of books and cooking, so I think we're even.'

'Ah, yes, the gardens,' Ainsley grinned. 'May I give you both a tour?'

As Susannah excused herself and returned to the lifestyle center, Ainsley led Tish and Jules down the central hallway of his two-story duplex townhouse, into the kitchen, and out a set of sliding glass doors.

Stepping on to a small red-brick patio, Tish and Jules were treated to the view of a lush carpet-like lawn bordered on three sides by an irregularly shaped mature evergreen garden. There were no roses or trellises or tendrils of ivy, no delicate pink or ivory blooms, only shrubs of varying texture, height, and hue. Feathery blue point junipers mingled with compact, richly toned boxwood, yellowish, leafy Gold Mound spirea, and spiky, emerald-green arborvitae to create an invitingly luxuriant canvas against which well-placed Japanese maples, scarlet-and-purple-berried viburnum, and Rieger begonias in yellow, red, and orange provided warm pops of color that echoed those of the coming autumn season.

'Wow,' Jules exclaimed.

'It's like a painting,' Tish declared. 'What with all the layers and textures.'

'Thank you. I switch out the winter begonias for more seasonal plants in the spring and summer, but I like the depth I've created. Makes my sixty-by-eighty-foot plot feel bigger. It also helps block the unsightly stockade fence that came with the house.'

Jules's jaw dropped open in surprise. 'I didn't even notice there was a fence.'

'See what I mean?' Ainsley challenged with a satisfied grin.

'We've yet to see the other contestants' gardens, but I'd say you're a sure bet for an award this Sunday,' Tish opined.

'That's most kind of you, Ms Tarragon, but as president of the garden club and a judge for the event, I'm not allowed to compete.'

'What a shame,' Jules lamented.

'Not really,' Ainsley shrugged. 'This garden suits me perfectly. If I were to open it up to the scrutiny of a panel of judges, I might feel compelled to alter it somehow. No, I'd much rather enjoy it the way it is and let the opinions of others be damned.'

'Meanwhile, you're willing to share *your* opinions with anyone willing to listen,' came a jocular man's voice from the other side of the fence.

Ainsley sounded a mighty guffaw. 'My friends, the Abercrombies,' he explained to his guests. 'They live in the connecting townhouse. They're also competing in this year's event. Come on, I'll introduce you and let you see their garden.'

Rolling up the sleeves of his pinstriped button-down Oxford shirt, Ainsley led Tish and Jules back into the house, out the front door, and, cutting across the shared duplex lawn, to the Abercrombie's white picket garden gate which was framed by an arbor festooned with late-blooming yellow and orange roses. 'Tucker? Violet? It's Ainsley.'

A petite, fine-boned, delicate-looking woman dressed in a fine-gauge turquoise sweater, white Bermuda shorts, orange garden clogs, and a giant sun hat appeared at the gate. Her yellowish gray hair was pinned into an elegant bun at the nape of her neck and her hazel eyes sparkled with the joy that comes from a well-spent life. 'Hello, Jim. Don't be listening to that husband of mine. He's just sore because I've had him in the garden since breakfast.'

'Needs must. Competition's tight,' Ainsley replied before introducing his guests.

After an exchange of greetings, Violet Abercrombie swung open the gate and guided the group into a quintessential cottage garden. Native asters in an array of purple hues, plump zinnias in white, red, pink, and orange, pink turtleheads, sunny black-eyed Susans, and local coneflower grew in tidy rows along a gravel-lined path that led to a center birdbath and, a few feet beyond it, a white gazebo outfitted with a wrought-iron bistro set.

'Oh, my!' Tish exclaimed. 'And here I thought the patio at the lifestyle center was the perfect setting for *The Secret Garden* luncheon.'

'There will be no luncheon's hosted in this garden. Not after all the work we've done,' a familiar voice joked. From his weeding spot behind a tall patch of Japanese anemone, a salt-and-pepper-haired man dressed in a blue polo shirt and khaki pants tucked into a pair of work boots rose to his feet. He was somewhere in his mid-seventies, of athletic build, and his eyes were covered by a pair of wrap-around sunglasses of the kind that ophthalmologists provide. 'Tucker Abercrombie.' He extended a muddied glove to his guests.

Tish extended a hand and then quickly withdrew.

'Sorry.' Tucker, realizing his error, removed the glove and then offered his hand again. This time Tish accepted. 'I've been in this garden since the crack of dawn. Starts to play with a man's mind.'

'Crack of dawn?' Violet scoffed. 'You came out here at nine. You only rolled out of bed at eight thirty.'

'For me, eight thirty is the crack of dawn. I worked fifty years for the right to sleep late. Now that I finally retired last month, I plan to exercise that right on a regular basis.'

'And once the garden competition is over, I won't stand in the way of you doing so. But, as the woman who made your coffee and fixed you breakfast for forty-five of those fifty years, I'd like a trophy.' Violet folded her arms across her chest and gave a defiant wag of her chin.

'For making coffee and breakfast?' Tucker was deliberately obtuse. 'I admit both have always been very tasty, but a trophy?'

'For best garden.' Violet gave her husband a playful slap on the arm.

'Oh, that.' He broke into laughter. 'Well, I'm here to do my best to help make that happen. No one deserves the award more than you, my dear.' Tucker turned to his guests. 'My Violet has planned, plotted, dug, planted, and nursed this garden into the vision you see before you. It's been a true labor of love.'

'It's incredible,' Tish admired.

'Like something you'd see in a Jane Austen miniseries,' Jules added.

'You watch Jane Austen miniseries?'

'A few of them may have come on after the cooking shows.' Jules shrugged as he polished his sunglasses on a shirtsleeve. 'I only watched for a few minutes. For the scenery.'

'Tucker gives me all the credit, but I couldn't have done it without his support,' Violet went on. 'When I was uncertain of my designs, he gave me encouragement and input, and when I was unable to dig a section myself, he rolled up his sleeves and pitched in. Sometimes even after he'd been at work all day.'

'It was certainly worth all that hard work. The garden looks better than ever. It's really come into its own, Vi,' Jim Ainsley noted.

'I'm thrilled with the progress it's made. I just hope it's enough to win the trophy,' Violet wished aloud. 'Although part of me wonders if the prize shouldn't go to Wren Harper. Her garden won many times in the past and she's had a difficult spring, what with her husband passing away and now their son, Benjamin.'

'Honey, if you don't win, I don't care who does, just as long as it isn't Sloane Shackleford,' Tucker inserted. 'Man's won the past five years despite having pro gardeners and the moral fortitude of an alley cat.'

'Now, Tuck, you know I can't disqualify Shackleford.' Jim was quick to defend the garden club judges' past decisions. 'He designed and planted the garden himself and now he oversees the general upkeep. The only thing those "pro gardeners" you mentioned do is mow and weed, and that's because Shackleford's heart condition precludes him from doing it himself.'

'Heart condition, my eye. The way that fellow hops from woman to woman, the only physical ailment Sloane Shackleford could possibly suffer from is a social disease.'

'Tucker,' his wife chastised.

'Sorry, Vi, but I have absolutely no use for the man.'

'Nor do I, as you are more than fully aware. However, we have company, so mind your tongue.'

Tucker responded like a scolded child. 'Sorry.'

Violet rolled her eyes at her husband and pasted on a beatific smile. 'I suppose y'all are going to take a gander at some of the other gardens?' she inquired of Jim Ainsley.

'Yes, we're off to Wren's first and then on to Orson Baggett's and then, finally, Shackleford's. Thought it would be nice for Ms Tarragon and Mr Davis to see the top contenders before they get to work on the luncheon.'

'A lovely idea,' Violet proclaimed. 'I'm sure you'll be too busy to get away from the kitchen while the gardens are open for public viewing tomorrow.'

'Most likely,' Tish conceded.

'Just watch yourself at Shackleford's,' Tucker leaned in and advised Tish, sotto voce.

'Thanks. I will.' She resisted telling the older man that she could handle herself.

Tucker replied with a wink and a nod as his wife, once again, rolled her eyes.

After an exchange of goodbyes, the trio departed the Abercrombies' garden and proceeded down the road and around the corner. The houses in this area of Coleton Creek were not duplex townhouses, but expansive single-household structures. Featuring front porches and detached garages, the homes were also situated on larger plots of land.

'As you can see, this is the higher-rent district,' Ainsley joked as he led them to the garden gate of the fifth house on the left-hand side of the street. 'Funny thing is, folks here have to pass by our meager dwellings in order to get out of Coleton Creek. Well, unless they take the long way around. Still, it's a good thing the garden club doesn't judge by the size of the garden. Just the design and content.'

Ainsley gave a call over the garden gate. 'Hello? Wren? It's Jim.'

There was no reply.

'Hello? Wren, are you at home?' Again there was no answer.

'Let's try the front door. She might be inside having lunch.' Ainsley led them to the screen door of Wren Harper's enclosed porch and rang the bell.

Several seconds elapsed before a light-skinned black woman emerged from the main interior door of the home. She was approximately five feet nine inches tall and, despite the deceptively loose fit of her gingham-print camp shirt and navy-blue cargo pants, of average build. Her eyes were red and her face pinched from crying, but even with the puffiness, it was clear she was barely over Coleton Creek's mandatory minimum age of sixty years. 'Oh, hi, Jim. Sorry, I was taking a break from the garden. These darned allergies . . .'

'That's OK, Wren. I just stopped by to show these folks your garden. They're the caterers for our luncheon.'

'Oh.' Wren wiped her eyes, smiled, and opened the screen door of the porch to extend a hand. 'I'm sorry. It's so nice to meet you.'

Ainsley proceeded with the proper introductions. 'I know you're busy, Wren, but if you don't mind, maybe I could give these folks a quick glance at your garden. Your plants look fantastic this year.'

'Sure,' Wren answered meekly. 'I'll take you.'

'That's not necessary,' Ainsley continued. 'You stay here and tend to your allergies.'

'Yes, you should rest,' Tish chimed in. 'And, really, Mr Ainsley, we have lots of work to do at the lifestyle center. We can come back at another time.'

Jules agreed. 'Absolutely.'

'No,' Wren insisted, this time her voice more ardent. 'No, I'll take you out back. I enjoy showing off my garden.'

Wren's words sounded more like a pep talk for herself than a statement of fact. Still, she swung open the porch door and led her guests through the gate of the rustic, weather-beaten split-rail fence and into a sea of wildflowers. Blue bachelor buttons and lobelia, purple asters, rosy slender gerardia and common pinks, golden sneezeweed and crownbeard, and brilliant white snakeroot and boneset swayed in the breeze as they played host to a bevy of birds, butterflies, and bees. From the gravel walkway, a mowed grassy path stretched to the back of the yard and an apple-tree-flanked pond awash with water lilies. The scene instantly transported the visitor from a backyard in a suburban adult community to a quiet country meadow.

'Astounding job,' Ainsley praised.

'It's amazing,' Jules gushed. 'I can imagine Mr Darcy wading out of that pond, his white shirt clinging to his broad torso.'

'So you only watched for a few minutes, huh?' Tish arched an eyebrow in her friend's direction.

Jules folded his arms across his chest and stared off into the distance.

Tish smirked. She knew Jules couldn't stay silent for long.

'What's even more amazing,' Ainsley replied to Jules, 'is that this is the property just before a twist in the road, but you still get a sense of expansiveness.'

Tish surveyed the garden, amazed that she hadn't noticed the area overlooked three other yards: a thriving traditional colonial-style garden to the right, a lush modern garden of tall grasses and styled hedges to the left, and a standard yard featuring a patio, lawn, and potted plants to the rear.

'The house back there' – Ainsley pointed to the comparatively 'naked' lawn and patio to the rear of the wildflower garden – 'was recently purchased by Ms Zadie Morris, former cosmetics queen. Zadie isn't much into gardening, but given her artistic eye, I've asked her to be on the judging committee next year. Have you spoken to her much, Wren?'

'No, we've only waved to each other over the fence,' Wren replied.

'Too bad. You should go over and say "hello" once the competition is over. Zadie's a single woman, too. She's also sharp as a tack and has a terrific sense of humor. You'd hit it off well, I think.'

Wren nodded her head to indicate that she would follow Ainsley's advice, but her mind was elsewhere.

'That's Orson Baggett's garden to the right,' Ainsley continued as he gestured toward the traditional garden. 'We'll go visit him next. And the property to the left with the tall grass is Sloane Shackleford's.'

'Ah, yes, Mr Shackleford,' Tish noted.

'You know Sloane Shackleford?' Wren questioned, a note of alarm in her voice.

'Only that he's won the competition the past few years.' Tish thought it best not to repeat Tucker Abercrombie's aspersions.

'Yes, he has,' Wren frowned.

'From what I see here, your garden is the loveliest it's ever been,' Ainsley encouraged. 'I wouldn't be surprised if there was a comeback in your future.'

Wren Harper's eyes filled with tears. 'If y'all will excuse me, I need to lie down.'

'Of course,' Tish answered. 'May we help you at all?'

'Yes, how about we walk you back?' Jules suggested.

'No, I'll be fine. I just need to go inside. It was nice meeting you both.' She hastened back along the gravel path and through the garden gate.

Upon hearing the slam of the front porch door, Jim Ainsley leaned in close. 'Wren's husband passed away last year during open heart surgery, and several weeks ago, she got word that their only child, Benjamin, died while on maneuvers in Afghanistan. Ben leaves behind a wife and two young children.'

'Poor thing,' Jules lamented.

Ainsley gave a knowing nod. 'This wildflower garden has been the only thing keeping her going. She told me it's her haven where she can escape from life.'

Tish glanced around at the place of beauty Wren had created. 'Do you think she'll be OK? Should someone come by and check on her?'

'I'll call Violet after our tour. Vi will know what to do. She always does.'

Ainsley's faith in Mrs Abercrombie's capabilities hinted at a relationship more intimate than that of mere neighbors. 'Yes, Wren could probably use the company.'

'Indeed, she could. In the meantime, let's get over to Orson's. I told him we'd stop by sometime after twelve. Knowing him, he's probably been waiting for us since eleven.'

THREE

As predicted, Orson Baggett was waiting at his garden gate alongside a house identical to Wren Harper's: screened-in front porch, upstairs dormer window, and detached garage. Orson's appearance, however, was anything but cookie cutter. Tall, with silver hair, dark eyebrows, piercing blue eyes, and a hawk-like nose, he was finely turned out in a beige ensemble of pleated pants, button-down short-sleeve shirt with winged collars, and a wide, blue-and-burgundy printed tie the likes of which Bing Crosby might have worn in the *Road to* movies.

As they approached, Baggett received them with a scowl. 'About time you showed.'

'Good afternoon to you too, Orson,' Ainsley greeted.

'Afternoon,' Baggett tipped the brim of his straw panama hat in Tish and Jules's direction before continuing on his tirade. 'You might have called to say you'd be late.'

'We're not late. I told you we'd stop by around noon.' Ainsley checked his wristwatch. 'It's just gone quarter past.'

'Maybe so,' Orson allowed, 'but knowing I'd be waiting on you, you might have stopped here before visiting Ms Harper.'

'What kind of self-respecting Southerner are you? Of course we visited Ms Harper first. She's a lady. Where are your manners?'

A self-conscious Orson Baggett removed his hat and pressed it against his chest. 'Sorry, Jim.'

'That's all right, Orson. Now pull up your britches and show these folks your garden. They have a luncheon to put together, man.'

Baggett swung open the gate of the whitewashed French gothic picket fence and led the group into a classic, geometric four-square garden: four raised vegetable and flower beds crisscrossed by a brick pathway, at the center of which grew a circular patch of herbs, punctuated at the heart by an antique bronze sundial.

'That's rosemary, sage, thyme, lavender, calendula, hyssop, and winter savory in the center herb garden,' Baggett explained. 'The raised beds are all edged with china pinks, dianthus chinesis, and Sweet William. The second round of peas and lettuces are just finishing up and the tomatoes, summer squashes, and beans will soon be gone. That's when I'll swap 'em out for turnips, winter radishes, collards, kale, and cabbage. They'll join the carrots, parsnips, and salsify I planted earlier in the season.'

Tish eyed the raised beds with more than a touch of envy. They were a cook's dream. But just as impressive as the robust produce was the incredible attention to detail. Everything, from the choice of paving bricks to the woven willow branch trellis supporting the trails of pea plants, harkened back to colonial times. 'This is incredible. Those vegetables are picture-perfect.'

Orson puffed out his chest. 'Heirloom varieties. I looked specifically for seeds our forebears might have planted. Would you like to use some of my vegetables for the awards luncheon?'

'Oh, well, I received a delivery of vegetables and other supplies just this morning.'

Baggett's grin diminished.

'But I could use some of those things at my café,' Tish reconsidered. 'And that lettuce would be fantastic in my prawn cocktail with Marie Rose sauce. That is, if you have no use for it.'

Baggett's face immediately brightened. 'Oh, no, Miss Tarragon. Please take whatever you like. There's far too much here for me to eat on my own.'

'Rumor has it you haven't been on your own for months,' Ainsley muttered in a clear attempt to get a rise out of Baggett.

'You know better than to listen to rumors,' Baggett retaliated.

'It appears I'm not the only one who might have forgotten what it means to be a Southern gentleman.'

'Sorry, Orson. I should have known better than to ask you to kiss and tell.'

Ainsley's tone was apologetic, but his words – primarily the phrase 'kiss and tell' – had been carefully selected to incite the other man into disclosing more information. Baggett failed to take the bait. Pulling an army knife from his front trouser pocket and stepping over a row of china pinks, he set a boot down in a raised bed containing three luscious-looking heads of lettuce. 'Miss Tarragon, if you just wait there, I'll harvest up that lettuce for you to take back to the kitchen.'

'You needn't do that right now, Mr Baggett. Judging is tomorrow and your garden would look better with those vegetables still in it, wouldn't it?' Tish interjected.

'They would, but I want you to have them in time for Sunday lunch. My garden has never taken top prize, but having my produce served to the trophy winner would be quite the feather in my cap.'

'I understand, but you needn't rush. I don't assemble the prawn cocktails until Sunday morning, so there's plenty of time for you to show your garden *and* contribute your vegetables. Also, if I'm not mistaken, we still have another garden to tour.'

'Yes, Sloane Shackleford's garden,' Ainsley confirmed. 'Then there's the walk back to the lifestyle center. No sense in Ms Tarragon hauling armfuls of lettuce and a sack of tomatoes through the neighborhood.'

'Sloane Shackleford? Why are you bothering with that old scoundrel? His garden looks like something you'd see on those *Housewives* shows on the reality TV,' Baggett complained, placing the accent on the 'T' instead of the 'V,' 'and he lets that mongrel of his destroy other people's property.'

'First of all, Biscuit is a dog, not a mongrel. Second, I've already discussed Biscuit's behavior with Shackleford. He's promised to keep the dog on a leash whenever he's outdoors.'

'So you spoke with him, did ya?'

'Yes. Two weeks ago, after the Abercrombies caught Biscuit sniffing around their prized gardenia.'

'Two weeks ago, huh? Fat lot of good that did. Just last week I caught the mangy cur wandering through my heirloom pachysandra.' Baggett pointed to the plush carpet of green that grew along the base of the picket fence. 'I chased him away, but just a few days ago a yellow patch developed. I spent a good chunk of yesterday pulling out the dead pachysandra and filling in with plugs I made by thinning the healthier plants.'

'I'm sorry you had to go to all that trouble, Orson.'

'No reason for you to be sorry. It's Shackleford's fault. Why, I think he instructs that dog to piddle in our gardens as a way of ensuring he wins the competition.'

'Don't be ridiculous,' Ainsley urged. 'The man just needs to get his dog under better control, that's all.'

Tish watched silently as Orson gripped the army knife until his knuckles went white.

'When you see Shackleford, you tell him he'd best do that. Otherwise, the next time I see that poor excuse for a canine near my property, I'm going to shoot him,'

'Orson. He's only a little dog. It's not as if he knows any better.'

At this, Orson fell silent and it appeared that Ainsley's calm reasoning was successful. Appearances were deceiving, for seconds later Orson threw his knife, blade first, into the ground. 'You know what, Ainsley? You're right. You tell Shackleford that if he doesn't lock up that dog of his, then his head's apt to meet the blunt end of my hammer.'

'I must apologize for Orson Baggett's behavior,' Ainsley expressed. 'He's always been on the ornery side, but never more so than when he feels his garden is under fire, be it from garden club judges, locusts, or wayward pets.'

'That's understandable,' Tish allowed. 'He nurtures those plants from seed, waters them every day, pulls weeds, prunes them when necessary. That's a tremendous investment of time, energy, and cash. It would be like me cooking for a three-hundred-person event, only to have something go hideously wrong.'

'Oh, don't even joke about that, Tish,' Jules exclaimed. 'Could you imagine?'

A slack-jawed Tish stared in utter bewilderment at her clueless friend. 'Yes, actually, I could.'

Jules's mouth formed into a tiny 'o.' 'The Binnie Broderick fundraiser. That was an engagement for three hundred, wasn't it?'

'It most certainly was.'

'Ah, well, compared with that, this should be easy-peasy,' Jules giggled awkwardly.

'Mmm,' Tish sounded in agreement.

'Thank you for being so understanding, Ms Tarragon.' Ainsley led Tish and Jules away from Wren Harper's house. 'Orson Baggett has always been something of the town grump, but he's liked well enough. Indeed, everyone here at Coleton Creek gets along quite fine. Quite fine. There are neighborhood potlucks, community picnics, and dozens of group activities. The only thorn in people's side seems to be Sloane Shackleford. I hate to say it, but I truly believe the man derives pleasure from winding people up.'

'Any idea why?' Tish asked.

'If I had that answer, I'd be more successful in keeping his dog away from our contestants' gardens.'

Similar in scale and design to other adjacent homes, Sloane Shackleford's residence found uniqueness in the form of two bay windows on either side of the main entrance and an open, rather than enclosed, front porch.

Ainsley led his guests along the asymmetrical concrete walk, lined on either side with lollipop-shaped ligustrum privet topiaries, and on to the sleekly furnished and carpeted front porch, where he proceeded to ring the doorbell.

'One of those wireless door ringers,' Ainsley noted as a jazzy saxophone riff emanated from inside the house. 'Plays tracks from your phone or whatnot. As you can see, Mr Shackleford's tastes are rather contemporary.'

When there was no answer, Ainsley again pressed the bell, this time with a look of disgust. 'Saxophone in lieu of a doorbell . . . sounds like a singles' lounge.'

'And a sleazy one, too,' Jules offered.

Tish pulled a face at Jules, but Ainsley found the comment amusing. 'Yes, well . . . apparently, Mr Shackleford's not home.'

'That's fine,' Tish pardoned as they retraced their steps back down the walkway. 'We'd better get on with decorating, anyway.'

'Wait.' Ainsley pointed toward an opening in the horizontal wood-slat fence at the top of the driveway. 'Looks like the gate is open. Shackleford must be back there, preparing for the contest. Let's go.'

Tish and Jules exchanged wary glances. Although they had thoroughly enjoyed their garden tour, it was going on a quarter to one and there was still staging, decorating, and initial food prep to perform. Likewise, given his neighbors' descriptions of him, a meeting with Sloane Shackleford didn't promise to be the most enjoyable encounter.

As he had done at Wren Harper's, Ainsley leaned through the garden gate and made his presence known. 'Hello? You back there, Shackleford?'

Tish peeked around the stone columns that supported the gate, but the only movement she could detect was that of tall blades of pampas grass rustling in the breeze.

Several seconds elapsed before Ainsley called again. 'Shackleford?'

Still there was no answer.

'No wonder that dog of his gets into so much trouble. Going out and leaving the gate wide open like that. No sense. No sense at all,' Ainsley grumbled. 'Well, come along. Since we're here, I'll give you folks a quick look around.'

Tish was reluctant to trespass on a Coleton Creek resident's property. 'I don't think that's such a good idea, Mr Ainsley. What if Mr Shackleford comes home and finds us here?'

'Don't worry. We'll make it snappy.' Ainsley stepped on to the irregularly shaped concrete block patio and beckoned them to follow. 'We'll be out of here in two shakes of a lamb's tail.'

Despite Ainsley's reassuring colloquialism, Tish still had misgivings. 'Yeah, I don't know . . .'

'Oh, come on. I can handle Shackleford, and we won't be but a minute or two.'

With a heavy sigh and a quick glance at Jules, Tish relented and followed Ainsley on to the patio. From the paved sitting area, a series of staggered square stones in varying sizes formed a path along the left lawn of the wedge-shaped property and culminated in another, smaller seating area, this one surrounded with rounded box hedges and perennials, and backed by a solid stone wall over which cascaded a gentle waterfall. To the right, lined by the swishing pampas grass and slender silver birches, a narrow canal of water glistened in the sunlight and led to a circular pool populated by lotus blossoms and a school of well-fed koi.

It was a spot of such supreme tranquility that, for a short while, Tish stopped fretting about the workload awaiting her at the lifestyle center. Indeed, Shackleford's garden possessed such beauty and serenity that it seemed at odds with the character of the man who built it. 'So, Sloane Shackleford designed this garden himself?'

'That's what he says,' Ainsley replied. 'I looked into it myself – I'm retired Virginia State Police – and couldn't find any evidence to refute his claim. In fact, he showed me the plans and drawings. They all bear Shackleford's signature in the corner. I'm aware that doesn't mean much, but how far am I supposed to go with it? It is, after all, just a garden competition.'

Tish nodded, although she suspected that many of the residents of Coleton Creek would have objected to the word *just*.

'Besides,' Ainsley grumbled, 'I have absolutely no doubt the man's guilty of far worse things than fudging his horticultural credentials.'

Given what she had heard thus far about Mr Shackleford, Tish couldn't disagree, but something about the vehemence in Ainsley's delivery gave her a chill.

'Well, we'd best be getting to work, Mr Ainsley.' Tish turned on one heel to begin to make her leave back to the lifestyle center. As she did so, she noticed a square, highly modern wicker seating set positioned several yards behind her and to the left. Resting upon the lounge chair lay the highly tanned figure of a man clad in white shorts, a tropical-print shirt, a pair of brown leather loafers, and a navy-blue ball cap that was tilted over his face.

The man was slumped, with his left arm folded across his lap and the other dangling at his side, his fingers nearly grazing the ground below.

Ainsley followed Tish's gaze and smiled brilliantly, albeit somewhat nervously. 'Oh, Shackleford. There you are. I hope you don't mind, but these folks were eager to see the winning garden and I just couldn't let them . . .'

Ainsley's voice trailed off and Tish soon saw why. The concrete beneath the chaise lounge was puddled with fresh blood.

'Oh my God!' Jules shouted. 'I'll call nine-one-one!'

Tish charged forward to check on the man, only for Ainsley, ever the policeman, to push her aside. 'I'll handle this, Ms Tarragon.'

Tish ignored the order and followed Ainsley across the patio, where he promptly removed the ball cap from the man's face.

Shackleford's forehead had been smashed open, creating a sickening tangle of hair, blood, flesh, and bone. His mouth was agape as if caught in mid-scream, and his eyes, now dilated and unseeing, were wide as if he had noticed too late the fate about to befall him.

'It's Sloane Shackleford,' Ainsley cried as he dropped the hat and staggered backward. 'H–he's dead.'

Tish brought a hand to her mouth and tried not to gag. As she looked away, she noticed a series of blood spatters and then a trail of droplets leading off the cement and toward the lawn. There, just twenty feet from the dead man's body, an object lay partially obscured in a patch of exceedingly plush ryegrass.

It was a bloody garden spade.

FOUR

As neighbors, alarmed by Jules's and Ainsley's shouts, milled about on the road outside Shackleford's house, Jules placed an arm around the shoulder of his friend. 'You OK?'

Tish screwed up her mouth and gave a silent shrug.

'At least Shackleford died before tasting your food,' he offered.

Tish said nothing.

'You've also done some successful catering jobs where people celebrated and no one died. Even that ninetieth birthday party. Which, to be honest, was a crapshoot.'

Again, Tish gave no response.

'Your café seems to be a hit, too. And everyone who's eaten there has survived, so I reckon you're ahead of the game on this one.'

'Jules?' Tish started.

'Yes.'

'Please stop talking.'

'Sorry. Defense mechanism. If there were food here, I'd be eating, but since there isn't—'

'Jules,' Tish reminded.

'Got it. Shutting up.'

From the house next door with the 'plain' garden, a petite woman emerged via a sliding glass back door. She strode across the lawn and through Shackleford's gate. 'Jim, what's going on?' she asked breathlessly, setting a canvas-tennis-shoed foot on to the concrete patio. 'I'd only just got back from my walk when I heard you and someone else shouting.'

'Zadie.' Ainsley received the woman by grasping her hands. 'Don't come any farther. It's Sloane Shackleford. He's been murdered.'

At the mention of the woman's name, Tish did a double take. Zadie Cosmetics had been a part of Tish's life since she was a girl. Both Tish's mother and grandmother had been, as advertising executives coined, *Zadie's Ladies*, saving their leftover grocery shopping money to treat themselves to the newest seasonal shade of Zadie lipstick at the local Woolworth's or splurging on fruit-flavored lip balm or bubble bath to put in Tish's Christmas stocking. Years later, while attending her senior prom, Tish complemented her strapless, full-skirted black-and-white early-1990s gown with a pair of fingerless black gloves and an electric shade of fuchsia Zadie lipstick dubbed *Magenta Madness*.

In the two-plus decades since that warm June evening, Tish's grandmother and mother had both passed away, the local Woolworth's had closed, and Tish had moved on from drugstore fuchsia lipstick to upmarket reds and mauves, but the thought of Zadie Cosmetics still conjured up nostalgia.

That's why, although still in shock at the discovery of Sloane Shackleford's body, Tish stood transfixed by the diminutive figure currently engaging Ainsley in conversation.

'Murdered?' an incredulous Zadie repeated. 'Oh! I'll run back home and dial the police.'

'We've already called. They're on their way.'

A distraught Zadie brought a hand to her forehead. 'You're sure he's been murdered? This is a retirement community. None of us are spring chickens any longer.'

'No, it's murder all right,' Ainsley confirmed. 'Someone whacked him in the head with a garden spade.'

'What? Here in his backyard? In broad daylight?'

'I know,' Ainsley commiserated. 'It beggars belief, but it appears that's what happened.'

'Oh,' the woman sighed.

Zadie Morris bore little resemblance to Tish's idea of how a successful cosmetics mogul might appear. Standing before her was not a brash Anna Wintour lookalike – an immaculately styled, coiffed, suited, and shoulder-padded executive – but a genteel woman with a pleasant voice and elfin-like charm. She was sporting a designer-made, yet decidedly low-key, nautical-inspired ensemble of half-sleeved navy-and-white-striped boat-neck tee and white French-terry cropped pants. Her hair, once quite dark, was now predominantly silver and cut into a simple bob, and her face, miraculously lineless for a woman in her late seventies, bore no traces of the product her company once formulated, manufactured, and sold. Ms Morris's only concession to glamour was the double strand of pearls around her neck. 'Who would do such a thing?' she asked, clearly confounded by the information she was receiving. 'And why? Was it a burglary gone wrong?'

'We don't know. But I'm sure the police will get to the bottom of it,' Ainsley stated with an air of confidence. The sound of sirens tore through the unusually warm, early-autumn air. 'There they are now. You'd best go on back home, Ms Zadie. No need for you to get in the middle of all this.'

Zadie waved a set of pink polished fingertips in the air. 'I live right next door, Jim. I *am* in the middle of it. It's only a matter of time before the police ask me what I did or didn't see.'

'If you're not up to answering their questions, I can try to put them off,' Ainsley offered.

'I don't mind them asking. I have nothing to tell. I went out for my daily walk and came back to hear shouting. I looked out my kitchen window and saw you all here. In fact, after the police ask *me* what I know, I would like to ask *them* how they plan to protect us from whomever did this.'

'Perhaps you shouldn't stay here tonight,' Ainsley proposed. 'The Abercrombies have a guest bedroom.'

'I never once got chased out of my apartment in New York, Jim. I'm not about to let that happen now. Hmph . . . funny to think I moved back to Virginia because I thought it was safer.' She looked up to see Tish and Jules lingering a few feet away. 'Who are they?'

'Oh, they're the caterers for Sunday's luncheon. I was giving them a tour of the gardens when we came upon . . .' He gestured in the direction of the chaise lounge containing the body of Shackleford.

Tish took the liberty of introducing herself and Jules. 'I'm sorry we're not meeting under better circumstances.'

'I didn't know Mr Shackleford well at all, but to think someone – well, it just doesn't seem real,' Zadie lamented. 'I was so looking forward to your luncheon, Miss Tarragon. It's been ages since I've been to the southwest of England and I was hoping to taste a real cream tea again. But now, well . . .'

'Don't be silly,' Ainsley admonished. 'Mr Shackleford's death is unfortunate, and I'm sure the community will be in shock for some time, but I see no need to cancel the garden competition or the luncheon.'

Tish, Zadie, and Jules shared expressions of disbelief.

'But, Jim,' Zadie began to argue.

Ainsley wouldn't hear it. 'Now, I appreciate that this is a sensitive issue, but you need to understand that this is a major event for the residents of Coleton Creek. Participants have been tending their gardens the past year in hopes of taking this year's trophy. The judges have been reading up on plant varieties and garden styles. And Susannah Hilton has put a lot of time into selecting and purchasing trophies and plaques and hiring our catering team. I'm sorry Sloane Shackleford is dead, but I think it would be hypocritical to toss all that hard work aside for some feeble display of mourning, when no one in this community thought much of him while he was alive.'

'Well, that makes my job a lot tougher,' deadpanned the man who had entered Shackleford's backyard while Ainsley spoke.

A startled Ainsley twirled about in horror. 'I beg your pardon, sir.' He eyed with suspicion the spiky-haired man wearing a black T-shirt and motorcycle boots.

'Sheriff Clemson Reade, Hanover County Police.' The man drew a badge from the rear pocket of his jeans and held it aloft for all to see. His eyes suddenly fell on Tish. 'Ms Tarragon, I'm surprised to see you here. The dispatcher didn't mention anything about poison.'

Tish ignored Reade's feeble attempt at humor. 'I'm here to cater a garden competition luncheon on Sunday,' she explained.

'Here in this backyard?' Reade pointed at the ground beneath his feet.

'No, over at the lifestyle center. Mr Ainsley was just giving us a tour of this year's top gardens when we found . . .' Her voice trailed off.

Reade's eyes then fell on Jules. 'Mr Davis. I trust I'll find no sandwiches in the trunk of your car today.'

'Of course not. I'm here helping Tish. I'll be serving the plonk.'

All eyes immediately turned toward Jules.

'The plonk?' Reade asked.

'The booze. I'm the bartender for Sunday's party.'

Reade's gray eyes narrowed. 'OK. Leave your statements with Deputy Croft and then you can get back to work.'

Tish and Jules thanked the sheriff and went off in search of Deputy Croft.

Thirty minutes later found them walking back to the lifestyle center.

'Plonk,' Tish mocked.

'It's British slang.'

'Yeah, I figured that. Problem is you're Southern, Jules. You were born in North Carolina, raised in Charlottesville, your dad has a room full of Roll Tide gear, and your mother was Miss Georgia 1970. The only way you'd be more Southern is if you were somehow related to Robert E. Lee.'

'No relation to Lee, but my crazy great-aunt used to pass herself off as Margaret Mitchell so she'd get a better table in restaurants.'

'Close enough.'

As Tish and Jules entered the glass front doors of the lifestyle center, Susannah Hilton rushed from her desk to meet them. 'I'm so glad you're both back. Is it true? Are the rumors true? Is Mr Shackleford . . .'

'Dead?' Tish completed the sentence. 'I'm afraid so.'

'I can't believe it. He was here at the lifestyle center just this morning. What happened?'

Reade had warned Tish and Jules against discussing details with the public before he could issue a statement. 'Well, the police need to analyze the scene, of course, but it appears Mr Shackleford may have been murdered.'

'Murdered? How? By whom?'

'As I said, the police are on the scene. I'm sure they'll release information as soon as they have it.'

'And you?' Susannah asked timidly. 'Are you launching your own investigation?'

'No, I have enough on my plate trying to get this luncheon together.'

'So the garden competition is still on?' Susannah's voice was hopeful.

'As of this moment, yes. Mr Ainsley is highly committed to moving forward with the event and, at the moment, the police seem to have no objections.'

'That's good. Oh, I hope that doesn't sound callous, but the people in this community live for the competition. Women plan for months what dress and hat to wear to the luncheon, men take odds on this year's winner, and the gardeners . . . well, I happen to know quite a few of them who would no longer be with us if it weren't for the competition. Many of our residents are widowed and retired. Their families have moved far away and rarely visit. Tending their gardens is often the only thing keeping them going.'

'Yes, Mr Ainsley touched upon the importance of the competition to the residents of Coleton Creek. He also mentioned how hard you work organizing it each year.'

Susannah rejected the praise. 'All I do is make a few phone calls. It's typical of Mr Ainsley to talk it up, though. He's an old-school Southern gentleman through and through. He's also got a soft spot for us ladies. In a respectable way, of course.'

Tish wondered if Ainsley's tenderness toward the opposite sex was behind his comment about Violet Abercrombie, but she thought it best to remain quiet about something that might start a potential scandal.

Before either Susannah or Tish could continue their conversation, the telephone at the front desk rang.

'Distraught residents, no doubt.' Susannah ran back to her desk to answer the device. 'If you find out anything at all from the police, Tish, could you let me know? I'd like to be able to put people's minds at ease.'

Tish agreed and led Jules past the desk and down the corridor that overlooked, via a series of glass doors and windows, the outdoor pool area. At the end of the hall stood a solid metal fireproof labeled *INDOOR POOL & SAUNA* and, beside it, a glass door that led outdoors to a brick-paved area surrounded by ten-foot-tall rose trellises and topped by a pergola covered with brilliantly blooming tendrils of bougainvillea.

Jules pulled open the door to the brick area and allowed Tish to enter. Stepping on to the basket-weave patterned brick, she was immediately greeted by the sight of a woman seated alone at one of the patio's delicately curved wrought-iron bistro tables. She was dark-haired, approximately sixty-five years of age, and quite attractive, if rather heavily made up. She wore a red off-the-shoulder dress, a pair of platform espadrilles tied high upon her calves, and an elaborate pair of red metal chandelier earrings that rattled as she sobbed into a lace handkerchief.

Tish was reluctant to intrude upon the woman's grief, but she also had to make a start on the decorating if everything was to be ready in time for Sunday afternoon. She stood, frozen to the spot, deliberating whether she should clear her throat to announce her presence or quietly back away without being seen.

Jules inadvertently settled the matter. Oblivious to the presence of the crying woman, he closed the glass door behind him and immediately whirled around to face Tish, his hands on his hips. 'Well, I don't know about you, but I've had enough Shady Pines drama for one day. Let's doll this place up and then get the heck out of here. There's a glass of Chardonnay out there screaming my name.'

As Jules spoke, Tish attempted to divert his attention toward the mysterious woman, but to no avail. The woman's startled gasp, however, finally did the trick.

Jules echoed the gasp and spun around. 'Who are you? What are you doing here?'

'I'm a resident of Coleton Creek looking for some peace and quiet,' she sniffed with indignation. 'What are *you* doing here?'

Tish stepped forward. 'I'm Tish Tarragon and this is Julian Jefferson Davis. We're catering Sunday's garden club luncheon. We came out here to get a start on the decorating.'

'You're wasting your time,' the woman announced. 'A man's been murdered. Hit in the head with a shovel. The luncheon is off.'

The woman's assertion that the luncheon was cancelled, combined with her detailed knowledge of Shackleford's death, threw Tish off-kilter, but she quickly recovered. 'Um, with all due respect, Ms . . .?'

'Aviero. Pepper Aviero.'

'With all due respect, Ms Aviero, we just came from the scene. Mr Ainsley assured us that the competition and awards luncheon are to go ahead as planned. The police gave us their blessing as well.'

'Jim Ainsley told you it was still on? I should have guessed,' Pepper scoffed.

'What do you mean?' Jules interjected. 'Why wouldn't Mr Ainsley tell us to go ahead with the luncheon? He is president of the garden club, isn't he?'

'Yes, Mr Ainsley is president of the garden club. He's also clearly a man without conscience; otherwise, he'd cancel this ridiculous competition. A man's been killed, for God's sake.' Pepper's olive-skinned countenance turned red hot with anger. 'Then again, Jim never did care much for Sloane Shackleford. I shouldn't be surprised at all that Jim's going ahead with a party instead of planning a memorial service.'

Pepper's assessment of Ainsley's feelings toward Shackleford seemed in direct contrast to the fair, even-handed way he dealt with the various allegations garden club members hurled against Shackleford, his dog, and his garden. 'Why didn't Mr Ainsley like Shackleford?'

Pepper shrugged. 'I can only guess he was jealous. Jim and I dated for a time, but lately I had been seeing Sloane.'

'I suppose that would make any man jealous. A woman breaking up with him to date someone else.'

'Oh, no. I didn't break up with Jim. He broke things off with me. It was all for the best, though. Sloane had great taste in food, great taste in music, great taste in art. You saw his garden. Light years beyond Jim Ainsley's suburban shrubbery,' she added, quite cattily.

'Sounds as though you'd found your dream man.'

'Yes, until Callie Collingsworth got in the way.'

'Callie Collingsworth? Sounds like the name of a soap opera actress,' a tickled Jules remarked.

'She's probably had as much plastic surgery as one, too,' Pepper frothed. 'I was out of town, visiting my sister in Mexico, when Callie threw herself at Sloane. She had the nerve to bring him dinner at his house. Sloane loved my *arroz con pollo*, so Callie brought him fried chicken. He raved about my *tres leches* cake, so Callie made banana pudding. How the evening ended, I can only imagine, because when I returned home, Sloane no longer wanted to see me.'

'If Callie knew you and Sloane were dating, then why would she throw herself at him?' Jules asked.

'Money. Sloane is – was – a very wealthy man. In addition to his home here in Coleton Creek, he had apartments in Paris and New York and a vacation villa in the Bahamas.'

Tish did her best not to roll her eyes. Although Callie's behavior was less than principled, the onus was on Shackleford to rebuff her advances. 'Not to speak ill of the dead, but just because Callie threw herself at him, doesn't mean Sloane was required to reciprocate.'

'You didn't know Sloane,' Pepper excused. 'He was a man's man. Extremely red-blooded. Before he retired, Sloane was a successful businessman with great instincts. He was a man of action, not words, and he always seized opportunity. You can't expect a man like that to look the other way.'

Tish thought it best to let the subject drop. 'You seem to have understood Mr Shackleford quite well.'

'I did. Or I thought I did.' Her eyes welled with tears.

'I'm very sorry, Ms Aviero. Jules and I offer our deepest condolences.'

'Thank you. I'd say I don't know what I'm going to do without him, but the fact is I've been doing without him for a while now.' Pepper rose from her seat and trudged toward the door. 'The bastard,' she whispered beneath her breath before letting herself in.

'Nice job not investigating Shackleford's murder,' Jules quipped when Pepper was out of earshot. 'The guy's not even cold yet and you've already uncovered a suspect.'

'It's not as if I went looking for her, Jules. She just happened to be here when we arrived.' Tish set about untangling a strand of party lights with birdcage shades on each bulb. 'That said, it was odd how she knew Shackleford was bludgeoned with a shovel.'

'Weird,' Jules agreed as he removed the plastic wrapping from a dried rose garland. 'Not surprising if this place is a hotbed for gossip. I mean, a guy or gal needs something to do between *Judge Judy* and the five o'clock news.'

'You're awful,' Tish scolded. 'Seriously, though, only you and

I, Ainsley, and Zadie Morris saw Shackleford's body and the police have yet to issue a statement. So how did Pepper Aviero know about the shovel to the head?'

'Someone must have told her,' he shrugged.

'But who? Ainsley or Morris?'

'Why didn't you just ask Pepper while she was here?'

'Because,' Tish nearly sang, 'I already told you, I don't want to get involved with the investigation.'

FIVE

After three hours of concentrated effort, Tish and Jules had transformed the patio at the lifestyle center at Coleton Creek into a romantically styled walled garden. The bistro sets had been replaced with long banquet tables which Jules and Tish covered with rolls of dried moss and scatterings of rose petals in various hues. At the center of each table Tish positioned a row of miniature topiary plants – prizes that would be raffled off to table members at the end of the luncheon – and at each setting rested a gold key with a place card attached with tulle ribbon.

The buffet and bar tables bore the same dried-moss covering as the banquet tables, but in lieu of topiaries, they were ornamented with miniature rose bushes, tall pots of lavender, and decorative Victorian birdcages. Adding to the garden-party charm were vintage china platters and tiered cake servers in a variety of floral patterns. And, above it all, entwined with the bougainvillea along the pergola, rows of party lights added an ethereal twinkle.

'Looks fabulous, honey,' Jules complimented his friend. 'But where do these rose garlands go?'

'They're to decorate the backs of the chairs. I have some white tulle chair covers I rented. I thought we'd pin short sections of garland to the back of each one. We'll do that tomorrow, though, just in case there's a stray shower overnight.'

'Or a dirty bird.'

'I hadn't thought of that,' she laughed.

The glass door leading to the lifestyle center suddenly swung inward. A couple in their late thirties and clad in business attire stepped on to the patio. He was short – just a tad taller than Tish's five feet five inches – athletically built, and his skin ridiculously bronzed. The tan suit he wore blended regrettably with the color of his hair, giving him a washed-out, homogenous appearance, and the ill-fitting dress shirt beneath his jacket lent him the air of a used-car salesman. The woman with him was curvaceous, ivory-skinned, and nearly a head taller than her companion – her height only amplified by the short hemline of her navy-blue skirt and the tumble of chocolate brown hair that fell down her back and ended a few inches above her waist.

'Nathan and Mariette Knobloch,' the man introduced with an outstretched hand. 'We're the developers and managers of Coleton Creek.'

'Tish Tarragon. And this is Julian Jefferson Davis. We're the caterers in charge of Sunday's luncheon,' Tish clarified after she, Jules, and Mariette had exchanged greetings and limp handshakes.

'Yes, we know,' Nathan Knobloch acknowledged. 'That's why we're here.'

'I'm not sure if either of you are aware, but one of Coleton Creek's residents is dead,' Mariette inserted.

'Murdered,' Nathan whispered, with an appropriate pucker to his brow.

'Yes, we're aware. Jules, Mr Ainsley, and I were the ones who discovered the body.'

'You were? Oh, my!' Mariette drew a hand to her bosom to denote her shock.

'Well, then, the two of you, perhaps more than anyone else in this community, must understand why this luncheon – indeed, this entire competition – needs to be cancelled,' Nathan presumed.

'Mr Ainsley's decision to go ahead with the luncheon seemed in bad taste at first,' Tish conceded, 'but then I learned just how important this competition and the garden club are to the residents here.'

'Too important!' Mariette's tone was sharp. 'Just look at what happened to Mr Shackleford.'

'Wait a minute.' Jules stepped forward. 'You're not implying that Mr Shackleford was killed because of the garden competition, are you?'

'Implying? We're not implying anything. We're telling you that's precisely what's happened.'

'You honestly think one of the residents killed Shackleford because he won the garden competition?' Tish was skeptical.

'Shackleford didn't just win the competition,' Nathan corrected. 'He won it the past five years straight. You can just imagine how that went down with the other members of the garden club. They're obsessed with the idea of winning the trophy.'

'I've met the residents here, and they do appear to be focused on the competition, but I think that's more about the pride they take in their gardens than winning the prize itself.'

'If this were your average village situation, I'd agree with you,' Mariette prefaced, 'but many of the residents here aren't quite – well, let's just say they're starting to feel the effects of the aging process. Some of them may not be entirely in touch with reality. When you take someone like that and tell them their garden – the thing they've been so obsessed with all these months – isn't good enough to win a trophy, well, you're playing with dynamite, aren't you?'

'Mariette and I have been afraid something like this might happen for years now. Not murder, of course,' Nathan Knobloch was quick to correct himself. 'Maybe an act of vandalism or assault, but we were certain someone would eventually lash out at Mr Shackleford for his winning streak. And now they have.'

'If only we'd come forward with our concerns about the competition sooner,' Mariette bemoaned.

'Even if you're right and Mr Shackleford was murdered by an irate gardener, I fail to see what either of you could have done about it,' Tish reasoned.

'We would have done what we're going to do now: disband the garden club.'

Tish and Jules fell silent as they digested Mariette Knobloch's announcement.

'But the residents here love the garden club as well as the competition,' Jules argued after several seconds had elapsed. 'You can't let one man and one incident mar something that's brought only good to this community.'

'Jules is right,' Tish rejoined. 'Even those who don't garden enjoy viewing their neighbors' efforts, and then there's the fun of the awards ceremony and luncheon.'

'They'll just have to find another event to take its place.' Mariette shrugged off their objections.

'And what about the gardeners? For many of these people, preparing for the competition is their reason for getting out of bed each morning.'

'Well, that's the beauty of our plan,' Nathan grinned. 'We're going to ask them to help us launch a community garden. Instead of digging their own individual garden beds alone in their back-yards, they can share their love of gardening with others on a plot just outside the Coleton Creek development which everyone, including the public, can enjoy.'

'I like the idea of a community garden,' Tish conceded, 'but you can't expect people to give up their own garden plots.'

'Why not? The whole point of this exercise is to eliminate the competitiveness that led to Sloane Shackleford's murder.'

'You can't control what people do on their own property,' Jules challenged.

'Sure, we can. We just need to get the homeowners' association to pass it into the bylaws. Given what's happened to Mr Shackleford, that shouldn't be too difficult.'

'Banning residents from having gardens is a bit drastic, don't you think?' Tish attempted to speak the voice of reason. 'And what about the people who can't drive to the new garden? Won't they feel isolated? Maybe you should give things some time to calm down before—'

'Calm down?' Mariette screeched. 'What, and take the chance of another gardener being murdered? We need to protect our residents.'

'I appreciate you wanting to protect your residents, Mrs Knobloch, but this isn't a nursing home or assisted-living facility. The people who live here are responsible homeowners. They have the right to a certain amount of personal freedom.'

'The residents of Coleton Creek sacrificed that right when they started pitting their gardens against each other and fighting with each other like petty school children. Now, I'm sorry you and Mr Davis put so much work into decorating this patio, but I'm afraid everything's going to have to come down. The garden competition, as well as Sunday's luncheon, is cancelled.'

'I'm afraid I can't abide by your request. You and your husband didn't hire me, and therefore you can't fire me.'

Nathan Knobloch leapt to his wife's defense. 'We can if the event in question is being held on our property. This patio is maintained by our management company.'

'Even so, my contract is with the garden club. They're the ones paying us to cater this event. They're the ones who need to make the call about cancelling it, not you.'

'Well, Jim Ainsley is going to hear about this,' Nathan declared before storming off through the lifestyle-center door.

Mariette followed closely behind but not before casting a withering glance in Tish's direction.

When the Knoblochs were safely inside the center and out of earshot, Jules turned to Tish excitedly. 'Great job standing up to those two.'

'Yeah, for all the difference it'll make. You just know they'll be back again.'

'Perhaps Ainsley will talk some sense into them.'

'I certainly hope so. I just don't get it, Jules. Why are the Knoblochs so opposed to the residents having gardens? Protecting against another crime is one thing, but they're being completely unreasonable.'

'I think they're just being plain ol' straight-up mean.'

'Maybe, but it's still very odd.'

'So is matching your suit to your spray tan,' Jules remarked with a shudder.

'Nathan Knobloch is rather monochromatic, isn't he?'

'Monochromatic? You're too kind. The man's so brown, if you set him loose in a UPS warehouse, even the FBI wouldn't be able to find him.'

Tish let out a hearty laugh. 'Well, I think we're done for the day. How about we get out of here?'

'Oh, Lord, yes.'

'Good. I'm just going to check with Susannah about overnight security. I don't quite trust the Knoblochs not to return and take down the decorations themselves.'

'Yeah, but they own the place. How will you stop them?'

'I'm not sure, but after I speak with Susannah, I'm going to put in a call to Schuyler to find out.'

'Ooh,' Jules cooed. 'Having a hunky attorney boyfriend has its perks.'

'Schuyler Thompson isn't my boyfriend. We're keeping things casual and seeing where our relationship might go.'

'Uh-huh,' Jules blatantly 'yessed' his friend.

'Neither of us wants to rush into anything right now,' she continued as she led Jules back into the lifestyle center and toward the main entrance of the building.

'Uh-huh. Keep telling yourself that.'

'What do you mean?'

'I mean that Mr Thompson is so into you that I'm surprised his law partners haven't sent out a search party for his brain.'

'Don't be ridiculous. Schuyler and I are—'

Tish did not complete the sentence for she was so busy reprimanding Jules that she hadn't been looking where she was walking. As a result, she bumped directly into a platinum-blond resident traveling down the corridor from the opposite direction.

'Oh!' the woman exclaimed as a pair of oversized sunglasses tumbled from the bridge of her nose and on to the tiled floor of the lifestyle center, a casualty of the collision.

'I'm so sorry,' Tish apologized and knelt down to retrieve the glasses.

'That's all right, darlin',' the woman replied with a thick Southern drawl. 'Had I taken my dang glasses off, I might have seen you in time to avoid you.'

'No, this was totally my fault. I was busy talking and not watching where I was going. I'm sorry.'

'I won't hear another word,' the woman insisted and placed her sunglasses atop her head where they came to rest in a tall tangle of cotton-candy-esque platinum hair. 'Say, you're that catering woman, aren't you?'

'Tish Tarragon, yes. And this is—'

'That is Mr Julian Jefferson Davis,' the woman sang with glee. 'My favorite weatherman in the world.'

Jules, who had been standing silently behind Tish, stepped forward and, in one sweeping motion, took the woman's braceleted and bejeweled hand in his and bowed. 'Thank you, Mrs . . .?'

'Collingsworth. Ms Callie Collingsworth.'

At mention of her name, Jules let both his jaw and Ms Collingsworth's hand drop.

'Is everything all right?' she asked as she brought said hand to the deep V-neck of her caftan-cum-swimsuit-cover-up. 'Mr Davis, you've lost all the color in your face.'

'It's been a long, difficult day,' Tish explained, eager to smooth over her friend's blunder.

'Yes, it has been.'

'I'm sorry, Mrs Collingsworth. I was told you and Mr Shackleford were close.'

'As close as anyone could be to Sloane Shackleford.' She frowned. 'Are the rumors true? Was he – was Sloane killed with a garden spade?'

So, Callie Collingsworth knew about the garden spade, as well, Tish mused silently. News of the manner of Shackleford's death really had spread quickly. 'Yes, I'm afraid he was,' she replied.

'Sounds as though someone from the garden club finally took their revenge on Sloane for winning all these years.' Callie gave a sardonic laugh. 'Should have figured it would catch up with him some day, but Sloane couldn't help it. He was such a competitive bastard.'

At Callie's use of the word 'bastard,' Tish and Jules's eyes doubled in size.

Callie Collingsworth took obvious delight in their surprise. 'That's right. I called him a bastard. Because he could be an awful one if he put his mind to it. Still, he had many good points. You know how he won the garden competition? By understanding all the different angles his competitors might use to take the trophy from him. Orson Baggett's garden was full of history, so Sloane made the classic English rill the center of his garden and surrounded it with privet hedges. Wren Harper prided herself on her pond and apple trees, so Sloane put in a koi pond and silver birches. The highlight of the Abercrombies' garden is their gazebo, so Sloane built a stone patio with a waterfall. He was brilliant.'

'And clearly quite wealthy,' Tish remarked.

'As my daddy used to say, it's just as easy to love a rich man as a poor one,' she gleamed. 'So is the luncheon still on for this Sunday?'

'Yes. Jim Ainsley is committed to ensuring everything goes ahead as planned.'

'Good. Sloane would have wanted that. He always enjoyed the competition and the luncheon. Mostly because he relished the opportunity to wind people up, but he also genuinely liked the event: the food, the cheesy trophies, the women in their tacky dresses and hats. Of course, he loved winning, as well. He would have won this year's competition too, I'm sure.'

'But Mr Ainsley told us it was anyone's competition.'

'Of course he did,' Callie defended. 'And to be fair, Jim wasn't entirely wrong. He just wasn't aware of Sloane's secret weapon.'

Tish's face was a question.

'Biscuit, Sloane's pet Bichon Frise. The little doggie's taken a liking to visiting other people's gardens.'

'Earlier today we heard Orson Baggett complain about a nocturnal visit from Biscuit that destroyed an entire patch of pachysandra,' Jules stated.

'Are you telling us that Mr Shackleford encouraged Biscuit to engage in that kind of behavior?' Tish was aghast.

'No, I wouldn't say he encouraged Biscuit, but he certainly didn't stop the dog either. Every night, instead of walking Biscuit, Sloane would leave the back gate open to let him roam free. Not only did it free Sloane's time for, ahem, other things, but he loved to hear the complaints the next morning. As I said, Sloane enjoyed winding people up.' Callie stared off at a spot somewhere behind Jules and Tish and narrowed her eyes as if straining to recall something. 'Funny thing is, when I talked to him about it, Sloane vehemently denied that his dog caused the yellowing in Orson's and the Abercrombies' gardens.'

'Well, if Mr Shackleford openly admitted that he knew his dog was sabotaging other people's gardens, he might have been kicked out of the competition,' Tish reasoned.

'Yeah, but it was just me asking him. He had no reason to lie or cover up. He knew I'd never report him. I couldn't care less about the garden competition. A contest where someone wins a trophy for most beautiful magnolia blossom or largest zucchini? I'd rather shear a pig.'

Tish had no doubt the woman was telling the truth. Callie Collingsworth was clearly more interested in money and all its trappings than horticultural pursuits. 'So if Biscuit wasn't responsible for the lost plant life in the neighborhood gardens, who or what was?'

'How in Sam Hill should I know? Do I look like Mrs Green

Jeans?' Callie mocked. 'All I can tell you is that Sloane went to the management about it.'

'The management? The Knoblochs?'

'If you mean Morticia and Gomez Addams, then yes.'

At Callie Collingsworth's description of Coleton Creek's developers, Jules howled with laughter. 'Morticia and Gomez. O. M. G. That is perfect!'

Even Tish had a giggle. 'What did he discuss with them?'

Callie screwed up her mouth 'Other than the fact that Biscuit wasn't to blame for the other gardeners' complaints, I haven't the foggiest.'

'Hmm, it's odd you mention the Knoblochs. They're two of just a handful of people who are against the luncheon and competition going on as planned.'

'I'm sure I can guess who else is opposed to the idea,' Callie sneered, but she didn't wait for confirmation. 'The fact of the matter is Pepper Aviero didn't know Sloane the way I did. She didn't accept him for the way he was, the way I did. Sloane Shackleford was a scalawag, rogue, and liar, but he was my scalawag, rogue, and liar.'

Tish was at a loss to known to how to respond, but Callie Collingsworth did not give her the opportunity. She flipped her giant sunglasses down on to the bridge of her nose, hiked her swim bag higher on to her shoulder, and prepared for departure. 'You stick to your guns regarding the luncheon, Miss Tarragon. The competition and award ceremony should go on as if nothing has happened. If it had been any one of us lying in their backyards, murdered, I can guarantee you Sloane Shackleford wouldn't have even stopped for a moment of silence. You can take that to the bank.'

SIX

'What do you mean, you won't take the case?' Jules asked as Tish navigated the Matrix back into Hobson Glen.

'Simple. There is no case for me to take.'

'A retired businessman has been beaten to death with a garden spade. If that isn't a case, I don't know what is.'

'Yes, but it's a case for the police, not me. "Taking the case" implies that someone asked me to investigate when, on the contrary, Sheriff Reade asked me not to get involved.'

'That's just because he's sore at you for solving the last murder,' Jules pooh-poohed.

'I highly doubt it, but whatever his reason, I plan to respect his request. Between the café, the garden luncheon, and other catering jobs, I have enough on my agenda. Besides, there's no legitimate reason for me to get involved. Last time, my business and reputation were at risk. This time around, no one outside Coleton Creek or our little circle of friends even knows I'm working there.'

'Oh, I wouldn't be surprised if Enid Kemper knew something. Not only is she the town eccentric, but I swear she sends that parrot of hers out on reconnaissance missions. Kinda like the Wicked Witch of the West and her flying monkeys.'

Tish chuckled and drove on to the café, where she noticed a familiar silver minivan in the parking lot. 'That's odd. It's after five o'clock. Celestine was supposed to close up two hours ago.'

'We were also supposed to be back two hours ago. Maybe she got swamped at the last minute. You know how customers always come in just as you're starting to clean up.'

'Yeah, but that shouldn't have taken two hours.'

'Maybe they were messy. Or chatty. You know Celestine – she can't leave untidiness behind, or a conversation.'

'True, but still . . .' As Tish pulled the Matrix into the Cookin' the Books parking lot, she still couldn't let go of the feeling that something wasn't quite right. A feeling borne out as she and Jules climbed the front-door steps to find the main door wide open, but the screen door latched.

'Celestine?' Tish peered through the screen into the darkened café.

No sooner had the words left her lips than Tish's trusty assistant and dessert-maker appeared in the doorway and unhooked the latch. Her substantial frame was clothed in her customary uniform of denim capris, loose-fitting floral blouse, and a black Cookin' the Books apron, and her short, cherry-tinted hair was layered and gelled for maximum volume. 'Sorry, I wanted some fresh air without all the foot traffic,' she explained over the top of her hot-pink reading glasses.

'That's fine. Is everything OK? It's awfully late for you to still be here.'

As Tish swung open the screen door and entered the café, Celestine stepped aside and gestured to the row of tables nearest the windows. There, at the table farthest from the door, sat Mary Jo Okensholt, her face puffy, tear-stained, and red. At the sight of Tish and Jules, she stood up and rushed toward her friends.

'MJ,' Jules addressed her as he gathered the T-shirt-and-legging-attired Mary Jo in an embrace. 'What's going on? You weren't in an accident, were you? Your car isn't in the lot.'

'I parked around the corner. I got here when the café was busy. I forgot you two were prepping for Coleton Creek today.'

'OK, but something's wrong. What is it?'

Mary Jo gazed down at the floor, her lips trembling.

'Is it the kids?' Tish quizzed before taking her turn hugging Mary Jo. 'Please tell me Gregory and Kayla are all right.'

'They are. It's . . . it's Glen.' Mary Jo broke into sobs, dampening the shoulder of Tish's dress.

'Oh my God, what's happened?'

'H–h–he asked me for a divorce. He says he doesn't love me anymore.'

Jules and Tish gaped at each other. This was not the answer either of them had expected to hear.

After several moments' silence and several more embraces, they accompanied Mary Jo back to the table near the window. Celestine, in the meantime, had wandered off to the kitchen.

'I just can't believe it,' Jules muttered, taking a seat to Mary Jo's left.

'I can't either,' Tish agreed in astonishment, as she sat in the seat opposite Mary Jo.

'Is Glen going through a midlife crisis or something?' Jules asked.

'Yeah, I mean, this doesn't sound like the Glen we know at all,' Tish echoed.

'I wish it were just a midlife crisis,' Mary Jo sniffed. 'Glen stayed home from work this morning, said he would go in to the office later for some meetings. I did my usual morning stuff, made sure the kids got off to school and had what they needed for the day. When I got back home, Glen had made my favorite breakfast. Poached eggs on toast with smoked salmon. I thought he had taken the morning off so we could spend some time together. Just last weekend we'd discussed how, with this being Greg's last year of high school and with Kayla turning sixteen soon and needing us a bit less, we could take some time to go on dates again. I thought breakfast was Glen's way of saying he was looking forward to the next chapter in our lives, but instead . . .'

Mary Jo paused and extracted some tissues from a nearby box. As she blew her nose loudly, Celestine returned from the kitchen with a pitcher of lemonade and four glasses and proceeded to serve.

'It was after breakfast, when I was clearing the table, that Glen told me he had some news,' Mary Jo continued. 'He told me he'd been seeing someone else. Someone who made him feel young and exciting and alive again. Someone he wants to be with from now on. All the time. Forever.'

'Good Lord!' Jules exclaimed. 'What is wrong with that man?'

'Oh, I'm so sorry, Mary Jo.' Tish felt a lump form in her throat, but knew that crying alongside her friend wouldn't help matters.

'All those nights he said he was working!' Mary Jo's mood swiftly progressed from grief to anger. 'All those weekends he was "at the office" instead of being home with his family. All the business trips. It was all a lie. He was with her.'

'He lied about his work schedule? He actually admitted it?' Jules was horrified.

Mary Jo nodded. 'Yes, but only after I asked him, the coward.'

'Oh, just let me go to my car and grab the tire iron out of the trunk. I'm going to drive to Glen's office and whack him right in the knees.'

Tish kicked Jules beneath the table. 'Shh. You're not helping, Tonya Harding.'

Mary Jo laughed through her tears. 'No, it's OK. I thought of doing worse than that, but, in the end he's still Kayla and Gregory's father.'

'Speaking of which, do the kids know yet?'

'Gregory does. He came home for lunch while Glen and I were right in the middle of everything. Gregory completely lost it. He's furious at his father for breaking up our family, and although I did my best to defend Glen as a father, I can't defend or explain what he's done. Not to Gregory, not to anyone.'

'And Kayla? Does she know?'

Mary Jo shook her head. 'She went to her shift at Chick-fil-A right after school. She gets off at eight.'

'Well, we'll go meet her. Together.'

'All three of us,' Jules asserted. 'She and Gregory can always rely on their Uncle Jules and Auntie Tish.'

Tish nodded. 'Have you and Glen made plans for the house?'

'He's offered to let me and the kids stay there, but if I decide I don't want it, he's happy to stay there . . . with her.'

Jules's face flushed crimson. 'He wants to move that hussy into your house? The cad! The fiend! The blackguard! The rotter! The utter—' Beneath the blank stares of Celestine, Mary Jo, and Tish, Jules became self-conscious. 'Sorry, I've been watching the BBC to get some gin cocktail recipes.'

'And indulge in period dramas. You know,' Tish teased, 'if you hurry, you might catch Glen at his office so you can slap him across the face with your white glove and challenge him to a duel at daybreak.' The remark lightened the mood of the table considerably.

Jules thrust his tongue in Tish's direction, but everyone present at the café knew he never minded being the brunt of a joke, especially if it served to make a good friend smile during a difficult time. 'Only if you serve as my second.'

'Caterer by day, gun-for-hire at night? I'm thinking that might not be good for business.'

'Can't be any worse than someone dropping dead after eating your prime rib,' Jules reminded.

'Or someone being bludgeoned to death with a garden spade two days before *The Secret Garden* luncheon you're catering,' Tish added.

'What?' Celestine and Mary Jo cried in unison.

Tish briefly described the day's events.

'Girrrrrrl,' Celestine sang. 'What's with all these people dying around you? Mr Rufus has an aunt and uncle celebrating a sixtieth wedding anniversary this February and I'd love to have you do the food for their party, but I'm afraid if I hire you, it'll be the last anniversary they celebrate.'

Mary Jo pulled a face. 'Hmm, makes me want to throw a divorce party and hire Tish to cater it. You know, just to see what happens.'

'Better hold that party before the final papers are signed. That way you can still collect on his life insurance,' Celestine cackled before rising from her seat. 'And on that note, y'all, I'm going to mosey on home.'

'Oh, Celestine. I got so caught up in Mary Jo's news that I forgot you've been here all day,' Tish apologized. 'Please get home. And thank you. I'll put the extra time in your next check.'

'Nah, no need. Y'all are more like friends to me than co-workers. Besides, none of us are immune to heartbreak in our lives. Next time it may be me and I know y'all would do the same.'

Mary Jo stood up and, after depositing a wad of used tissues on the table, threw her arms around Celestine's plump torso. 'I don't know how to thank you.'

'You take care of yourself, that's how. And please know you're welcome at my house at any time. Your kids, too. I know your folks are out in California, but if Kayla and Gregory need some grand-smothering, as I call it, I'm always up to the challenge.'

'That's very kind of you. Kayla and I might take you up on that offer someday. As for Gregory, who knows . . .'

'Don't you worry now. You've gotta let that boy feel what he's feeling. He has a right to be angry and hurt. He'll figure it out eventually. When he's ready.'

'I hope you're right.'

'I know I am,' Celestine asserted with a reassuring smile and then went on to address Tish. 'So, what's the schedule for tomorrow? Want me to help with the café?'

'That would be lovely, but I don't want to overload you.' Tish was appreciative, but cautious. 'Wait. I think Charlotte Ballantyne is here visiting her dad for the weekend. We could call her in.'

'I'll stop by their house on my way home,' Celestine announced.

'No, no,' Mary Jo spoke up. 'There's no need for Celestine to be here. Or for you to call in Charlotte. I'm on the schedule for the day, so that Celestine can bake cakes for the luncheon.'

'It's fine, honey. I'm baking the cakes with my daughters and granddaughters tonight. Tomorrow, I'm piping on the icing. I'll have plenty of time to come and pitch in here.'

'That's too much work for you. And on top of you playing nursemaid to me today. No, I should be fine by myself.'

'Nothing doing. What if Kayla and Gregory need you? Or what if he-who-shall-not-be-named stops by to talk? Nope, you need some leeway and support in your life right now.'

Tish was in complete accord. 'Celestine's right. Neither of us doubts you can handle the work, but with everything going on, you don't need to be worrying about the café. You need to be looking after yourself and the kids. If working here for the day will help you get your mind off things, then, by all means, do it. But if, at any point, working here makes you feel tired, or uncomfortable, or worse, you need to be able to get out and take a walk or go upstairs for a nap. Besides, you know how Charlotte loves helping out here.'

'And to help take pressure off everybody,' Jules added, 'I'm available all weekend to help with the luncheon. I can meet you at Coleton Creek first thing, Tish.'

'Really? Are you sure? You're already helping with the bartending.'

'I know but, aside from assembling the garnishes, there's not much for me to do until Sunday morning. I can meet you at Coleton Creek and help you get a jump-start on Sunday – that way, there's less for you to do at the last minute.'

'That would be helpful,' Tish acknowledged. 'Thank you.'

'Yes, thanks Mr J,' Celestine said with a smile.

'Just one of the many services I offer.' He blew on the fingernails of his left hand and polished them on the collar of his linen shirt.

Celestine grabbed her oversized wicker purse and made her way to the door. 'Night, y'all. Try to get some sleep and I'll see ya tomorrow.'

Tish, Jules, and Mary Jo bade Celestine farewell and poured themselves another round of lemonade before re-entering into conversation. 'So, have you given any thought to your next move?' Tish asked Mary Jo.

Mary Jo ran a hand through her shoulder-length frosted brown hair with a sigh. 'Only that I should probably call an attorney on Monday.'

'I can ask Schuyler if he can recommend someone, if you'd like.'

'That would be great. I'm also thinking that I can't stomach facing Glen right now. It might sound foolish, but the thought of getting into things with him again makes me feel physically ill. Do you mind if I stay here with you for the weekend?'

'Of course not. And it's not foolish. You and the kids can stay here as long as you want.'

'I'm not sure about the kids. Gregory's staying with a friend tonight. Whether he'll be there all weekend, I don't know. I spoke to his friend's mother about Glen and me – she's going to keep an eye on things and report back to me.'

'That's very kind of her,' Jules noted.

Mary Jo nodded. 'Kayla doesn't know what's going on yet, so I can't say whether she'll be here or not. I hope she comes with me instead of staying with her dad at the house, but she needs to make that decision herself.'

'I totally agree,' Tish stated as she took a sip of lemonade. 'Just know that until things are sorted out, I want you all to feel as though this is your second home.'

'My place is open, too,' Jules invited. 'I don't have as much space in my apartment as Tish has upstairs, and I can't cook worth a damn, but if anyone wants to crash on my sofa or Netflix and chill with a pizza—'

'Or BBC and unwind with a cuppa,' Tish joked.

'*Mi casa es su casa.*'

'You guys are awesome.' Tears rolled down Mary Jo's cheeks. 'You know that, right?'

'Meh, we're OK. You're the one who's truly awesome. I can't count the number of times you've bailed me out of a jam,' Tish reflected.

'Tish might be modest, but I'm not,' Jules broadcast. 'You're dang skippy I'm awesome. Work hard at it, too.'

Mary Jo chuckled at Jules's lack of humility. 'You don't need to work too hard,' she said as she leaned over and placed a hand on his shoulder. 'Now, if you two don't mind, I think I'm going to go upstairs and lie down.'

'Absolutely. You can have your pick of my room or the guest bedroom,' Tish instructed.

'No, no. Guest bedroom is fine by me,' she stated as she trudged through the kitchen and up the stairs.

'We'll wake you for dinner,' Jules shouted after her.

'We? You're staying for dinner?' Tish quizzed.

'Staying? Heck, I'm ordering it for delivery. I was thinking the Thai place Mary Jo likes so much.'

'Ooh, good idea. Kayla loves the pad Thai from there, too. Maybe we can order a pint, just in case she comes back here?'

'Of course. In the meantime . . .' Jules wandered into the kitchen and reached into the cupboard alongside the sink. From it, he extracted a tall green bottle and held it aloft. 'It's wine o'clock.'

'I have a Pinot Grigio chilling in the fridge, too,' Tish offered.

'Nah. Murder and a divorce in the same day? It's a red night. How about you?'

'I still have some things to do for tomorrow, so white for me, please.'

Jules opened the refrigerator and collected the Pinot Grigio from the shelf in the door. 'What could you possibly need to do right now aside from sitting on the front porch and drinking a glass of wine with your friend after a grueling, terrible, horrible, no-good day?'

'Well, I suppose everything is on track for tomorrow, isn't it? I do have to call Schuyler, though, and get his thoughts on the Knoblochs and a good divorce attorney for Mary Jo.'

'Divorce attorney.' Jules grabbed two wine glasses from the cupboard nearest the sink. 'I can't believe it.'

'I know. It's surreal. Everything about Mary Jo – including her marriage – has been dependable and stable.'

'Only to have the rug suddenly pulled out from under her. Poor MJ. Mark you, I did say at their wedding that she and Glen would never last.'

'Never last? Their marriage lasted twenty years and produced two children. I'd say that's more successful than most,' Tish argued.

'And yet here we are. Makes you wonder if it wouldn't have been better to find out about Glen right at the start. Oh, speaking of start, when you call Schuyler, why don't you ask him to join us?' Jules suggested as he popped the cork from the chilled Pinot and poured it into one of the two glasses he had collected.

'That's thoughtful of you, Jules, but I think I need to focus on Mary Jo and Kayla tonight.'

'True. It is difficult to focus with those piercing blue eyes gazing back at you.' He presented Tish with her glass of wine. 'I'm jealous of y'all.'

Tish accepted her glass and, grabbing her phone from her handbag, stood up and wandered toward the porch door. 'Yes, you've intimated as much,' she smirked.

'No, I don't mean about Schuyler – although, by any standards, he's a hunk. I mean, I'm jealous of you and, yes, although it seems weird, Mary Jo.' Jules poured his glass of Malbec and carried it out of the kitchen and into the café, where Tish awaited. 'Y'all have had loves and losses and have moved on to other things, and I'm still just Jules.'

Tish led the way out to the porch and plopped on to the cushioned swing. 'Some might say you were smart for not wasting your time on the wrong person. You've placed your efforts into building the career and the life you want.'

'But some might also say my life has been safe and boring,' he volleyed as he perched on the porch rail alongside a vibrant red hibiscus plant.

'An aspiring news anchor and journalist who works as a television weatherman, moonlights as a bartender, and who, until a few weeks ago, had a disco ball in the trunk of his car could hardly be described as boring. And, for the record, you've never been and you never will be "just Jules."'

'I appreciate your kind words, but—'

'I knew there'd be a "but" in there,' she laughed and took a sip of wine.

'But I think I need to experience life a little more.' He took a large swig of his red wine and then sighed. 'Oh, that's better.'

'Well, you're doing a bit better financially, what with the new responsibilities at the TV station and your bartending work. How about some travel? There's nothing like exploring the world to broaden your mind and break you out of your routine.'

'I *have* always wanted to see Paris,' he thought aloud, 'but it will be a while before I've saved enough for that.'

'There's plenty of places you could visit on a long weekend,' Tish suggested.

Jules crinkled his nose. 'I've been put off road trips since that bus trip we took to Savannah.'

'Well, considering it was a single gay men's tour company, you might have had a better time had you gone alone.'

'What? And risk being assigned a roommate who snored or shed hair all over the shower? No, I loved having you as a roomie. And I think we made the best of the trip, even though that nasty coach driver wouldn't stop at The Lady and Sons restaurant.'

'It wasn't on the itinerary, Jules,' Tish sighed.

'Itinerary, i-shminerary. This is Paula Deen we're talking about here. Remember how I dressed up as her for Halloween one year?'

'How could I forget? By the end of the night, the sticks of butter you brought as part of your costume had melted all over my hardwood floors. I slid across the dining room while serving dessert and wound up with a sprained ankle.'

'Oh, that's right. The party was at your house, the first year you were married to Mitch, wasn't it?'

At the sound of her ex-husband's name, Tish felt her blood pressure rise and her eyes tilt ever so slightly toward the back of her head.

'Sorry,' Jules apologized. 'Anyway, the Lady and Sons incident was bad enough, but when the driver made me get rid of my Wet Willie's tequila sunrise slushie before getting back on the bus, that ended the trip for me.'

Tish was tempted to point out that a beverage made from 190-proof grain alcohol, even if presented in a child-friendly manner, was a flagrant violation of the bus company's zero-tolerance liquor policy, but she no longer possessed the energy for such pointless debate. 'Well, if you don't want to travel, what *do* you want to do?'

'I don't know just yet, but if Sloane Shackleford's murder and Mary Jo's separation have taught me anything, it's that the unexpected is always right around the corner. None of us know what lies in store. So, from this point forward, I'm going to live life with greater intensity and purpose. I'm going to embrace each day and live it as though it might be my last.'

'Life is, indeed, short and uncertain,' Tish quietly agreed.

Jules took a sip of wine and then placed his glass on the wicker table near Tish. 'Do you have a menu for that Thai place? I don't feel like straining my eyes looking at my phone.'

'It's in the kitchen. There's a binder of menus in the second drawer to the right of the sink. But don't you usually order the same thing?'

'Yes, but the first step in savoring life is branching beyond my usual order of phat si-io,' he announced and disappeared behind the screen door.

When he had gone, Tish took a sip of wine and repeated her friend's new mantra, 'Julian Jefferson Davis. Living life with greater intensity and purpose . . . Heaven help us all!'

SEVEN

Tish awoke on Saturday morning at six o'clock, a full thirty minutes prior to the sounding of her alarm clock.

It had been a late and restless night. Following a tasty Thai dinner that Mary Jo scarcely ate, Tish, Mary Jo, and Jules drove to the Chick-fil-A outside of town to collect Kayla from her after-school and weekend job and break the news of her parents' split.

Kayla's reaction was as expected: shock, tears, anger, and uncertainty for the future. The trio did their best to convince the fifteen-year-old that, although her family dynamic might be shifting, the love and support she had experienced in her short life was unwavering.

Unfortunately, Glen's absence during the discussion (when asked by Mary Jo if he would like to be present when informing Kayla of their separation, Glen claimed to be too busy catching up on the morning's paperwork) did little to convince Kayla of her father's continued affection and commitment to her care and wellbeing. It was, therefore, not surprising that Kayla opted to stay at Tish's apartment with her mother.

It was a tearful night that ended just before one in the morning, when Kayla had finally settled enough to eat some reheated pad Thai and then turn in to bed.

In the five hours since, Tish had tossed, turned, and sporadically snoozed, but never entered the kind of deep sleep that refreshed the senses. Opting to get out of bed rather than attempt a last-ditch grasp at slumber, she tiptoed to the spare bedroom, where Mary Jo and Kayla were snuggled together beneath the duvet, both fast asleep.

Quietly closing the guest bedroom door so as not to disturb them, Tish then padded to the bathroom where she took a quick shower, dried off, and applied her daily moisturizer before returning to her bedroom to dress for the day. After sliding into a pair of dark denim capris, a flowing black floral kimono-styled top, and a comfortable pair of hot-pink canvas sneakers, she made her way downstairs to brew a pot of coffee and enjoy a slice of seeded wholewheat toast with a smear of peach butter she and Schuyler had purchased from a Charlottesville farmers' market.

As Tish finished her second cup of coffee and set about getting the café in order for the day's business, Celestine let herself into the kitchen with her back-door key. 'Hey, lady,' she greeted.

'Hey, yourself. You're here early.' She grabbed an additional mug from the cupboard above the coffee maker and poured Celestine a cup.

'Thought you could use a hand with the morning baking.' She accepted the mug of coffee, to which Tish had added both sugar and half-and-half. 'Thanks, darlin'.'

'That's sweet of you, but aside from the biscuits, the baking is done. We were up late with Mary Jo and Kayla last night, so I figured . . .' She shrugged. 'Some people drink when stressed; I bake and cook.'

'So Kayla decided to stay here with her mama?'

'They're upstairs, sound asleep.'

'Probably need it, the poor darlin's. How are you holding up?'

'I'm fine. Focusing on people and tasks as they present themselves. How about you? You were here all afternoon with Mary Jo, then you baked the cakes last night, and now you're here early. You must be tired.'

'January nineteenth, 2003,' Celestine answered matter-of-factly.

'Huh? What's that?'

'The last time I slept more than five consecutive hours in one night.'

'You've had insomnia for over fifteen years?' Tish glanced at the steaming mug of coffee in Celestine's left hand. 'Did you try switching to decaf?'

'Honey, I've tried everything, but it's my darned hormones. I've given up caffeine, I've taken up green tea, I've replaced sweet tea with lemon water, I've tried those relaxation tapes. Nothing. I even tried to increase my soy intake by eating edamame beans. I made my old-fashioned layered salad – you know, the one with iceberg lettuce and topped with Miracle Whip – and stuck 'em in between the bacon and cheese layers, right where the peas should be. Didn't do a thing.'

Tish had called the state of Virginia home for over twenty years, but the Southern predilection for frying, pickling, or smothering otherwise deliciously fresh vegetables with mayonnaise still confounded her. Even Jules, despite his otherwise cosmopolitan tastes, had once argued that his mother's sour cream, cheese, and Ritz cracker squash casserole could be categorized as health food because it was a plant-based dish.

Not wishing to insult her friend and employee's deep culinary roots, Tish overlooked the method of preparation of Celestine's edamame and instead expressed her regret that her menu modifications had failed to produce a good night's sleep.

'Aw, it's OK. Nothing that thousands of other women haven't experienced since time immemorial. So, you gonna be OK at Coleton Creek today?'

'Yeah, Jules is meeting me there in an hour. So long as no one's bothered the patio overnight, I should be fine.' Tish described the trouble with the Knoblochs.

'Oh, that's all you need right now. Not enough you have a party to cater, a heartbroken friend to tend to, and a murder investigation right at your feet.'

'I know. Fortunately, I have Schuyler on alert. Should the Knoblochs try anything, I'll just give him a call and he should be able to sort it out quickly.'

'Handsome and handy. Nice to have a lawyer you can actually trust. Personally, I'd always hoped one of my girls would marry a doctor – you know, for all the free medical advice – but it wasn't in the cards. Still, my one son-in-law works for town maintenance, which has its own benefits. Why, just last week the streetlight at the end of our road went out. My son-in-law made a phone call to his boss and it was repaired within the hour. Normally, we'd have waited days.'

'It's always good to have connections,' Tish smiled before making her departure for Coleton Creek.

She arrived in the lifestyle-center parking lot approximately fifteen minutes later. Grabbing a bag containing several sets of potholders, a pair of Cookin' the Books aprons, and some favorite kitchen tools from the passenger seat of the Matrix, she stepped out of the driver's side door and on to the blacktop-paved lot only to be greeted by the sound of Lady Gaga's 'Bad Romance' blasting from the outdoor pool area.

It was an odd time for a pool party, Tish thought to herself. Deciding to explore the source of such early-morning frivolity, she approached the fenced area and let herself in through the gate.

As she stepped on to the brick-paved poolside patio area, she was completely unprepared for the scene that met her gaze. Approximately thirty women of varying shapes and sizes and skin and hair colors, all clad in swimsuits of every description, stood at the shallow end of a vast swimming pool, waving their arms, bending their legs, splashing in time with the music, and engaging in what was, evidently, a water aerobics class. This in itself would not have come as a surprise, except that the person leading the class was none other than Julian Jefferson Davis, wearing swim trunks and Ray Bans.

'OK, girls. Stretch your arms over your head as far as you can reach. Remember, you're caught in a bad romance and you need help. That's right. Good. Now, let's alternate bringing our hands to our foreheads in distress. First right. Then left. Now right, left, right. Very good. Now let's—'

Jules's instructions came to an abrupt halt as he spied Tish standing near the fence, her blond head framed by the archway of the gate behind her. 'Take five, ladies.' He immediately jumped out of the pool and disconnected his phone from a nearby boombox. 'What are you doing here?'

'I was about to ask you the same thing,' she stated as she glared over the top of her sunglasses.

'I got here bright and early to help you and happened upon these lovely ladies about to embark upon their weekly water aerobics class and thought I'd add a little spice to their routine.'

'And you just happened to bring your swimsuit?' she challenged.

'I thought, perhaps, we might be able to talk Susannah Hilton into letting us take a dip after all our prep work today.'

'Uh-huh.'

'You must be Tish,' greeted a woman from the front row of the water aerobics class. 'You're just as lovely as Jules described.'

'Oh, well, thank you,' Tish blushed.

The woman raised a hand to shield her mouth from Tish's view. 'You're right, Jules. She is a little uptight.'

Jules gave a brief nod toward the woman before officially ending the class. 'OK, ladies. That's enough for today. It was a good one.'

As the women exited the pool, Tish followed Jules into the lifestyle center as he toweled off. 'You know you're not allowed in the pool, Jules. It's for residents only.'

'Residents *and* their guests. I was just passing by when those ladies invited me to join them. When I saw just how slow-paced and sad their workout was, I couldn't help but add some sizzle.'

'I know you meant well, Jules, but what if one of those women had a heart condition? What if someone slipped in the pool and injured herself? We might have been sued.'

He pulled a turquoise T-shirt from his gym bag and yanked it over his head. 'Well, if Coleton Creek want to protect their residents, they should provide them with an actual water aerobics instructor. Those gals organized that whole exercise class themselves.'

Before Tish could respond, a group of water aerobics students entered the lifestyle center singing 'Bad Romance.' At the top of her lungs, one of them cried out about being a bitch, baby, at which the rest of the group broke out in hysterics.

When the women had disappeared down an adjacent corridor, Tish turned to Jules. 'Look what you've done. That's someone's grandmother.'

'Sorry, but you can't get your heart rate up exercising to Barbra, and my entire Kylie Minogue catalog seems to be missing. I swear, if I find out someone at the newsroom deleted Queen Kylie from my phone . . .'

'I wasn't criticizing your music selection, Jules. I was just noting that you're usually not this careless.'

'I was not careless. I was simply sucking the marrow out of the bone of life.'

'OK,' Tish sighed, realizing that Jules was on yet another crusade of self-realization. 'Maybe I'm being too harsh. Many of these people do seem lonely and I'm sure you're like a breath of fresh air to them. However, right now we have a job to do, so can you refrain from sucking marrow while we prep for tomorrow? I promise, if you get hungry, I'll make you a ham sandwich.'

'Deal. In other news, I peeked through the door to the patio before class started and everything seemed to be in order.'

'Really?' Tish hurried down the corridor to see for herself. 'Wait a minute, I thought you said you happened to be "passing by" those women in the pool?'

'Did I?' Jules emitted a nervous giggle.

'Jules, I really—'

'Hey, how are things?' came a familiar voice from behind Tish.

She spun around to see Schuyler Thompson, freshly shaven, and looking positively delectable in a blue-and-white chambray shirt and jeans. 'Schuyler,' she greeted him with a hug and a quick kiss on the lips. 'What are you doing here? Not that I don't want you here, but I just didn't expect you to show up while I'm about to work.'

'Whoa, whoa,' Schuyler urged with a broad grin. 'Whoa there. Slow down.'

'Sorry,' Tish breathed heavily. 'There's quite a bit going on at the moment.'

'I know. That's why I'm here to help you. Well, and also to make sure the property managers didn't give you any grief today.'

'I haven't seen them yet,' Tish remarked.

'But everything we set up yesterday seems fine,' Jules added.

'Good,' Schuyler deemed. 'I actually put in a call to Reade after I spoke with you, Tish. I thought he should know about the Knoblochs' odd behavior, especially since their desire to shut down the garden club competition could be a motive for murder. While I had him on the line, I mentioned we thought they might try to sabotage the event. Reade had his officers include this place on their patrol last night.'

'Wow. Nice work,' Tish praised. 'I'm sorry I didn't think of calling Reade myself.'

'You have a lot on your mind. Speaking of which, how are Mary Jo and the kids?'

'Gregory called last night. He's hanging in there. Mary Jo and Kayla were asleep when I left this morning. Celestine's keeping tabs on them today.'

'Then they're in good hands. Look, if it's OK with you, I'm going to suggest I take care of dinner tonight. We can go out or, if Mary Jo's not up to it, we can get some Italian from that place in Ashland. I'm fine with anything, just as long as you're not adding dinner to your existing duties.'

'That would be lovely,' Tish smiled. 'Thank you.'

'No problem. Tell Mary Jo to call Gregory. And if he and Kayla each want to invite a friend, that's fine. Oh, it should go without saying, you're included in that invitation too, Jules.'

'Aww, thanks, Sky. I should be able to join y'all for a little while but I may have to leave early. I promised Mrs Newman I'd pop by her place for a little Mahjong with the girls. She needed a fourth player so I volunteered.'

'I didn't know you played Mahjong,' Tish said with a note of surprise in her voice.

'I don't. They're going to whip up a pitcher of Mai Tais and teach me.'

'Who's Mrs Newman?' a confused Schuyler asked.

'One of the ladies here at Coleton Creek. Jules just taught a water aerobics class this morning.'

'Mrs Newman was in the front row. The one who said you were "lovely,"' Jules described.

'And "uptight,"' she reminded.

Jules immediately colored. 'You showed up at just the right time, Schuyler.'

On this point, Tish could not argue. 'You really did.'

Schuyler remained humble. 'Just trying to help. I know how worried you both are about Mary Jo and her family. I've never gone through a divorce, but I know, first hand, how it is to not have a father present all the time. Those kids need to know that they're supported. To that end, Glen's invited to our dinner too, if he wants to come. He is Gregory and Kayla's dad, after all.'

'I'll run that past Mary Jo, but I think she needs a little more time before she can bear facing Glen at a family-style supper. Still, I'll mention it to her. Thanks.'

'Of course.'

'No, I mean it. Thank you for being so wonderful.' Tish leaned forward and bestowed upon Schuyler a far less chaste kiss than the one she had given him earlier.

'My pleasure,' he smirked when she had finished. He then caught sight of Jules beaming at them. Awkwardly clearing his throat, he asked, 'Shall we go check on the patio before getting to work in the kitchen?'

Tish nodded and led the way down the hall. Jules, his gym bag in tow, sidled up alongside of her and whispered, in a sarcastic tone, 'Oh, no, Schuyler Thompson is *totes* not your boyfriend.'

EIGHT

As the lifestyle-center kitchen filled with the aroma of baking scones, Schuyler chopped mango for the Coronation chicken salad, Jules set about peeling and deveining several pounds of shrimp for the cocktail of prawns and Marie Rose sauce, and Tish, with a mindful eye on the oven, set about mixing the spicy pork filling for the sausage rolls.

Feeling the stress of the past few hours melt away, Tish contentedly chopped an onion and then several cloves of garlic into the bowl of a food processor. She was always astonished at how quickly the act of cooking set both her heart and mind at ease.

After roughly tearing some fresh sage leaves and adding them to the onion and garlic, Tish moved to the refrigerator to retrieve the package of organic sausage meat she had ordered from a local butcher. When she returned to her station, she spotted Orson Baggett standing in the kitchen door.

'Good morning, Mr Baggett,' she welcomed, noting that the man was wearing a similar outfit to the one he had been sporting the day before, only today his tie was yellow and featured a repeating pattern of red and blue feathers that floated against the bright backdrop as if shed by a passing bird.

Baggett removed the straw fedora from his head. 'Mornin'. I'm not interrupting, am I?'

'Not at all. Come on in.'

'Be careful, though,' Schuyler warned. 'She might put you to work.'

Tish introduced Orson to Schuyler.

'Pleased to meet you, sir,' Schuyler greeted.

'Likewise.' Baggett approached the counter at which Tish was working with a smile. 'I brought over that produce you had your eye on yesterday.'

'How sweet of you,' Tish declared, 'but you didn't need to do that. I thought we agreed you should keep it in the garden until the judging was finished.'

'Yes.' Baggett pulled three lusciously green heads of Cos lettuce from a reusable canvas shopping bag and plopped them on to the counter. 'But that was while Sloane Shackleford was still in the running.'

The lettuces and the dozen or so tomatoes that tumbled on to the counter behind them were some of the finest-looking heirloom produce Tish had seen in a long time, but Baggett's remark about Shackleford no longer being in the competition left her feeling somewhat loath to accept them. 'So, you're confident you're going to win the top prize?'

'I wouldn't say confident. The race will be close as cat's breath, but I believe I might just squeak it out.'

'I would think having Shackleford around would have driven everyone to make their gardens better.'

'We did make them better,' Baggett snapped. 'But Ainsley was blind in one eye and couldn't see straight out the other when it came to Sloane Shackleford. The man let his dog wander town and destroy our plants, and Ainsley did nothing about it. Then there's that whole nonsense about Shackleford personally designing his garden. You're going to tell me a retired insurance salesman designed that ritzy set-up he had there? Hogwash.'

Tish conceded that Shackleford's garden was a rather sophisticated piece of landscape design. 'Mr Ainsley said the plans Shackleford provided appeared to be genuine.'

'Of course they did. Man was a grifter. Can't trust anyone who makes their money off selling insurance.' Like a true Southerner, Baggett pronounced the word as *en*-surance. 'He was a real masher, too. Grabbin' them one minute and treatin' them like trash the next. Why, he drove poor Susannah Hilton to distraction.'

'Susannah?'

'Yes. He was always pawing at her, and when she finally told him to stop, well, he became nasty. Made it his personal vendetta to upset that poor girl. Why, he was always on her about the pools being dirty, or the grass outside not being mowed, or that she didn't answer the phone quick enough.'

It was becoming abundantly clear to Tish that Orson Baggett's visit was less about delivering produce than it was about ensuring Shackleford's untimely death didn't afford him martyr status. If, in the process, Baggett happened to divert suspicion away from himself, that was just an added benefit.

'Did Susannah complain to the property managers?' Schuyler asked.

'What, the Knoblochs? Heck, no, those two ain't worth two cents.'

Tish reflected upon their arrival yesterday morning. Was Sloane Shackleford the resident with whom Susannah experienced so much difficulty? If so, it gave her quite a motive for wanting him dead.

'Poor Ms Morris,' Baggett continued with a heavy sigh. 'Living next door to such a villain. And now a murder's been committed practically in her own backyard.'

'Don't forget about Wren Harper,' Tish reminded. 'Her property neighbors Shackleford's as well.'

'Oh, yeah, Wren, too,' he answered absently. 'She's on her own now, isn't she? Poor woman. But, well, if you haven't guessed, I'm kinda sweet on Ms Morris.'

'So Jim Ainsley was telling the truth yesterday,' Jules smirked.

'He was. Ms Morris and I have been enjoying each other's companionship. But try not to let it get around too much, will y'all? There's some in this town who can be a hair more than catty.'

'Of course,' Tish agreed. 'Although you should probably discuss your concerns about Ms Morris with the police, don't you think?'

'No, I don't think. There's a big difference between worrying over Zadie' – in his annoyance, Baggett suddenly did away with any formalities – 'and killing a man.'

'I wasn't suggesting you killed anyone, Mr Baggett,' Tish prefaced, although Baggett certainly wasn't short on motives, 'but if Shackleford had a history of harassing women, that opens up a whole new set of suspects and circumstances that the police need to examine.'

'It's up to Ms Hilton and those women to say something, not me.'

'But you just said you were concerned about Ms Morris living next door to Shackleford because of the way he treated women. I think that information should be shared, don't you?'

'I don't know about that.' Baggett stared at a spot on the countertop. 'Many of the women round here seemed to enjoy flirting with Shackleford.'

'Meaning?'

'Meaning, I'm not set to raise a fuss over two consenting adults acting like the tomcat's kitten.'

Tish narrowed her eyes. 'Mr Baggett, are you sure you weren't simply jealous of Mr Shackleford?'

Baggett looked up from the countertop at Tish, his eyes flashing with anger. 'Jealous? Of a cad like Sloane Shackleford? Never.'

'So you weren't afraid that Ms Morris might, like the other women you mentioned, enjoy Mr Shackleford's attentions?'

'No. Never. I mean, Zadie is a gorgeous woman. And kind. A real gem. She's definitely someone Shackleford would have gone for, but she wouldn't have put up with his manhandling or manufactured charm. She told me she'd known a man like Shackleford in the past and she had absolutely no desire to socialize with his sort ever again.'

'Ms Morris might not have wanted to socialize with Mr Shackleford, but that doesn't mean he didn't try to socialize with her,' Tish said as delicately as possible.

'I understand what you're getting at, but you don't know my Zadie. She's like a diamond – beautiful, but tough. If that swine had said or done anything off color, she'd have put him in his place. My Zadie has sass and class, unlike some other women here at Coleton Creek who fought over Shackleford like two mules fighting over a turnip.'

'But still you were worried,' Tish noted.

'Yes, I was worried. I didn't trust Sloane Shackleford. I just plain ol' didn't trust him. I had good reason too, but you might want to ask Jim Ainsley about that,' he quipped as he gathered up his reusable bag.

'Ask me about what?' Ainsley, as if by magic, had materialized in the kitchen doorway, looking dapper in a white dress shirt, white trousers, and a gray pinstriped blazer.

'Oh, Ms Tarragon had some questions.' Baggett was intentionally vague. 'I see you're wearing your judging outfit.'

'Yes. Less than two hours to go. We'll be starting at Wren Harper's, as usual, and working our way through the neighborhood.'

'I'll be ready and waiting,' Baggett assured, placing his fedora back on his head at a jaunty angle.

'Oh, Mr Baggett,' Tish spoke up before the man could make his leave. 'What do I owe you for the produce?'

'Not a cent. Just make sure to give me credit in the dish.'

'Will do and thank you.'

Baggett leaned toward Ainsley so that their faces were mere inches apart. 'I can't wait to see everyone's reactions when they bite into the lettuce and tomatoes raised by the winner of the competition. Won't that be a scream? Ha!'

With a tip of his hat, Orson Baggett marched out of the kitchen, still chuckling over his imminent success.

'Honestly, that man,' Ainsley grumbled. 'I hope he wasn't too much of a nuisance.'

'Not at all,' Tish replied.

'Good. I stopped by to see how you were getting on and whether you needed anything.' Ainsley flashed a sly smile. 'I was also wondering if there might be a chance of sampling a sausage roll.'

Tish laughed and wandered over to the oven. 'Sausage rolls won't be ready until this afternoon, but the scones are done. I can fix you one with clotted cream and jam, if you'd like.'

'That sounds like a mighty agreeable substitute.'

Tish grabbed an oven mitt and went about pulling the two baking sheets of scones from the oven and stacking them on a rolling rack with the others. 'So, going back to your first question, everything is moving along well. However, I did have a bit of a run-in with Nathan and Mariette Knobloch yesterday afternoon.'

'Really? What were they doing here?'

'Simply put, they were here to stop the luncheon.' Tish removed a cooled scone from one of the lower tiers of the rolling rack and placed it on a plate.

'Really? Why?'

Tish split the scone in half and wandered to the refrigerator. 'They claim the garden competition is responsible for Mr Shackleford's death.'

'That's ludicrous. What did you tell them?'

'I told them that I was hired by the garden club and, as such, they would need to talk to you if they wanted to stop the luncheon.' Tish, having fetched a container of clotted cream and a jar of her homemade strawberry preserve from the refrigerator, placed a dollop of each on the plate, added a knife for spreading, and presented it to Ainsley.

'Ooh,' he moaned as he sniffed the still-warm scone. 'Well, the Knoblochs didn't say "boo" to me. I was in all evening. My phone never rang and no one came knocking at my door.'

'Strange, because they seemed to be dead set on cancelling the competition and shutting down the garden club. I even thought they'd come back at night and tear down the decorations I put on the patio.'

'Yeah, I called Sheriff Reade to have his officers keep an eye on the place,' Schuyler corroborated.

Ainsley spread some cream and jam on a half of scone and sunk his teeth into it. 'Mmm,' he moaned once again. 'Scrumptious. Simply scrumptious.'

'Thank you. So, even though the Knoblochs didn't contact you last night, you must have known about their disapproval of the garden club.'

Ainsley chomped on a large bite of scone, sending crumbs cascading down the front of his shirt. When he had swallowed the mouthful, he spoke. 'I'd heard some rumblings indicating that Mariette and Nathan weren't fans of the garden club or our annual competition, but they themselves never once spoke to me directly. Their communication with you is the first time they've openly tried to stop our event. Not that I'm too surprised by that either. The Knoblochs were never in favor of the residents having gardens in the first place.'

He popped another bit of scone into his mouth and licked his fingers.

Tish moved to the other end of the counter and prepared to roll out the pastry casing for the sausage mixture. 'If the Knoblochs weren't in favor of residents having their own gardens, then why is it permitted? This is their development. They set the rules, don't they?'

'To a point. Any regulations the Knoblochs propose are subject to the approval of the Coleton Creek Homeowners' Association. The development actually started out with a non-garden clause in the bylaws – imposed, of course, by the Knoblochs – but as the community grew and developer-appointed board members were slowly phased out and replaced with members of the community, the mandate came into question. The board voted unanimously to reverse the non-garden clause. The Knoblochs immediately tried to overturn the ruling, but to no avail.' Ainsley punctuated this statement by taking another bite of scone and cream.

'What about the garden club and competition? Did the Knoblochs propose a regulation to outlaw them?'

Ainsley replied in the negative. 'Like I said, all I've ever heard are rumblings and rumors. And even those didn't start until a few months ago.'

Tish glanced at Jules, who raised a questioning eyebrow. The Knoblochs claimed that Shackleford's murder had spurred them to take action against the garden club, but Ainsley's words suggested they had been trying to undermine the club for several weeks. 'Can you think of what might have provoked the Knoblochs' disapproval?'

Having finished his scone, Ainsley wiped his mouth with a paper napkin and disposed of it on his empty plate. 'I can only speculate, of course, but I think it was Biscuit.'

'Biscuit?' Tish retrieved her favorite rolling pin from her bag of tools. 'The dog?'

'Again, I'm guessing, but I've gotten the distinct impression that the Knoblochs had been fielding several complaints about Sloane Shackleford and how his dog was turning contestants' lawns and gardens yellow.'

'I thought contestants complained to you about Biscuit,' Tish stated, recalling Orson Baggett's account of Biscuit's late-night travels.

'They did. And I, due to their complaints, spoke to Shackleford on their behalf. But when Biscuit was still seen marauding, some folks went over my head.'

'I know Orson was furious that you didn't toss Shackleford out of the club,' Tish remarked as she dusted the counter with flour.

'I know he was. But how could I? There was no proof Shackleford set Biscuit loose with a command to destroy other gardeners' properties. What folks don't realize is that Shackleford's garden was compromised just as much as anyone else's – perhaps more so. Just back in July, Shackleford had some yellow patches dug up from his lawn and replaced with sod.'

Tish stopped in her tracks. 'Shackleford's garden had yellowing problems, too?'

Ainsley nodded. 'Shackleford was convinced something other than Biscuit was at the root of the problem.'

'Did he mention what he thought it might be?' Tish returned her attention to the pastry.

'No. Shackleford wasn't much of a conversationalist, unless he happened to be the central subject of discussion.' Ainsley watched as she shaped the dough into a loose rectangle. 'That sure looks buttery.'

'It is.' Tish realized that as long as Jim Ainsley was eating, he'd be happy to keep on talking. 'Would you like some mango, Mr Ainsley? I'm using it in a chutney for the Coronation chicken salad, but we can spare a small cup of it for you.'

'Really? That would be excellent.'

Tish approached Schuyler's work area and scooped a handful of the gloriously orange pulp into a small ramekin, which she presented, with a fork, to a delighted Ainsley.

'So, with Shackleford no longer in the competition, Orson Baggett seems confident he's going to take the garden-of-the-year prize. Is he really the favorite to win this weekend?'

'I wouldn't call him the favorite, but he's certainly in close contention for top prize. Wren Harper's garden will probably score high for overall design. And the Abercrombies will take top rank as the most colorful. However, judges will probably award Orson extra points for his heirloom plant varieties and for recreating a historic colonial garden. All in all, it will be a very tight race.'

'Much tighter now that Mr Shackleford is no longer in the competition?'

'Yes,' Ainsley begrudgingly admitted as he slurped down a chunk of mango. 'Look, I see what you're getting at, Ms Tarragon, but I don't think a gardener killed Sloane Shackleford. Gardeners start life from seed and nurture plants to grow. They don't hack a life down for some foolish trophy.'

'Even if they believe that trophy has been won by treachery and deception?'

'Even if that trophy was won by treachery and deception for five years straight.' Ainsley thrust his hands into the pockets of his striped blazer and stared down at the floor. 'No, if you're looking for Shackleford's killer, you're better off looking at the unsavory elements of his life.'

'Such as?' Tish asked, although she was fairly certain she already knew the answer.

'Among other things, the endless parade of women entering and exiting his bedroom door.'

'From what I hear, Shackleford was single and the women were willing,' Jules offered. 'Not sure we should pass judgment.'

Ainsley looked up. 'I'm not judging Sloane Shackleford for his lifestyle, Mr Davis. I'm objecting to the collateral damage that lifestyle left in its wake. The women Shackleford used for profit, for sex, even his daily meals, and then discarded as if they were meaningless, worthless entities.'

A long, dark silence drew over the kitchen as Schuyler, Jules, and Tish focused on their individual tasks.

Ainsley, meanwhile, collected himself. 'I apologize for my outburst, Ms Tarragon. I just . . .'

'It's OK,' Tish excused. 'Between the murder and the competition, emotions are running high right now.'

'There's that, but I might as well tell you as you'll eventually hear about it from someone else. One of Shackleford's "conquests" was a lady friend of mine.'

Tish's mouth formed a tiny 'o.' She had learned of Ainsley's relationship with Pepper Aviero straight from the lady herself, but it would interesting to get his take on things.

'Pepper and I had been seeing each other for almost a year. It wasn't a serious relationship by youthful standards. There was no talk of marriage or moving in with each other. We both enjoyed our own homes and valued our independence, but we met on a regular basis for dinners, walks, movies, conversation.' He smiled wistfully. 'It was all about caring and companionship. Or, at least

I thought it was.' Ainsley's smile faded. 'Pepper started to cancel dates at the last minute. The first time it happened, she claimed she was ill. I offered to bring her soup at her home and to pick up whatever medication she might need from the store. She refused – said she just needed a good night's sleep. I respected her wishes and didn't think much of it until a week later, when she delayed our dinner date by nearly two hours. When I asked her why she needed to move the time, she said she was busy with children and grandchildren. What had occurred to make her so much busier than usual, she could not say. This pattern of behavior went on for several weeks. Pepper was unavailable to meet certain days of the week, whereas previously she'd been free. And when we did manage to make plans, she would arrive late or she'd reschedule entirely. Whenever I'd try to talk to her about it, she claimed that things were the same as they always were and I was being paranoid or insecure.

'Shortly after Ben Harper's funeral, I paid a visit to Wren. I wanted to see how she was getting along and whether there was anything I could do to help. I also wanted to convince her to focus on her garden as I felt it could serve as therapy. I was pleased to hear that Wren was, of course, continuing her garden and had ordered several bags of manure from the nursery. Only problem was the nursery had delivered the manure in fifty-pound sacks, which she couldn't lift. Happy to have found some small way to help, I went out and moved the bags from the driveway, where they had been dropped, and spent several hours working with Wren to rake the manure on to the grounds. We were halfway through the spreading when I glanced over the fence to see Pepper exiting the back door of Shackleford's house. He was standing in the doorway in his bathrobe and she gave him a kiss before sneaking off through the hedges.'

'I'm so sorry,' Tish sympathized.

'I'm over it now.' Ainsley raised his shoulders as if to divest himself of the ugly affair. 'That evening, I broke things off with Pepper. I didn't tell her I'd seen her at Shackleford's. Didn't see the point really. She'd only make excuses or tell me I was imagining things. Nor did I ask what I had or hadn't done to push her into another man's arms. Most likely out of fear she'd give me an honest answer.

'And so,' he went on, 'we parted ways. Well, as far apart as two people can be in a tightknit community like this. I did, however, break the news about Shackleford to her yesterday. I didn't want her finding out from the police or the Coleton Creek rumor mill. For some reason, I felt I owed her a little bit of compassion. When I spoke to her, she told me Shackleford had done to her what he'd done to dozens – if not scores – of other women. He threw her over for someone else.'

'Karma,' Jules commented and flung a peeled, deveined shrimp into a chilled bowl with added verve.

'There was a time when I would have shared that viewpoint. But right now I feel sorry for her. Pepper threw away what we had – something that I thought was sweet and good – for a man who tossed her aside at the first opportunity. She should have been smarter than that. She *is* smarter than that.

'As president of the garden club, I try to remain above the fray of neighborhood affairs. I try not to allow my personal thoughts and feelings to interfere with our competition or how the club is run,' Ainsley explained. 'As such, I pleaded with our members to keep a cool head and to give Sloane Shackleford the benefit of the doubt. But beneath it all, I've always thought he was a monster, a manipulator, a megalomaniac. Being done in with a garden spade is far better than the man deserved. Far better.'

NINE

'Nice job not interrogating Mr Ainsley,' Schuyler remarked, shortly after Ainsley had left the kitchen for his judging duties.

'See?' Jules pointed his shrimp-deveining knife in Tish's direction. 'Even your boyfriend thinks you're on the case.'

'He's—' Tish was about to shout that Schuyler wasn't her boyfriend, but then noticed the ecstatic grin that had crept steadily across the attorney's visage. 'I'm not on the case.'

'Is that why you questioned Orson Baggett, too?'

Schuyler tossed the last of the chopped mango into a bowl and presented it to Tish. '"Questioned" is putting it mildly. What I saw was more like grilling. It reminded me of when we learned how to cross-examine witnesses back in law school.'

'I didn't question or grill anyone.' Tish punctuated the statement by shoving a tray of sausage rolls into the oven and slamming the door shut behind them. 'I'm a cook. I nurture people and, therefore, they open up to me. It's similar to people chatting to a bartender, except the people who share their stories with me spew crumbs rather than slur their words.'

'Spewing aside, don't you think you ought to check in with Clemson Reade and tell him what you've learned?' Schuyler asked.

'No, the sheriff is quite capable of running his own investigation. Besides, he's probably already unearthed everything I know.'

'Are you kidding?' Jules exclaimed. 'Baggett hated Shackleford because he won the competition and might have tried to steal his girl. Ainsley hated Shackleford because he stole his girl and dumped her. Pepper Aviero hated Shackleford because she was charmed and then dumped. Susannah Hilton hated Shackleford because she dissed him and he harassed her—'

'According to Orson Baggett,' Tish clarified. 'We don't know that as a fact.'

'Whatevs. That's some serious information to acquire in just a few hours.'

'If you add in the wandering dog and Shackleford's history of abusing women, I'd say you've come up with a motive for practically everyone in this development,' Schuyler rejoined.

'But if I go to Reade with all that information, he's going to think I'm on the case,' Tish disputed.

'You *are* on the case,' Schuyler and Jules shouted in unison.

'I'm not. All I want to do this weekend is serve a successful luncheon, get my check from Mr Ainsley, run my café, and console the friend who's taken up residence in my spare bedroom. But if you both insist I speak with Sheriff Reade, I will.'

'Good,' Schuyler approved.

'Those sausage rolls take thirty minutes to bake,' Tish directed. 'I should be back before they're done, but if I'm not, could you take them out and put in the next tray?'

'Sure. Anything else?'

'We have lots of lettuce to wash. How are you with a salad spinner?'

'The last time I used a salad spinner was in 1984 in my mother's kitchen. I put my *Star Wars* and G.I. Joe action figures in it, gave it a spin, and transported them to an alternate universe.'

'Ah, well, if you could try to keep our salad greens here at Coleton Creek and in the present day, I'd appreciate it.'

'I'll do my best, but if a time portal happens to open up before I can hit the brake, I can't be held accountable,' he grinned.

'Duly noted,' Tish replied with a smile.

'Y'all need to get a room and geek out in private,' Jules complained. 'Seriously. Take some quiet time alone to watch your *Doctor Who* and *Quantum Leap* and *The Big Boom Theory*.'

'*Bang*,' Schuyler corrected.

'See?'

'We'll be sure to sign up for a joint Netflix account first thing in the morning,' Tish deadpanned before exiting the kitchen and hastening down the corridor toward the main entrance of the lifestyle center. She passed the reception area just as Susannah Hilton was settling in for the day's work.

'Good morning, Susannah.'

'Morning, Tish. Just the woman I wanted to see.' Susannah's voice was breathless.

'Oh?' Tish stopped in her tracks and leaned her elbows on the tall countertop that served as Susannah's desk.

'Yes, is everything OK for you this morning? Kitchen functioning all right? Do you have everything you need?'

'Yes, everything's buzzing right along. Thank you.'

'And you don't need another set of hands for anything?'

'No, I actually have a set of hands I hadn't initially counted on, so we're in good shape.'

'Are you sure? Because I have a light workload today and I'm sure you must be super busy, what with both the luncheon and the whole Shackleford thing.' At the word 'thing,' Susannah's voice lowered and she visibly cringed.

'Oh, I'm not working on the Shackleford case. All my time is devoted to the luncheon.'

'You're not on the case?'

'No, the police are perfectly capable of handling things on their own,' Tish explained.

'Oh.' Susannah stepped out from behind her desk, her face registering disappointment. 'Well, may I come back and see what progress you've made with the food? In case the garden club members come by to ask, I want to be able to answer them. Some of them can be awfully nosy.'

'Of course, but can it wait a few minutes? I'm just off to meet with Sheriff Reade to discuss a few things. After that I'll be back to cooking.'

Susannah's eyes narrowed. 'So you *are* on the case?'

'No, I just have some information to give to the sheriff. That's all.' Tish frowned as she realized just how ridiculous her statement sounded.

Susannah grasped Tish's upper arm and whispered, in a furtive manner, 'May I speak with you first?'

Tish, albeit confused, agreed. 'Sure. What's going on?'

'I . . .' Susannah nervously smoothed the skirt of her sage-green sundress and cast an eye heavenward as if searching for the right words. 'I should probably talk to the sheriff directly, but I haven't told my story to anyone before and I'd feel more comfortable confiding in you first. As a woman.'

'OK.'

'The resident who was giving me such a difficult time yesterday, the one who had me completely flustered when you and Julian arrived? It was Sloane Shackleford.'

Tish feigned surprise. 'Oh, how terrible. I'm so sorry.'

'Not as sorry as I am.'

'What happened?'

'What always happened when Mr Shackleford came to the lifestyle center.' Susannah covered her eyes with her hands. 'I can't believe I let the whole thing go on for so long. But, then again, what was I to do?'

Tish patted the woman on the shoulder while urging her to continue. 'Shh. There's no sense in looking back. Just tell me what happened.'

'It was my first day working here when Mr Shackleford came in to introduce himself. He brought me a bouquet of flowers – daisies – to welcome me to Coleton Creek and told me if I needed to know anything about the residents or the facilities, I should ask him because he knew everything there was to know about the place. I thought he was sweet, if perhaps a bit too presumptuous for my liking. However, I wrote that off as a generational issue, and still viewed his behavior as being motivated by kindness.'

'And that changed?' Tish presumed.

Susannah nodded. 'Deteriorated is more like it. Deteriorated rapidly.'

A Coleton Creek resident wearing a swimsuit and flip-flops entered through the glass doors. Susannah pasted on a sunny smile of welcome. 'Good morning.'

The female resident gave a wave and continued on her way to the indoor pool. Only when she was safely ensconced behind the insulated door did Susannah continue to recount her tale. 'Less than a week later, Mr Shackleford stopped by and asked if he could take me out for lunch. I declined, explaining that, as a Coleton Creek employee, I was not supposed to venture off the premises with residents.

'Mr Shackleford backed off for a few days,' Susannah went on, 'only to come back with an Indian lunch for two he had had delivered to the lifestyle center. Seeing as the food was already here and I wouldn't be, technically, breaking policy, I ate the meal with him, but afterward stipulated that the situation could not occur again as the nature of our relationship might be misconstrued by other residents. That's when he put his hands on my waist and pulled me close to him. He was crazed. He told me that he found me beautiful, sexy, and how he just had to have me. Then he tried to kiss me. I pushed him away and told him, in no uncertain terms, that I did not wish to be alone with him again. To say I was completely repulsed by the incident would be putting it lightly,' Susannah explained as she blinked back tears.

'He assaulted you. You could have called the police on him.'

'No. I wasn't sure the Knoblochs would believe me. Plus, I felt too ashamed for having been in that situation in the first place. I'd only been working at Coleton Creek a short time and here I was, allowing a resident to serve me lunch. Stupid.'

'You were trying to be kind,' Tish excused. 'You'd only just met Shackleford. You gave him the benefit of the doubt.'

'I'm sorry I did. From that day forward, Sloane Shackleford

endeavored to make my life here at Coleton Creek a living hell. No matter how petty or trivial, the slightest variance here at the lifestyle center or elsewhere on the grounds became the cause for an onslaught of abusive complaints. A leaf floating in the outdoor pool hours after the pool technicians cleaned it, the Jacuzzi tub motor still running because the last person who used it forgot to switch it off, the television remote in the gym gone missing – most likely because someone had put it in their gym bag by mistake. All of these minor incidents resulted in Sloane Shackleford berating me and threatening to have my job taken away.'

'Did you tell the Knoblochs about Shackleford's harassment?'

'No. I wasn't sure how'd they'd react and I didn't want to be fired. Aside from Mr Shackleford's abuse, I love my job. I enjoy helping the residents here to lead a more fulfilling life. And, most of the time, I could even get through Mr Shackleford's behavior without too much of a meltdown.'

'And yesterday morning?' Tish prompted.

Susannah cast a watchful eye over her surroundings before answering. 'Yesterday morning I called Mr Shackleford to notify him that his appointment with Mr and Mrs Knobloch that afternoon was cancelled. Well, he was livid. Absolutely livid. Typically, he'd wait until I was alone before verbally attacking me. Yesterday, after my call, he marched straight down here and instantly began shouting at me in front of some of the members of the craft club. He called me such vulgar names and was so completely incensed that I nearly called the police. I only hesitated to do so because the garden competition was this weekend and I was afraid it might cast a shadow over the event. Fortunately, two of our male residents were playing bocce on the lawn and overheard Mr Shackleford's outburst. They came in and talked him into going back home.'

'So you're saying Shackleford was irate because the Knoblochs cancelled their meeting?'

Susannah's hazel eyes grew large. 'Irate? Oh, he went through the roof. There was absolutely no reasoning with him.'

'Do you know what the meeting was about?'

'No idea. Mr and Mrs Knobloch don't typically involve me in their business matters. They have an assistant who handles their appointments and paperwork. I was only asked to make the call to Mr Shackleford because the situation involved a Coleton Creek resident. I can, however, tell you that their last meeting didn't end well.'

'So if the meeting had occurred, would it have been the second one to transpire between Shackleford and the Knoblochs? Or have there been more?'

'No, it would have been the second meeting. The first took place in the conference room two doors down from the kitchen. I couldn't hear what was being said, but it wasn't long after the meeting started that I heard raised voices. Ten, maybe fifteen minutes later, Mr Shackleford came storming out of the meeting room. Mr and Mrs Knobloch emerged a few minutes afterward and drove back to their office in Richmond.'

'And there was nothing unusual about the meeting? I mean, apart from the way in which it ended?'

'Nothing at all.' Susannah was absolute in her appraisal of the event, until moments later when she added, 'Well, aside from the plastic bag of building rubble Mr Shackleford brought with him.'

'Building rubble?' Tish repeated.

'Bits of concrete, steel mesh, nails, screws, even some scraps of vinyl siding, all in a clear trash bag – the kind you'd use for collecting leaves or garden clippings.'

'That's strange. He obviously brought it along to show to the Knoblochs, but why?'

'A complaint of some sort, no doubt,' Susannah huffed. 'And one for which I would invariably be blamed. Except . . .'

'Except what?'

'Except Mr Shackleford didn't say a word to me as he walked past my desk on his way out of the meeting room. It wasn't like him to pass on an opportunity to berate or intimidate me, yet he stormed out of the lifestyle center without even a glance in my direction.'

'Do you think Shackleford met with the Knoblochs in order to get you fired?'

'Nothing's impossible, I suppose, but I highly doubt it. Otherwise, he would have told me, just so he could watch my reaction. Also, I don't think Mr Shackleford's aim in harassing me was to have me fired. Asking the Knoblochs to do so would have put the power he possessed into someone else's hands. No,

Mr Shackleford derived pleasure from pushing me closer and closer to the edge, until the day I went to the Knoblochs and quit.'

'Did you ever consider quitting?'

'Only every single morning I've come to work,' Susannah recalled, her upper lip quivering. 'If I'd been away for a few days or for a long weekend, sometimes I'd lie awake the night before, filled with dread, praying I wouldn't see him in the morning.'

'All that fear and angst, yet you're still here,' Tish noted.

'Because I love my work. I received my degree in geriatric care management and, since then, I've either worked or volunteered in nearly every nursing home and assisted-living facility in the Richmond area. Although some of those facilities paid me a far better wage than I'm earning now, I found their treatment of the patients to be less than ideal. But whenever I spoke out against the quality of care we were providing, my complaints got lost in a bureaucratic vacuum. It was, to put it mildly, depressing. That's when I saw the ad in the paper looking for an administrator for Coleton Creek' – Susannah's lip stopped quivering and her face brightened – 'it was like an answer to an unspoken prayer. Here, I've been able to put my management skills to use while assisting our residents on a personal level. It's been satisfying to watch them try new hobbies and function as a community instead of isolated homeowners. My only wish is that the Knoblochs would allocate more of the development's operating budget toward hiring teachers, trainers, and motivational speakers. It would be nice to broaden our residents' horizons even farther than they're currently being stretched.'

Tish smiled. Susannah's vision of Coleton Creek was a bold one. 'As one who's recently followed her heart to uncover her true vocation, I'm happy you've found your dream job. Still, it must have been difficult having the specter of Shackleford's harassment looming over your head.'

'It was exceedingly difficult and, as I said, there were times when I was tempted to call in sick and never return, but when I thought about the residents and how they're like family to me, I knew I had to stay on. No matter what Shackleford said or did to me, he was never going to force me to quit. My place is at Coleton Creek, with the people who need me.' Susannah's eyes grew cold and steely. 'No, if anyone was going anywhere, it was goddamn Sloane Shackleford.'

TEN

'Thanks for the information, Ms Tarragon,' Sheriff Reade acknowledged once Tish had summarized her discussions with Orson Baggett, Jim Ainsley, and Susannah Hilton. He was dressed in his law-enforcement-meets-motorcycle-gang uniform of dark T-shirt, blue jeans, boots, spiky hair and several days' worth of stubble. 'Have you been distributing baked goods again?'

At Reade's allusion to her mode of investigation of Binnie Broderick's murder, Tish pulled a face. She hadn't walked to Sloane Shackleford's garden in ninety-plus-degree heat to be mocked. 'No, I've been at the lifestyle-center kitchen cooking and prepping for tomorrow's luncheon. I'm far too busy to be roaming the neighborhood in search of clues and motives.'

'And yet, less than twenty-four hours after Shackleford's murder, you've already found both,' Reade smirked.

'I can't help it if people swing by the kitchen to chat.'

'Nor, it would seem, can you help but ask them about the murder.' Reade's smirk broadened.

'Well, it does come up in conversation. I mean it's a shocking thing to have happen in a community like this. Everyone is so tightly knit.'

'Perhaps a little too tightly.'

'Why? Did you discover something?'

'No, I was simply going by your report. Shackleford stole one man's girlfriend, drove another man insane with envy over both his garden and his sexual prowess, while simultaneously harassing, preying upon, hitting on, and manipulating practically every woman within a mile radius. Sounds like a soap opera.' Reade flashed a toothy grin. 'Nice try to get me to disclose my findings, though.'

'I wasn't trying to get you to disclose anything.'

'Yes, you were. Perhaps not directly, but you were.'

Tish heaved an exasperated sigh. 'I'm far too busy with my catering business and café to even think about Sloane Shackleford's murder, let alone investigate it. That's why I came here to share what I discovered. So that you and your team could follow up as necessary.'

'Thank you for your generosity, Ms Tarragon.'

'I wouldn't call it generosity. I'm simply trying to do the right thing.'

'Still, thanks. And if you hear anything else, please be sure to keep me in the loop,' Reade instructed, an amused expression on his face.

'Oh, I doubt I'll hear anything else. I have a flock of chickens to poach and shred for a salad, and a billion other little things to finish before tomorrow morning. I'll be in the kitchen the rest of the day.'

'Yep.'

'I mean it. I'll be flat out this afternoon and all day tomorrow.'

'So you've told me.'

'Oh, I don't know why I even bother to argue,' Tish huffed. 'Have a good day, Sheriff, and if you need me, I'll be in the lifestyle center. All. Weekend. Long.'

'I'll keep that in mind. In the meantime . . .' Reade pointed over Tish's shoulder at Wren Harper, who was leaning over the fence that divided her property from Sloane Shackleford's and gesturing wildly at Tish.

'Ms Tarragon,' Ms Harper yelled.

Tish turned around and waved at Wren to indicate she had seen her. 'I'd better go. See you around Hobson Glen.'

This time Reade waited until she was outside hearing distance. 'Sure.'

Tish approached Wren with a gentle smile. Despite being outfitted in a smart, light-blue floral-printed, cap-sleeve dress with empire waist and full skirt and matching pumps, Wren Harper looked more tired than she had the previous day. 'Hello, Ms Harper. You wanted to speak with me?'

'Afternoon, Ms Tarragon. Yes, I wanted to apologize to you and your colleague for my emotional outbursts yesterday. I'm not sure what got into me. Must have been the pressure of the competition.'

Tish was gracious. 'There's no need for you to apologize. I'm sure you've been under a great deal of stress lately. I can't even imagine what it takes to plan and raise a garden as breathtaking as yours. Have the judges been by yet?'

'They just left for Orson Baggett's. I think I stand a good chance this year.' Talk of her garden was the only thing that seemed to ignite a spark in Wren Harper's dull, weary eyes.

'Yes, now that Sloane Shackleford's out of the way, it sounds as if the playing field has been leveled considerably.'

At the mention of Shackleford, the light in Wren's eyes was extinguished. 'Mr Ainsley told me you solved that murder in Hobson Glen last month. Are you looking into Sloane Shackleford's murder, too?'

Tish was thoroughly aggravated by being posed the same question wherever she went, but she also recognized that poor Wren Harper did not deserve the brunt of her frustration. 'No. Simply focusing on making tomorrow's luncheon as delicious as it can be. Wouldn't it be lovely if the luncheon celebrated your win?'

'Yes, it would. Um, pardon me for asking, but if you're not looking into Sloane Shackleford's murder, then why were you speaking with Sheriff Reade just now?'

Tish struggled to find an innocent explanation. She found one and went overboard. 'What? That? I was just telling Sheriff Reade about next week's specials at my café. He comes in every morning for coffee, but the only breakfast product I've ever managed to sell him is my *Portrait of the Artist as a Young Ham* – ham (natch), egg, Irish farmhouse cheddar, and grilled tomato served between two slices of toasted soda bread. This week, I'm testing out my *Children of the Corned Beef Hash* recipe and thought he might want to give it a whirl, but, alas, no. I swear, if my ex-husband had been as committed to me as the sheriff is to that breakfast sandwich, we might still be together.'

Tish chided herself for enacting such an obvious deception; however, she didn't want to frighten off Wren Harper by telling her what she and Sheriff Reade had actually discussed. Besides, Tish rationalized, the description of Sheriff Reade's daily coffee run was – aside from the one odd morning when, while nursing a stomach bug, he ordered a bowl of *Danielle Steel Cut Oats* – entirely accurate.

Tish drew a deep breath and awaited Wren Harper's response,

but there was none. The woman stared back, her mouth agape, her face blank, and her eyes unblinking.

'I, um, I'm not sure if Jim Ainsley informed you, but I'm a literary caterer . . .' Tish's voice trailed off.

Still, no response.

'I create dishes inspired by authors and their works. That's why tomorrow's luncheon has a *Secret Garden* theme.'

'Oh,' Wren Harper snapped from her reverie. 'OK. Whew. I was wondering why you were talking about recipes and books all of a sudden. I thought for a moment the heat had got to you or something.'

'No, I'm perfectly healthy.' Tish laughed aloud. 'Although I suppose I do sound a bit like a nut with all my punny menu items, don't I?'

Once again, Mrs Harper fell silent. And that said more than words ever could.

'So' – Tish shifted her weight from foot to foot and smoothed the back of her hair – 'what was it you wanted to talk to me about?'

'I don't know,' Wren shrugged. 'I feel as though I should talk to someone, but I don't want to get anyone in trouble.'

Tish glanced over her shoulder at Sheriff Reade, who was watching them with avid interest and more than a trace of amusement. 'May I come into your garden? We'd have more privacy there.'

Wren nodded and waved Tish around the fence and through the back gate. There, they wandered to the brink of the lily pond, beneath the shade of one of the miniature apple trees. 'What is it you need to talk about?'

Wren Harper erupted into tears. 'I don't want to get anyone in trouble.'

'How do you know someone will get into trouble?'

Wren reached into the pocket of her dress, pulled out a wad of tissues, and blew her nose into them. 'I don't know. I don't know anything anymore.'

Tish placed a consoling hand on the woman's shoulder as her body convulsed with sobs. 'Look, whatever you have seen or heard might have an innocent explanation. The only way someone would get into trouble is if they had committed a crime or are concealing the truth.'

This line of reasoning only intensified Wren's cries.

'Mrs Harper,' Tish soothed. 'Mrs Harper, please talk to me. I want to help you.'

'No one can help me,' she wailed.

'That isn't true. It may seem that way right now, but it isn't true.'

'Hello,' a bright, singsong voice resonated from the garden gate, serving as stark contrast to Wren's mournful sobs. 'Hello, Ms Harper? It's Zadie Morris, your neighbor. Jim Ainsley said today was an open garden day so I thought I'd use that as an opportunity to introduce my—'

Zadie, looking terribly glamorous in wide-legged navy trousers, an orange wrap-front blouse, and a white wide-brimmed hat, stopped a few feet inside the gate. Her face was exquisitely made up, from her foundation to the brilliant copper lipstick that complemented the olive undertones of her skin.

'Oh, my goodness, Ms Harper.' Zadie approached the lily pond. 'Are you all right?'

Wren continued to sob, albeit less violently.

'Ms Tarragon,' Zadie addressed, 'what's going on here?'

'I'm not exactly sure. Mrs Harper wanted to tell me something, but then she broke down. Said she's afraid of getting people in trouble.'

'Nonsense. If you have something to tell us, Ms Harper, then say it. I promise, you are among friends.'

Wren Harper, who had until now been slouched over and crying into a soggy clump of tissue, stood erect and blurted, 'I saw Pepper Aviero and Callie Collingsworth enter Shackleford's house yesterday morning.'

'When was that?' Tish quizzed.

'Around eleven o'clock. I was working in my garden. They went in the back door carrying casserole dishes.'

'What?'

Zadie passed a clean tissue to Wren who used it to blot her eyes dry. 'Shackleford was surprised to see them, but he let them into the kitchen. Not long after that, there was shouting and yelling to beat the band.'

'Did you hear what the dispute was about?'

'No. I felt funny being outside in my garden while they were carrying on like that. It felt like I was eavesdropping, so I came inside and poured myself a glass of water.'

'What happened then?'

'I don't know. I had the windows closed and the air conditioner on. The heat must have gotten to me because I started in with a headache. So, I went to my bedroom to lie down. I was there until Jim Ainsley came round with you and Mr Davis.'

'And we arrived a little after eleven thirty.' Tish turned to Zadie. 'Did you happen to see Ms Aviero and Ms Collingsworth stop by Mr Shackleford's yesterday?'

'No, but of course I couldn't have. Although I can see Sloane Shackleford's garden perfectly well from my kitchen window, his kitchen door is at the other end of the house. I can't see it unless I'm standing at the far back of my yard which, considering I pay someone to mow the lawn, doesn't happen very often.'

'Did you hear the shouting Mrs Harper described?'

'No, I didn't, but I would have been out of the house on my daily walk at that hour of the morning. I'd only just returned home from that walk when I heard you, Mr Ainsley, and Mr Davis raising a ruckus.'

'Hmm, how strange that Ms Aviero and Ms Collingsworth should have shown up together.'

'Yes, well, I'm new to the neighborhood, but even I've heard the rumors,' Zadie disclosed.

'What rumors are those?'

'That Shackleford was having a ding-dong with the both of them.'

Tish assumed the term 'ding-dong' was a colloquialism for an affair. 'Have you heard that rumor as well?' she asked Wren Harper.

Wren nodded. 'More than that. I've seen both of them coming and going from the house on more than one occasion. Sometimes bringing food in the evening. Other times leaving early in the morning.'

'Sounds like Mr Shackleford found himself in a bad spot yesterday,' Zadie remarked. 'Stringing along two women in the same neighborhood. No wonder the man's been murdered.'

'As much as I agree that both women have a very strong motive for murder and that the timing is quite close, it doesn't quite add up.' Tish voiced her opinion. 'We found Mr Shackleford dead in his lounge chair, apparently killed while sunning himself. I'm no psychologist, but I doubt he'd have taken to his chaise lounge to work on his tan while two furious women screamed like banshees in his kitchen.'

'No, I suppose not.' Zadie pulled a face. Several seconds later, she snapped her fingers. 'What if they murdered Shackleford together and then dragged his body outside? One woman might not be able to move a man of that size, but two could.'

'Just as I'm not a psychologist, I'm also not a forensics expert. However, I'm fairly certain Mr Shackleford was killed in that chair. Everything seems to . . . line up with that theory.' Tish took great care not to be overly graphic in her explanation.

'Then I won't get Pepper and Callie in trouble if I tell the police I saw them?' Wren's voice was hopeful.

'That's entirely up to the police,' Tish advised. 'Still, you should talk to them and tell them what you saw.'

'I will,' Wren promised as tears returned to her eyes. 'I'm just so scared.'

'Of course you are. That's to be expected under the circumstances.'

'Would you like me to go with you when you speak with the police?' Zadie offered.

'Oh, that's most kind of you, Ms Morris, but we've only just—'

'Nonsense. We gals need to stick together.'

Wren wiped her tears and nodded again. 'Is it OK if I take a quick nap before we go to the police? I feel a headache coming on again.'

'Absolutely. I was just going out for my walk when I stopped by to say hello. I'll come back here when I'm finished.'

'Thank you. Thank you both.' A still-tearful Wren wandered through the garden and into the back door of her home.

'I thought you were going out somewhere special for the day,' Tish commented upon Zadie's makeup and attire as the pair walked back up the garden path toward the gate.

'No, I just like looking my best when I go out, even if it's just for a walk or to run some errands. A leftover from my working days, I suppose, but having my face on and wearing decent clothes makes me feel pulled together, no matter what might be going on in the world. Also, I'm at that point in my life where saving your best dress or finest perfume for a special occasion is rather ridiculous. Best to enjoy it while I can.'

'You also have more than a bit of a reputation to uphold in regard to glamour.'

'Oh, you're not old enough to remember that, are you?' Zadie was skeptical. 'You couldn't possibly be.'

'My moisturizer must be working,' Tish joked. 'My grandmother and mother were both Zadie's Ladies. They wore your lipstick all the time. My grandmother's shade was shell-pink. My mother gravitated toward corals and mauves.'

'And you?'

'Oh, my first lipstick was an embarrassingly eighties shade of fuchsia to match my non-Zadie hot-pink eyeshadow.'

'Funny how trends change, isn't it?' Zadie laughed as they exited the gate and closed it behind them. 'And now? What do you wear?'

'Reds, mostly, with the occasional mauve and neutral. I'm afraid I no longer have any Zadie products in my possession.'

'Nor should you. The company that purchased Zadie hasn't the same meticulous standards I did. Their lipstick is too waxy, their mascara too goopy, and their eyeliner smudges if you blink too hard.'

'Have you confronted them about it?'

'I wrote them a letter a few years back, when I started noticing the changes. But they'd already paid me for the name. There's not much else I can do.'

'But the name they bought – it's yours.'

'It is, but it's not the same company. The Zadie Cosmetics in drug stores now is mass-produced by computers and machines using cut-rate ingredients – that's why it's side by side with Wet and Wild and Rimmel. The Zadie Cosmetics of old – the one that was handmade using natural waxes, scents, and oils and shared the shelves with Max Factor, L'Oréal, and Revlon – is still mine.'

'I don't understand.' Tish followed Zadie as they walked past Orson Baggett's house, where Jim Ainsley and his fellow garden judges were gathered in the backyard.

'Oh, I hope Orson wins. He is a dear man,' Zadie announced to no one in particular. 'When I sold Zadie Cosmetics, I did, indeed, sell them my name. But it was only the name. The bestselling products of my company – the shell-pink and coral that your grandmother and mother loved – became what were called Zadie Classics. I hold the formulas for those items and retain the right to produce them again should I ever desire to do so. Sadly, I don't think your magenta made the cut.'

'Ah, well. I've managed without it this long,' Tish chuckled. 'So why sell them the name and not the products?'

'Because I knew the company buying Zadie would eventually cave to technology. They were about slick advertising and maximizing the bottom line, whereas I wanted a personal relationship with my customers. I got to know the women buying my products. They weren't about setting trends. They wanted to try the latest styles and fads, but they wanted to be able to fall back on their favorite products – the tried and true items that made them feel confident. My customer didn't have a lot of money, but a five-dollar tube of lipstick was inexpensive enough to fit in the budget yet still just expensive enough to feel decadent. The new owners have made their products so cheaply that it's young girls just getting into makeup snatching them up. Not that there's anything wrong with that, necessarily, but that wasn't my business model. Zadie wasn't something you outgrew when you had more money, style, and sense. It was something you could always rely upon to make you feel beautiful.' Ms Morris paused and flashed Tish an apologetic smile. 'Forgive me for rambling on like a crazy woman. My business was like a baby to me.'

'No need to apologize. I got involved in a murder investigation to save my business.'

'Yes, Jim Ainsley told me about that and it's not crazy. That's instinct. Just as new mothers don't need to be taught to protect their children, a fledgling businesswoman doesn't need to be taught to protect her investment.' Zadie Morris stopped in her tracks.

'Are you OK, Ms Morris?' Tish stopped walking and turned to check on her companion.

'Yes, yes,' Zadie swatted aside any suggestions to the contrary. 'The entire time we've been talking, I've been thinking to myself that you remind me of someone. I just figured out who it is. You remind me of myself when I started my company.'

For the first time in her life, Tish was genuinely speechless. 'I–I don't know what to say,' she finally articulated after several seconds had passed. 'I don't think I've ever received such a compliment.'

'It's not a compliment,' Zadie stated as she commenced walking. 'It's the truth. You're a smart woman, Tish Tarragon. And if you don't mind, I have something back at home I'd like to give to you.'

'You've already given me enough with your kind words.'

'At least hear what it is before you turn me down,' Zadie chuckled. 'I have a tube of lipstick I'd like to share with you. It's a limited-edition shade inspired by my life's mantra and it would look fabulous on you.'

'Oh, I couldn't,' Tish protested. 'Not a limited edition. Not when it's no longer being produced.'

'I have more than just the one tube, Ms Tarragon. Heck, I have the formula if I need to make more. I want you to have the lipstick. Not only will you love the color, but I'd love to see someone like you wear it. Someone strong and smart. Someone who's been self-sufficient most of her life. You see, my mother died when I was young, too.'

'Too?' It was Tish's turn to stop in her tracks.

'Am I wrong?'

'No, but how did you—?'

'Same way I knew what Zadie products would sell and what would be a flop. Same way you know what menu items your customers will enjoy. Same way you solved that murder case you mentioned. We observe and analyze and understand the people with whom we are interacting.'

'OK,' Tish relented. 'I'll stop by your house when I've finished for the day, but I'm not coming empty-handed. You mentioned how you'd love to have a cream tea again. How about I provide you with your own private tea in your home?'

'That would be delightful. Are you sure you have enough?'

'As long as Mr Ainsley didn't stop by the kitchen while I was talking to you, yes.'

'Good to see I'm not the only one with a weakness for scones. I'll see you later, then?'

'You will. It may be after five or six o'clock if that's OK.'

'I'll be home. Oh, and Miss Tarragon, speaking of observing and analyzing, Pepper Aviero and Callie Collingsworth still might have murdered Sloane Shackleford, you know. One or both of them could have left his house and double-backed to perform the deed. But, of course, I'm sure you'd already thought of that.'

'At the risk of sounding arrogant, the thought had crossed my mind. However, Ms Harper was so frightened of getting those women in trouble that I thought it best to keep that possibility to myself; otherwise, we may never had gotten her to agree to speak with the police.'

'Good girl.' Zadie Morris nodded her head in approval before strolling down the shady street to continue her daily walk, a mysterious smile upon her face.

ELEVEN

Tish was deep in thought as she hastened along Coleton Creek Way on her way back to the lifestyle center. Meeting Zadie Morris – the legendary Zadie Morris, Cosmetic Queen – had led her to reflect upon her childhood. The long, sweet summer evenings when her mother, dressed in her best *Saturday Night Fever* disco attire, would apply a coat of glossy coral Zadie lipstick and leave Tish in the care of her grandparents for the night and most of the following day.

Sundays spent at her grandparents' house were the days Tish loved best. Waking to the smell of coffee, Tish would get dressed, pad downstairs, and meet her grandfather in the kitchen, where they'd both enjoy a 'cup of joe' – his milk and no sugar, hers all milk and a tablespoon of sweetened brewed coffee. Upon drinking their respective beverages, grandfather and granddaughter would gather the week's stale, leftover bread pieces into a paper bag, buckle themselves into the cream-colored 1978 Buick LeSabre sedan parked in front of the house, and drive to the local duck pond. Once the bread was gone and the avian population of the pond was carb-filled and content, Tish and her grandfather would then travel to their favorite bakery for rolls and pastries for breakfast.

Post-breakfast meant the dull routine of church, followed by

Sunday lunch. Years later, after her grandfather had passed away, Tish's grandmother, her faith in God and will to live eroded, would do away with church entirely. But Sunday lunch, invariably in the form of a stringy old roasting hen and overcooked vegetables, always prevailed.

Then, when the lunch dishes had been washed and put away, came the highlight of the weekend – the Sunday drive. For Tish's grandfather, who had been raised in a cold-water flat in New York City during the Great Depression, the Sunday drive was an opportunity to show the world that the grimy kid from the Bowery had achieved the American dream. For Tish's grandmother, who for the rest of the week stayed home and tended to household chores and yard work, the Sunday drive was a chance to switch her housecoat for a colorful dress, apply a few pats of Emeraude dusting powder, and swipe on her favorite shell-pink Zadie lipstick.

For Tish, those halcyon afternoons were the only part of the week when her nuclear family and her extended family combined. There, in the giant backseat of the LeSabre, she'd start sing-alongs, enjoy the scenery outside the open windows, play 'I Spy,' and laugh.

A car drove past, snapping Tish back into the present day. She had lost so much since those untroubled, sun-dappled days. A grandfather. A grandmother. A mother. A marriage. A home.

Tish blinked back her tears and drew a deep breath. There was no use in dwelling on the past. It was the present and future that mattered, and Tish's future looked very bright, indeed, unless she failed to meet the Coleton Creek Garden Club's expectations.

And there was a growing chance she might. There were still chickens to poach and shred, sandwich fillings to prepare, and several hot beverage dispensers to wash and sterilize. The workload awaiting Tish bordered on daunting, yet Sloane Shackleford's murder was making it increasingly difficult to concentrate on catering, recipes, and mundane kitchen tasks.

Was someone at Coleton Creek responsible for Shackleford's death? As Tish learned of motive after motive on the part of Coleton Creek's residents, it seemed exceedingly likely. She recalled Susannah Hilton's account of Shackleford's harassment and both Pepper Aviero's and Callie Collingsworth's final, vulgar assessment of the man as a bastard. Had Shackleford been taken down by a vengeful woman? Or maybe even two? The scenario Zadie Morris suggested was not outside the realm of possibility.

Or had Shackleford met his fate at the hands of one of the gardeners from whom he had snatched victory? Both Orson Baggett and Wren Harper seemed confident that Shackleford's presence was the only thing standing between them and the trophy for best garden.

And then there was the suspicious screaming match between Shackleford and the Knoblochs. Why did Shackleford bring a bag of construction materials to the meeting? Did he know something scandalous about the Knoblochs? And what, if anything, did the Knoblochs know about Shackleford?

Tish closed her eyes in an effort to clear her mind. Such questions only served to divert her from her true purpose. She needed to focus on the luncheon, get through the weekend, and then get back to the café, she determined as her pace quickened and her fists clenched. As Zadie Morris would agree, Tish's livelihood depended upon it.

Having decided to ignore the murder case for the rest of the afternoon, it was with great apprehension that Tish encountered Violet Abercrombie pacing in the lifestyle-center parking lot.

She was wearing a bright magenta cotton-knit sheath-cut dress with a floral-printed hem and a coordinating bolero jacket for modesty. On her feet, Violet Abercrombie chose a pair of comfortable canvas sandals in the same shade of pale pink as the flower she had tucked into the tightly fastened blond bun at the back of her neck. 'Ms Tarragon,' she greeted, her voice anxious and her face pinched with worry.

'Hello, Mrs Abercrombie.' Tish continued walking toward the lifestyle center in hopes the older woman might take the hint. 'Is garden judging over?'

'Not hardly. The judges are at our place right now, but I can't watch. I've never been able to bear the suspense, so I let Tucker show them around. I have too much invested in those little blooms to listen to any criticism of them.'

'I can understand that,' Tish sympathized before speeding the conversation to its conclusion. 'Well, good luck in the competition. I'll see you at the luncheon tomorrow.'

'Ms Tarragon, please.' Violet Abercrombie sounded panicked. 'I need to talk to you.'

Tish pulled a face and stopped walking. She wanted desperately to get back into the kitchen, but she couldn't turn Violet Abercrombie away without feeling as though she was completely heartless. 'What about?'

'Sloane Shackleford's murder, of course.'

'Sure, but for the record, I'm not on the case, Mrs Abercrombie.'

'But you were seen talking to the police at Sloane Shackleford's house just a short while ago,' Mrs Abercrombie argued.

Tish was stunned by how quickly the news of her meeting with Sheriff Reade had traveled. 'Yes, I did, but that was just to—' She stopped mid-sentence. She couldn't stomach the thought of telling another lie. 'OK, what is it?'

Violet Abercrombie glanced over each shoulder. 'I'd rather not speak about it out in the open.'

Tish nodded. 'Go into the courtyard. It's set up for tomorrow's luncheon so it's closed to through traffic. I have to put some chickens on to cook. I'll meet you there in a few minutes.'

With a nod of her head, Violet Abercrombie followed Tish into the lifestyle center and proceeded to the courtyard.

After apprising Schuyler and Jules of her meeting with Violet and assigning them their next tasks, Tish placed her chickens into the poaching liquid and set the alarm on her phone for the anticipated cooking time. With things humming along in the kitchen, she dashed to the courtyard where she found a nervous Violet Abercrombie pacing between banquet tables.

'Sorry to keep you waiting, but I'm a bit under the gun, what with tomorrow's festivities,' a breathless Tish explained.

'I'll try not to keep you very long, Ms Tarragon. Jim Ainsley told me about the wonderful job you did solving that murder in Hobson Glen a few weeks back.'

'I'm afraid Mr Ainsley may have overstated my importance in the case.' Tish pulled a chair away from the table closest to the buffet and took a seat.

Violet Abercrombie took the chair beside Tish. 'Regardless of what you did and didn't do to find the murderer, I come to you seeking help.'

'OK. I'm not sure what I can do, but tell me about your problem.'

Violet leaned forward in her chair and stared, unblinkingly, into

Tish's eyes. 'I want you to know that Tucker, Jim Ainsley, and I are innocent of having murdered Sloane Shackleford.'

Tish leaned back in her chair, eager for some – any – breathing space away from the intensity of Mrs Abercrombie's gaze. 'Um, OK. Why do I need to know that?'

'Just in case you may have heard otherwise.'

Ah, so Violet Abercrombie is using me to get an inside track on the police investigation. 'Why would the three of you be on the suspect list in the first place?' Tish shrugged.

'Because eight years ago I was diagnosed with stage-two breast cancer.'

'I'm so sorry. Are you OK now?'

'Yes.' The intensity in Violet's eyes slackened. 'I'm officially out of the woods, but I still need to remain vigilant. Which I do. Which I've always done. Which ultimately led to Tucker and me losing everything we own.'

'Once again, I don't understand.'

'When I received my breast cancer diagnosis, I was terrified. Then the doctors explained that, with proper treatment, there was a better than fifty-fifty chance that I would live to see the next five years and beyond. I was still terrified, but I was optimistic and determined to be one of the survivors. Tucker and I readied ourselves for a fight and we got one. But two months into it, we were quite heartened when we heard that the radiation and chemotherapy I was receiving appeared to be working. We were cautious, but relieved. Until we received the bill.' Violet's eyes flashed in anger. 'Because I had a benign cyst removed from my breast the year prior, the insurance company categorized my cancer as a pre-existing condition and refused to pay for treatment. Tucker and I visited the patient advocate at the hospital and told her our story. She put us in touch with some outside resources, but none of them could cover the nearly three hundred thousand dollars in debts we had accrued. We filed an appeal against the insurance company, but they held to their decision. Tucker and I had put both our son and daughter through college, so we didn't have much in the way of savings. We wound up selling just about everything we owned and foreclosed on our home just to get out from under our financial burden.'

'I'm so sorry, Mrs Abercrombie. No one should have the

experience you did, least of all when they're trying to get well,' Tish sympathized. 'But what does this have to do with the murder case?'

'The insurance company that stripped Tucker and me of our savings and home was owned by Sloane Shackleford,' Violet stated, her voice trembling.

'Wow!' Tish pondered the odds that would bring the Abercrombies and Shackleford together in the same neighborhood. 'Did you know he lived here?'

'When Tucker and I first arrived, he didn't. Coleton Creek was supposed to be a community of affordable townhouses and small, two-bedroom homes. When the developers got greedy, they decided to switch gears – that's why the rest of the neighborhood contains larger, higher-end homes with porches, bigger yards, and special finishes in the kitchen and bathrooms. Some of those, like Sloane Shackleford's and Callie Collingsworth's, are custom builds.'

That Mrs Collingsworth had sufficient funds to afford a custom-built home didn't come as a surprise to Tish. 'It must have been a shock to see Shackleford here.'

'We had no idea he was moving in until he was actually here. Even then, we only learned he was in the neighborhood when we saw a note posted in the homeowners' association newsletter welcoming Coleton Creek's new residents, and there was his name in big, bold letters. Although we wished otherwise, what are the odds of there being two Sloane Shacklefords living in central Virginia?'

'Given all I've learned about the man, let's hope very slim.'

'Hear, hear,' Violet Abercrombie seconded. 'When we finally came face to face with him, our fears were confirmed. Back when my treatment claim had been denied, we had seen Sloane Shackleford's photo on his company website. The man we met was older, grayer, and a bit heavier, but it was definitely the same person. Poor Tucker. For months, his stomach was a nervous mess.'

'Did you consider moving out of Coleton Creek?'

'We can't afford to move. We're lucky to be living where we are now. And even though Tucker finally retired, he's still doing some consulting work – as much as allowed – while we live off our social security checks. No, our only choice in dealing with Shackleford was to stay where we were and try to limit our interaction with him. It worked for a time, until he decided to join – or should I say *conquer*? – the garden club.'

'That must have been quite difficult,' Tish commiserated.

'We've spent the past couple of years avoiding garden club meetings, holiday parties, and community barbecues for fear of running into the man. Sometimes it feels as if we're hostages in our own home,' Violet Abercrombie cried.

Tish fell silent. If Violet Abercrombie was trying to exculpate herself and Tucker of any wrongdoing, she was failing miserably. 'So how does Jim Ainsley fit into all this?'

Violet turned her gaze from Tish to one of the boxwood topiaries that lined the table. 'Jim's a good friend,' she replied in a wooden tone.

'That doesn't quite explain why you think the police would suspect him of murdering Sloane Shackleford. If I were your friend, I'd be angry Shackleford caused you to lose your home and life savings, but I'd be talking the two of you out of seeking revenge. I wouldn't be committing murder on your behalf.'

Violet Abercrombie picked some invisible flecks of dust from the tablecloth and drew in her breath. 'Since I'm in this deep, I suppose I might as well tell you everything. Jim Ainsley and my husband have been friends since they were in grade school. They've always been more like brothers than best friends. Jim was the best man at our wedding and is godfather to our son, Finn. He's shared family holidays with us, sat at the head table with us at our daughter's wedding. He's always been there – for all of us.'

The tone of Violet's voice and her last-minute clarification – *for all of us* – was a clear sign to Tish that Jim Ainsley had likely been supportive to one member of the family above the rest. 'It's lovely that your husband and Mr Ainsley have such a close relationship. And I must compliment you for being so supportive of their friendship all these years. Many a spouse might have been jealous of all the time they spent together.'

'Truth is, there wasn't much to be jealous of, Ms Tarragon. In the early days of our marriage, Jim Ainsley probably spent more time with me and the kids than he did with Tucker.

'The company Tucker's worked for since the kids were young – the company from which he just retired – has clients all over the country,' Violet explained. 'These days, product information, specs, and product demonstration videos can be sent via email, but back then, when Tucker first started working for them, everything needed to be done by mail or in person, which meant Tucker spent half of his year traveling. Tucker hated leaving me alone with the kids, but it had to be done. I was working part-time as a kindergarten teacher and our children were small. Understanding that I was run ragged with laundry, grocery shopping, and jockeying my daughter, Lucy, to nursery school and my son, Finn, to elementary school and baseball practice, Tucker asked Jim to check in on me.'

Violet smiled. 'Having Jim around was a godsend. He'd come by with groceries or take-out meals. He'd toss the ball around with Finn and color and draw with Lucy. Thanks to him, I was able to get out and have my hair done or have lunch with a girlfriend on a Saturday afternoon.'

'How very kind of him to help out,' Tish remarked.

'Yes, Jim is and always has been a gentleman of the first order. Which is what made what happened next so very difficult for both of us.'

Tish raised an eyebrow as a prompt for Violet to continue.

'We'd gone on for about three years with Tucker traveling and Jim coming over to help with the kids. At that point, Jim would stay for dinner some nights and help me get the kids changed and ready for bed, then we'd watch television together. One night, Tucker called to say he was returning home early. You'd have thought I'd be excited to have my husband back home, but I wasn't. I felt disappointed. Like I was being cheated out of my time with Jim. When I told Jim, he confessed that he felt the same way. Never – and I mean never – had we kissed or touched each other inappropriately or even entertained the notion of pursuing a romantic relationship, but we had created a scenario where Jim was a surrogate husband. A surrogate husband who provided the things Tucker didn't.

'I went to bed that night and wondered how we might remedy the situation, but there was only one clear answer. I loved Tucker. I'd always loved Tucker. I always will. He was the father of my children and I needed to focus my energies on building our marriage. The next morning, I called Jim and told him he wasn't to come around the house when Tucker wasn't at home. I told him that he needed to go out and find a wife of his own with whom he could start a family.'

'Did he listen to you?'

'He did. He told Tucker that his work schedule – Jim was a police detective – was going to change and that he'd be working more night shifts. Jim also went out on a few dates and was engaged to be married for a time, but his fiancée eventually broke off the engagement. She said that Jim was emotionally distant. That his mind and heart were elsewhere.'

'With you and your family?'

A single tear trickled down Violet's finely etched countenance. 'Yes. Heaven knows my thoughts were with him on those lonely nights when Tucker was away, the kids had gone to bed, and I was by myself in front of the television, telling the dog about the highs and lows of my day. But I never broke down and called Jim. I knew if I did, it would put my marriage in jeopardy.'

'So, how did you wind up living next door to each other?' Tish inquired. 'That's obviously not in keeping with your need to keep your distance.'

'When I was diagnosed with cancer, Jim was there to help Tucker pick up the pieces. The treatment required overnight hospital stays, and even when I wasn't in the hospital, I wasn't able to do much. I was tired, sick, and thin. The children had lives of their own already. They'd visit me when they could, but running the house and taking care of bills became Tucker's responsibility. Just as he did for me, Jim would stop by the house with groceries and help with laundry. He'd also visit me in the hospital and watch over me at home so that Tucker could have an evening or afternoon off to play a round of golf or go fishing. When Tucker and I were forced to foreclose on our home, Jim was already living here at Coleton Creek and was searching for a tenant to rent the townhouse. He slashed the rent so that we could live here.'

'And living next door to Mr Ainsley hasn't compromised your marriage?'

'It's funny, isn't it? How passion fades as one gets older and comfort and security seem far more important,' Violet philosophized. 'We've lived so long this way that it's as if the three of us are a familial unit. Jim and I still care for each other, of course, but the flames that once existed are now warm embers. He found some love and companionship with Pepper Aviero for a time, and I was happy for him. I still love Tucker and look forward to a future together, doting over grandchildren and tending our garden, and Jim's happy for us. And Tucker's just so relieved to have me alive and to finally be able to retire, that having his best buddy living so close that they can drop by each other's place unannounced and watch the ball game on the TV is the icing on the cake.'

'The perfect living arrangement for everyone,' Tish commented.

'Yes,' Violet Abercrombie conceded. 'That's why I'm so concerned about the police digging around and asking questions about the past. Doing so would only serve to hurt Tucker – and to what purpose?'

'The purpose of finding a killer. The history you described gives all three of you a very strong motive for wanting Shackleford dead.'

'I know it does, but we didn't murder him.' Violet's mood turned frantic. 'Life is good now. Why would any of us wish to ruin that?'

Tish recalled Violet Abercrombie's comment that she and Tucker had felt like hostages in their own home. 'Mrs Abercrombie, I'm not privy to the police investigation, but it's only a matter of time before Sheriff Reade learns about your denied health insurance claim. When he finds out about your history with Shackleford, he's going to want to question you and Tucker, and probably Jim, too.'

Violet went into a full-on panic.

'What I can do,' Tish offered in an attempt to calm the woman, 'is impart to Sheriff Reade the delicacy of your situation and ask him not to expose the finer details of your friendship with Jim Ainsley if they're not relevant to the case.'

Violet brought her hands to her mouth and looked as if she might cry. 'Oh, thank you, Ms Tarragon. Thank you.'

'You're welcome, but, again, I can't promise anything.'

'I understand, but it helps to know that you're in our corner.'

As if by magic, the alarm on Tish's phone chimed. 'That would be my chicken.'

'I'd better leave you to it. I've already taken enough of your time. Thank you again, Ms Tarragon.'

Tish replied with a weak smile and watched as Violet Abercrombie returned to the lifestyle center via the courtyard door. Could the woman have murdered Sloane Shackleford? She certainly appeared to be more concerned about her husband learning of what amounted to emotional infidelity than being accused of murder. But was that simply a ruse? Clearly, Violet's hostage comment belied everything she described about her ideal home life.

Indeed, Violet Abercrombie's account of her picture-perfect 'family' arrangement struck Tish as naïve at best. It was, in Tish's estimation, extremely unlikely that, during their decades of personal interactions, Tucker never perceived that his best friend's feelings for Violet might go beyond simple friendship.

Having lost the family home and now working through what should have been his retirement, Tucker Abercrombie experienced additional humiliation when he was forced to rely upon the kindness of said best friend for affordable housing. Had Tucker Abercrombie snapped and murdered Sloane Shackleford – the man ultimately responsible for his current imprisonment – Tish wouldn't have been the slightest bit surprised.

Conversely, if Jim Ainsley still fostered feelings of love for Violet, witnessing her and Tucker's marriage grow stronger with each passing day could prove a difficult ordeal. Might Ainsley harbor a grudge against the person whose unadulterated greed delivered the Abercrombies on to his doorstep? And would Ainsley not be doubly embittered when Sloane Shackleford, whose indirect actions drove the inaccessible Violet Abercrombie closer, paradoxically wooed away Ainsley's sole female companion, Pepper Aviero?

Tish thought about Jim Ainsley, Tucker Abercrombie, their individual circumstances, and also their common bond. Had either man murdered Sloane Shackleford, would they have confessed their crime to Violet? And if they had, how far would she be willing to go to protect them and her perfect world?

As Tish pondered that last question, she recalled the words of Jim Ainsley: *I'll call Violet after our tour. Vi will know what to do. She always does.*

TWELVE

The alarm on her phone sounding its second alert, Tish entered the kitchen and walked directly to the stove. Lifting the lid of her oft-used blue enamelware stockpot, she grabbed a stainless-steel skimmer and used it to lift the quartet of roasting hens from the simmering white wine, leek, peppercorn, and herb-infused liquid and on to a platter. Using a fork, Tish pierced one of the chickens in the thigh and pulled away the skin. Despite her worst fears, the meat had been poached to perfection.

Tish gave a happy sigh followed by a tiny 'Yay,' but there was no one in the kitchen with whom she could celebrate. A salad spinner of lettuce sat beside the sink, waiting for an application of centrifugal force to separate water from leaves, and, on a nearby counter, hundreds of peeled and deveined shrimp filled a wide-bottomed saucepan filled with water and seasoned with sliced lemon, carrots, and celery in anticipation of receiving a gentle simmer, but the men tending to both vessels were nowhere in sight.

'Schuyler? Jules?' Tish's calls were met with the sound of a fracas just outside the fireproof metal kitchen door.

Throwing her weight against the stainless-steel crash bar, Tish pushed the door outward into an enclosed, concrete-paved area. From somewhere between the trash and recycling dumpsters, the quarrel continued. 'Get your filthy hands away from me,' a female voice with a thick Southern drawl shouted.

'My filthy hands? Yours are covered up to your elbows in blood,' a second female voice – this one with a slight accent – volleyed.

Tish followed the sound to find Schuyler and Jules holding back Callie Collingsworth and Pepper Aviero, respectively, from engaging in a physical altercation.

'Ladies. Ladies!' Schuyler urged as Callie struggled to break free of his clutch.

'And he's using that term loosely,' Jules quipped as he tightened his hold on the writhing fury that was Pepper Aviero.

'If you don't stop right now, I'll be forced to call the police.'

'I've already been asked to speak with the police later today because that old bat called them on me.' Although she could not gesture toward Callie Collingsworth, it was clear she was the old bat in question.

'I didn't call the police on you. You called them on me,' Callie argued.

'No, but I wish I had. I know it was you who snuck into Sloane's backyard and bashed his brains in.'

'The woman's obviously delusional,' Callie remarked to their captors. 'Don't you have better things to do than accuse people of murder, Ms Aviero? Shouldn't you be at home making burritos or chilaquiles or something?'

'At least men love my chilaquiles,' Pepper sneered.

'Really? Sloane told me they were dry and tasteless.'

'That's a lie. Sloane loved my chilaquiles.'

'Sweet baby Jesus, please tell me we're talking about Mexican food,' Jules pleaded.

Tish stepped forward. 'Mrs Collingsworth? Ms Aviero? What's going on here?'

Pepper pointed a finger at Callie. 'She murdered Sloane Shackleford so she could inherit his fortune.'

'Are you to benefit from Mr Shackleford's death?' Tish asked Callie Collingsworth.

'Yes, Sloane's attorney called me this morning.'

'Were you aware that he had made you his beneficiary?'

'Yes . . . no . . . I mean, Sloane might have mentioned it a couple of times, but I had no idea he was serious.'

'You liar,' Pepper seethed. 'You've been widowed twice. Both times your late husband left everything to you. It's how you've earned all your money, isn't it? You partner up with a wealthy man, get them to sign over their fortune, and then bump them off.'

'I never killed anyone. One husband died of a stroke while in bed with his personal assistant, and the other died in a car crash while driving over the legal limit.'

'And Sloane? What did you do to him to get him to sign everything over to you?' Pepper raged.

'Wouldn't you like to know. You're simply jealous that I get paid for what you give away for free.'

'You witch! If I give anything away, it's out of love.'

'Well, that either means that you're completely ignorant of your lowly status as a mature woman or you're just plain old dumb,' Callie sneered. 'Either way, how do we know it wasn't you who snuck back and killed Sloane? You hated Sloane for dumping you, especially after you gave up Jim Ainsley in order to be with him.'

'Or perhaps it was both of you,' Tish suggested before Pepper could retaliate.

Pepper, Callie, Jules, and Schuyler all turned to face Tish.

Tish continued, 'The reason you ladies were contacted by the police is because you were seen together at Sloane's kitchen door at eleven o'clock yesterday morning. You were both carrying casserole dishes and, shortly after being admitted, a disagreement was overheard by the neighbors. Neither of you were seen leaving the house. So what went on? Why were you there? Who left and when?'

The women instantly relaxed, prompting Jules and Schuyler to release their grips.

'We were there to make Sloane choose between us,' Pepper admitted as she shifted her gaze to her feet. 'It was stupid, really.'

'We did it because Ms Aviero couldn't accept that Sloane had thrown her over for me,' Callie added.

'And you did it to rub salt into my wounds. But, as things worked out, Sloane picked neither of us.'

Tish glanced at Callie Collingsworth to confirm.

'All right . . . yes. However, it was stupid on my part. I knew what Sloane was. I knew what I had with him. It was stupid to try to pin him down. I only demeaned myself in the process.'

'So, did you leave together?' Tish asked.

'Together? Hell, no.'

'But we did leave at the same time,' Pepper amended.

Callie Collingsworth grudgingly agreed. 'I even watched over my shoulder for a time to make sure she didn't go back to grovel. Of course, that doesn't mean she didn't go back later and give him the what-for with the blunt end of a shovel.'

'It doesn't mean *you* didn't either.'

'I didn't. I went home and sat in my yard for a spell before coming here for a swim. Why, you and Mr Davis caught me as I was leaving,' Callie said to Tish.

Tish nodded and looked at Pepper. 'And you?'

'I went home, flung myself on my bed, and cried. Then I ate a pint of chocolate ice cream before pulling myself together and taking a walk. That's when Jim called me with the news.'

'And what time, approximately, did you both leave?'

'How should I know?' Callie challenged. 'It's not like I was looking at my watch. Ms Aviero should know how long it takes to be dumped. She's had it happen to her before.'

'Oh, and having a husband die while in bed with his secretary isn't the ultimate rejection?' Pepper volleyed.

After bestowing upon Pepper a look that could slice a woman in half, Callie sighed. 'Oh, I'd say we were at the house maybe fifteen minutes.'

'Less,' Pepper corrected. 'Ten at the most.'

'Thank you, ladies,' Tish stated, glad to have gleaned even some information, given the circumstances.

'Well,' huffed Callie, trying to extricate herself from the scene, 'if you're through with all the drama, Ms Aviero, I'd best be on my way. I'm meeting a friend in Richmond for an early supper, followed by the theater, and I need to shower, dress, and put my face on.'

'You should have started an hour ago,' Pepper said beneath her breath.

'Keeping it classy, I see,' Callie dismissed as she dusted Schuyler's fingerprints off her paisley print scuba dress and opened the kitchen door. 'Gentlemen, Ms Tarragon, I'd say it's been real nice, but my mama taught me not to lie. *Ciao*.'

As the door swung closed behind her, Pepper fumed. 'Gah, that woman! Why does she bother me so?'

'She obviously knows the right buttons to press,' Tish observed.

'I feel like such a fool. I thought I was different from all those other women. I thought Sloane cared about me.'

'That's how men like him operate. They build up your confidence and gain your trust, only to smash both of them to pieces.'

'I can't believe I fell for his lines. I thought I was better than that. I thought I was smarter. I was in a relationship with someone who treated me like a queen and I threw it all away for an idiot.'

As Pepper proceeded to pour her heart out to Tish, Schuyler recognized it as his cue to return to the kitchen. 'Jules,' he prompted before clearing his throat and jerking his chin toward the kitchen door.

'What? But things were just getting juicy.' At the sight of both

Schuyler's and Tish's frowns, Jules amended his statement. 'I mean, you're right, Schuyler. I'd better cook that shrimp.'

The pair bid a dutiful retreat back to the galley.

'Do you miss your relationship with Jim Ainsley?' Tish asked.

'Only every day. I know I came across as being angry with Jim yesterday, but the truth is that I was angry with myself. He and I had been together a year and it was wonderful. He's a good man.'

'But?'

'But things started to get a little stale.'

'Stale?' Tish prompted and prayed Ms Aviero wouldn't disclose anything too intimate in nature.

'Jim and I had agreed early on that we weren't going to discuss commitment or marriage or anything like that. However, when we got near the one-year mark, it felt as though our relationship had plateaued. Even though I cared about Jim and didn't want to necessarily end the relationship, I became a bit bored with the arrangement we had.'

'Did you try talking to him about it?'

'No, I thought it might scare him off. As if I might be looking for him to propose marriage.'

'Were you looking for marriage?'

'No,' Pepper scoffed as she waved the notion away with the back of her hand. 'I've had a husband before. After twenty years, I finally divorced him and went back to my maiden name. I'll never do that again. No, what I wanted from Jim was to spend more time together. A long weekend at a bed-and-breakfast or in DC, roaming the museums and monuments. Or even a staycation scenario where I camped at his place for a couple of days, then he would stay at mine. You know, a little romance. A little break from the routine of dinner and movies and TV and playing cards with the Abercrombies.'

'That seems reasonable to me.'

'It would to most people, but Jim was always reluctant to leave town. I traveled to Mexico this past January to visit family and invited Jim to join me, but he declined. There was a chance of snow in the forecast and he wanted to be here to shovel out the driveway and walk for Tucker and Violet. Then, this May, I flew up to New York City for a high school reunion. I asked Jim to be my date. Again, he turned me down, claiming that he was needed to tend to garden club matters.'

'May is when gardens really start to take off,' Tish allowed.

'I know it's a busy time, but Jim is retired. He could have easily completed his garden club duties before we needed to leave that Friday evening. And New York is a short, easy flight. We'd have been back here early Sunday afternoon.' Pepper pulled a face, 'No, it's as if Jim doesn't want to leave Coleton Creek for any length of time because he'd be missing something.'

Tish's thoughts traveled to Violet Abercrombie, but she remained silent about the possibility that she and Ainsley shared a secret relationship. 'Would you get back together with Mr Ainsley, if given the chance?'

Pepper, her eyes pink and glassy, replied without hesitation. 'Absolutely. Not only would I jump at the opportunity to rekindle our relationship, but I'd thank God for that relationship each and every day and promise to never again take it for granted. But I'm afraid that chance won't come my way again, Ms Tarragon. I tossed aside the best man I've ever known for someone who, when confronted by two women who cared for him and wanted to go on caring for him, told them both to go to hell.' Pepper's sorrowful expression gave way to a sneer. 'And given all the pain I've caused Jim, that's exactly where *I* deserve to go.' She rushed off through the kitchen door as if it were the portal to the fiery underworld itself.

Tish was tempted to give chase but was distracted by a scratching sound radiating from behind the tall, plastic food-waste caddy in the farthest corner of the enclosed area.

Tish investigated the area, only to be met by the sight of a small dog, weighing approximately ten pounds and less than a foot tall, with long, curly hair, floppy ears, a rounded head, a soft, slightly rounded muzzle, and dark, shoe-button eyes. His paws were apricot in color, as though he had been traipsing through the soil of someone's garden, but the rest of his coat was pristinely white and well groomed.

He wandered to Tish's feet and gave a whimper before returning to the compost bin, where he stood on his hind legs and clawed at it, hungrily, with his front paws.

Acting on a hunch, Tish knelt down on the pavement and called to him. 'Biscuit?'

The dog confirmed his identity with a yip before rushing back to Tish and lavishing her hands and face with canine kisses.

'Well, now that we know who you are,' Tish told the Bichon Frise as she ran her hands through his fur, 'we'd better find out where you're going to stay.'

THIRTEEN

Biscuit, his belly filled with poached chicken and fresh water, and his collar secured to the top rail of the chain-link fence with a length of heavy-duty kitchen twine, snoozed in the shadows just outside the kitchen door.

Inside the kitchen, Tish, Schuyler, and Jules were finishing up the last of the day's chores and making plans for the evening.

'Thanks again, you guys. I couldn't have made it through this day without you,' Tish acknowledged her volunteers.

'What are friends for but to help out while you don't investigate a murder?' Jules teased.

'All joking aside,' Schuyler chuckled, 'there was nowhere I'd rather have been today than right here. With you.'

'Trying too hard,' Jules sang out of the side of his mouth.

Tish shot Jules a warning look and then bestowed Schuyler with a radiant smile. 'I loved having you around all day. Although I wish I'd actually been *here* more often than I was.'

'We're fine. You can relax and enjoy yourself tonight. And maybe we can make up for lost time,' Schuyler suggested.

'I would really like that.'

'Good. Speaking of tonight, I should get back to the café and touch base with Mary Jo and the kids to see who'll be joining us for dinner, who won't, and what everyone feels like doing. You two have any preferences?'

'Not cooking,' Tish joked. 'Apart from that, I'm up for anything.'

'Yeah, I'm sorry, but I won't be able to join y'all,' Jules excused himself. 'Mrs Newman sent me a text. Seeing as how I'm a bachelor, the Mahjong ladies decided to turn tonight's match into a potluck. There's going to be green beans, mac and cheese, fried chicken, banana pudding, and, instead of Mai Tais, Mrs Newman is trying her hand at mojitos.'

'Wow. Can we crash?' Schuyler teased.

'Seriously,' Tish concurred. 'We'll miss you tonight, but it sounds like you'll be in good hands.'

'Well, you know how grandmas are,' Jules posited. 'Everyone's too skinny.'

Tish was about to joke that Jules might need to lead a second water aerobics lesson to work off dinner, but was interrupted by the sight of Sheriff Reade peeking his head through the kitchen door.

'Hey, I'm glad I caught you,' he announced to no one in particular.

'We were just about to pack it in for the day,' Tish explained. 'Have you found a place for Biscuit to stay tonight?'

'That's why I'm here.' Reade stepped through the doorway and approached the stainless-steel counter where Tish stood. 'I called Richmond Animal Control, the SPCA, the Humane Society, and a few local shelters. They're all completely maxed out this weekend due to Richmond police breaking up a dog-fighting ring last night.'

'What are we going to do with him?'

'I can call some of the smaller nonprofit rescue groups out east if you'd like. I'm not sure they'd be able to pick him up tonight, but I can try.'

Tish thought of the small white dog outside the kitchen door and the trauma he'd already faced. She also thought of a certain young lady back home who might benefit from a furry distraction. 'No, he appears to be in very good health, but I'm not sure he needs to be traveling that far tonight. Besides, this isn't an emergency; it doesn't seem right to ask a tiny nonprofit group of volunteers to send someone out here on a weekend when another animal might need rescuing. I'll take him home with me.'

'Are you sure? I can ask one of our K-9 unit members to take him for the weekend.'

'That's OK. I have a teenage girl staying with me who will be thrilled to see his fuzzy little face, even if it is just until Monday morning.'

'You're right,' Jules agreed. 'Kayla would love him.'

'Especially since Uncle Jules won't be around tonight.' Tish slathered on some fake guilt.

'Hey, I'd be there if I could, but you do understand that turning down a Southern woman's offer of fried chicken could get you killed, don't you?'

'One murder at a time, please,' Reade half joked.

Jules mumbled a self-conscious apology. 'Sorry.'

'Well, if you're fine with the dog, Tish, then I'll wish you all a good evening. Oh, and thanks for your help today. I appreciate you getting folks to open up about Shackleford.'

'Open up? I can't get them to be quiet about him. All I want to do is cater the luncheon.'

Sheriff Reade exchanged commiserating glances with Schuyler and Jules. 'Uh-huh. Night, y'all.'

The trio bid Reade a pleasant evening.

'So, do you want to follow me back to Cookin' the Books, Tish? Or should I follow you?' Schuyler asked.

'Oh, I can't leave right now. I promised Zadie Morris I'd bring her scones and cream. If you want to go on without me, that's fine. Biscuit and I shouldn't be too far behind you.'

'Get out!' Jules exclaimed. 'You're meeting Zadie privately?'

'Yes, she's trading me lipstick for scones and cream. Why?'

'My mama used to love Zadie Cosmetics.'

'Well, if you bring along some of that tea you've been perfecting, I'm sure she wouldn't mind if you tagged along. That is, if Mrs Newman doesn't already have the limes cut for the mojitos.'

'I'm not due at Mrs Newman's for another hour. I'll get brewing.' Jules dashed to the teapot on the stove.

'If you and Jules have to deliver scones, I'll take Biscuit with me,' Schuyler reasoned. 'He'd be happier running around the café parking lot with the kids than stuck here, tied up outside the kitchen. I'll swing by the pet store and pick up some dog food and a proper leash on the way.'

'No, I couldn't let you do that,' Tish was quick to answer. 'Not with that gorgeous car of yours.'

'Why not? I'll put a towel down so the dirt from his paws doesn't get on the upholstery.'

'It's more than that. Biscuit . . .'

'Biscuit is like me when I was a kid,' Jules interjected as he filled the kettle with water. 'My mama always said she should send me for piano lessons because I was the *pianist* kid in town. Get it – *pee-in-ist*?'

'Oh,' Schuyler's brow furrowed. 'But he's been fine out there. Last I checked Biscuit hadn't gone at all.'

'Probably dehydrated,' Tish hazarded.

'Or maybe just being around that creepy Shackleford made him nervous,' Jules proposed.

'Either way, I'll figure out a way to get him to the café,' Schuyler vowed. 'Safe and dry.'

A man of his word, twenty minutes later Schuyler loaded Biscuit on to a makeshift, backseat wee-wee pad constructed, MacGyver-style, from plastic grocery bags, cardboard egg cartons, kitchen paper, and tea towels, and set off for Cookin' the Books.

Tish and Jules, meanwhile, locked up the kitchen and, with a tray of delectable scones in tow, walked to Zadie Morris's house. As they approached the boxwood- and perennial-lined front walk, Sheriff Reade waved to them from his position outside Shackleford's house. 'How nice of you to bring refreshments,' he exclaimed as he approached.

'We're bringing these to Ms Morris,' Tish replied.

'I thought you were leaving for the day, not bribing people with baked goods.'

'I'm not bribing, I'm *nurturing*,' she corrected.

'Ah, you know, we should talk about you doing some nurturing – I mean catering – for the Sheriff Office's holiday party this December.'

'You and your crew wind up at too many of my parties as it is, don't you think?'

'Maybe, but if you'd just cook for us in the first place, it would cut out the middleman. You know, the dead person.'

'That might be safer for all concerned. Sure, next time you're at the café, we'll discuss it.'

'Cool. Enjoy your, um, *nurturing*.'

'We will, thanks.'

As Reade returned to his post, Tish and Jules continued along the path to Zadie Morris's front door.

'Hmm,' Jules remarked.

'What's "Hmm"?'

'The sheriff was awfully chatty. And he's doing his hair differently. It's edgier. Sexier. Did you notice?'

'No, I can't say that I did,' Tish denied as they reached their destination.

'Think there might be a particular reason for that?'

'No.' Tish pressed the doorbell. 'People change their hair all the time.'

'But what about the chattiness? And the invitation to cater the Sheriff Department's party?'

'Sheriff Reade is a regular customer of mine. Why wouldn't he chat or hire me for a job?'

'I don't know. Still seems odd to me. Like maybe he's sweet on you.'

'Jules, just this morning you scolded me for not addressing Schuyler as my boyfriend. Now you're suggesting Sheriff Reade has a crush on me. You make me sound like the Helen of Hobson Glen.'

'No, but you are beautiful, smart, funny, a great cook, and a crime-fighting genius. Why wouldn't Reade find that absolutely irresistible?'

There being no reply to the first door chime, Tish pressed the buzzer again. 'Do you ever think of anything other than sex and romantic intrigue?'

'Of course. I also think of clothes, wine, and food. Not necessarily in that order.'

Tish rolled her eyes and awaited the arrival of Zadie at the front door. When several seconds had elapsed without a single sound from inside the house, Tish gave the front door a series of hard raps with her right hand. 'Ms Morris? Ms Morris, it's Tish Tarragon. I have your scones and tea.'

'I'm here,' Zadie's voice floated through a nearby open window. 'The door's open. Come on in.'

Following orders, Tish and Jules pushed open the front door and stepped inside. There, to the left of the entrance foyer, stretched an expansive living room painted a brilliant shade of crimson and featuring a clean-lined mid-century modern sofa upholstered in dark-gray linen and covered with a myriad of colorful pillows and cushions. Above said sofa hung a collection of black-and-white photographs in an assortment of frames.

Zadie, her face scrubbed clean, sat at the end of the sofa nearest the front window with her feet elevated on an oversized white ottoman that doubled as a coffee table. 'Sorry, I didn't hear you. I was watching a cardinal that took up residence in the crepe myrtle out front and must have nodded off.'

'No problem.' Tish instructed Jules to place the tray of goodies on the ottoman. 'However, I don't think it's wise to leave your front door unlocked at a time like this. Not when there's a murderer lurking in the neighborhood.'

'Locks only serve to keep out honest people.'

'Maybe' – Tish locked the deadbolt on the front door – 'but there's also no point in making things easier for the dishonest ones.'

'I can understand why you might have nodded off,' Jules commented. 'It's terribly warm in here. Do you want me to close the window and put on the air conditioning?'

'Oh, no. The heat doesn't much bother me and I rather enjoy the sound of that cardinal. They're messengers from the other side, you know.'

Tish had heard the legend about cardinals being the reincarnated souls of the departed, but she wasn't convinced of its veracity. 'Would you like your scone, cream, and jam now? Or would you like me to save them in the kitchen?'

'I would love them now, if you don't mind.' Zadie slowly lowered her feet from the ottoman so as to make more room for the tray and its contents.

'I brewed you a special Earl Grey tea blend,' Jules announced as he poured the hot beverage from an insulated thermos jug into a porcelain teacup. 'Do you want milk or sugar?'

'No, thank you. Perhaps just some lemon?'

'At your service.' Jules extracted a lemon wedge from a small sandwich bag.

Meanwhile, Tish sliced the scone, spread it with cream, and topped it with jam.

'You've both gone to so much trouble,' an appreciative Zadie remarked.

'We're not done yet.' Jules extracted his phone from his shorts pocket and, after a few points and clicks, a string-quartet rendition of 'Autumn Leaves' began to play, much to Zadie's delight.

'Oh, I feel as though I'm back at the Palm Court.'

'That was our goal.'

'You've succeeded. The tea is a wonderful blend of spice and citrus, and the scone is absolute perfection. Not dry at all, but tender and light.'

Tish and Jules sat in a pair of neighboring armchairs and watched as Zadie finished her repast with zeal, interrupting only to answer a question or to exchange observations about food, the weather, the neighborhood, and, of course, the garden club luncheon.

As Jules's phone moved on to the fourth song in a classic playlist, Zadie swallowed the last bit of scone, dotted the corners of her mouth with the linen napkin provided, and folded her hands on her lap. 'You've made an old woman very happy. Thank you. I'm afraid, as much as I hate the phrase "eat and run," I'm feeling rather exhausted at the moment.'

Tish was more than forgiving. 'That's fine, Ms Morris. We completely understand. It's been a difficult past twenty-four hours for everyone.'

'Yes. And as much as I don't mind the heat, it was a terribly hot day for September. I may have overdone things with my walk.'

'It's easy to do in this heat and humidity.' Tish closed the front living-room window while Jules went to the thermostat and switched on the air conditioning. 'We'll just pack up the tea tray and be out of your way so you can rest.'

'No, you two run along. You can fetch that in the morning. Unless you need it right away.'

'No, we won't need that tray until the afternoon.'

'Ah, then it's settled. I'll wash up the plates in the morning and get your lipsticks ready, too. Julian' – Zadie addressed Jules by his full name – 'what color did your mama wear?'

'What? Me? You mean you're giving my mama a lipstick?' Jules asked, his voice a blend of excitement and bewilderment.

'You said she was a *Zadie Lady*, didn't you?'

'Yes, but . . .'

'So what color did she wear?'

'I don't remember the name, but she was madder than a puffed toad when she couldn't get it any longer. It was pink. Not too light, not too dark – like the color of the roses that grow by the outdoor pool at the lifestyle center.'

'Ah, yes, that would be *Pink Organza*,' Zadie declared. 'I'll have a tube of it ready for you in the morning.'

'Thank you. Mama will love it!'

'Yes, thank you, Ms Morris.'

'No, it's I who thank you.' She rose from the sofa and brushed the crumbs from her lap. As she straightened up to take her first step, her knees buckled, sending her tumbling toward the ottoman.

Tish and Jules each grabbed one of Zadie's arms, preventing her from falling, head first, into the tea tray.

'Are you OK?' Tish asked.

'Yes, I'm fine. I guess I was sitting on that sofa longer than I thought. Blood rushed from my head.'

'Here, we'll help you sit down.' Jules began easing her back into her seat.

'No, I don't want to sit any longer. If you wouldn't mind, could you help me to my bedroom?'

'Of course not. Just tell us which way to go.'

Zadie led them across the living room and down a long corridor where, just past the guest bathroom, she rallied and pushed aside the helping hands of her escorts. Tish and Jules complied, but stayed close behind as Zadie shuffled along to the spacious master bedroom at the end of the hall.

With its thirteen-foot-tall ceilings, crown molding, and a set of French doors that opened on to the rear patio, the airiness of the room was, of itself, a marvel, but of particular interest was the king-sized, upholstered back bed that occupied three-quarters of the room.

Covered with a six-inch-thick quilted silk satin duvet in a glorious shade of blue-green and a bevy of pillows, Zadie Morris's nightly resting spot was more like something seen in an Arab odah or an old Hollywood mansion than a retirement community in central Virginia.

'Wow.' Tish breathed.

Jules echoed the sentiment. 'Oh, my.'

'Where did you expect a former cosmetics queen to sleep? In a fleece-lined sleeping bag?' Zadie teased.

'It's wonderfully glamorous.'

'This bed was my only concession to the "high life." Most of my things are well made, high quality, and not too flashy, but I figured since this is the room one last sees at night and first sees every morning, some over-the-top furnishings were permitted.'

'It truly is lovely.' As she watched Zadie perch on the edge of the bed and remove her shoes, Tish's eyes became drawn to a faded color photograph that rested upon the nearby nightstand. The photo, displayed in an elegant, vintage silver frame, depicted a boy, no older than six years of age, with an overgrown head of wavy, flaxen hair and a slightly mischievous, gap-toothed grin. He was standing on the front stoop of a yellow-shingled bungalow with a black Labrador retriever puppy in his arms.

Zadie followed Tish's gaze. 'That's my godson.'

'Aw, very sweet. How old is he now?'

'He's no longer with us. He was just sixteen when he passed. You're right, though. He was very sweet. That's why I've kept his photo all these years – to remind me that despite all the wickedness in the world, there is some good in it.'

'I'm so sorry.'

'Not as sorry as I am.'

Tish suddenly felt like a voyeur. A woman's bedroom was the secret chamber where she kept hidden love letters, family photos, and the ingredients of her daily beauty regimen. It was not a place for casual visitors. 'Is there anything else you need before we go? Would you like us to turn down the bed for you?'

Zadie stretched and yawned. 'No, thank you. No, I'm not turning in quite yet; otherwise, I'll be awake at three in the morning. I'm just going to take a little nap.'

Tish nodded. 'We'll lock the door on the way out.'

True to their word, Jules and Tish retreated down the hallway, through the living room, and into the foyer, where they turned the twist knob of the deadbolt and shut the front door behind them.

The pair remained close-mouthed for the first block of their walk back to the lifestyle center. It was Jules who finally broke the silence. 'I hope Ms Morris is OK. She was awfully wobbly.'

'I hope so, too. I tend to think it's all the excitement over Shackleford's murder. She lives right next door; it must be quite frightening.'

'Not frightening enough for her to lock her front door.'

Tish shrugged. 'That doesn't mean she wasn't scared. Just means she didn't give in to her fears.'

'People of her generation are resilient, aren't they? I have a great-aunt in her eighties who still insists on making chicken and dumplings for our Christmas Eve gathering. Everyone keeps offering to change the menu or even bring food in, but she won't hear of it. That's the way Christmas Eve has always been and that's the way it'll continue to be.'

'I wonder if we'll be that stubborn in our old age.'

Jules broke into hysterics. 'Old age? You're that stubborn now.'

'I suppose you're right. I can be rather tenacious.'

'Honey, you can be as tough as a pine knot.'

They had reached the lifestyle-center parking lot. 'When it comes to being tough, I don't hold a candle to Ms Morris. Still, I plan to check in with her first thing in the morning. Under the pretense of collecting our tray, of course.'

'Good call. Both the heat and stress can take a serious toll. And even though she loves her daily walks, she should probably take it easy until it cools off some.'

Tish agreed. 'So, I'd best be getting back to the café.'

'Yeah, I'm gonna dash to that convenience store just down the road and see if I can pick up a decent bouquet of flowers. I don't want to show up at Mrs Newman's empty-handed.'

'No, you could have your *Official Southerner Card* revoked.' Tish embraced her friend. 'Well, have a good time tonight.'

'Yeah.' He returned the hug. 'Say hello to MJ and the kids for me. I'll miss seeing them.'

'I know, but they'll be fine. I'll explain to them that you have another engagement. They'll totally understand.'

'I hope so, because I can't really turn down a night of Mahjong, booze, and good Southern home cooking, can I?' Despite the dazzling smile on his face, it was quite clear that the only person Jules was trying to convince was himself.

'You'd be foolish if you did.'

'I know, right? Well, I'll see you tomorrow morning. Seven thirty?' he asked as he climbed behind the wheel of his black Mini Cooper.

'Perfect,' she proclaimed and watched as Jules pulled out of the parking lot and turned left on Coleton Creek Way, toward the community's passcode-secured front gates.

When Jules was out of view, Tish opened the driver's side door of the Matrix and perched upon the front bumper of the car while the hot air trapped inside the vehicle escaped. With nothing but the sound of singing birds and a gentle breeze rustling the trees, the few minutes' quiet was exactly what Tish needed to clear her head.

In the midst of all the chatter, all the investigations, all the luncheon preparations, she could perceive that something wasn't quite right. There was, of course, the matter of Jules – his odd behavior and, beneath the surface, an impalpable sadness. But that, Tish determined, could be remedied after the luncheon by means of a candid discussion and her undivided attention.

No, Tish decided, there was something else. Something completely unrelated to Jules and his pool high jinks. Something she'd noticed but had since forgotten. Something she couldn't quite place.

FOURTEEN

Tish arrived at Cookin' the Books both exhausted and meditative, but her mood promptly lifted at the sight of Kayla Okensholt and Charlotte Ballantyne standing outside the café, laughing and smiling while playing with a highly animated, tail-wagging Biscuit.

Tish brought the car to a stop at the end of the parking lot and, tossing her car keys in her handbag, strode across the gravel-lined area to greet them. 'Hi, ladies. Is Biscuit behaving for you?'

'Oh my gosh, Aunt Tish, he's the sweetest little dog,' Kayla exclaimed as she threw her arms around Tish's torso. 'He's like the best medicine ever.'

'Good.' Tish returned the hug and planted a kiss on top of the girl's auburn head. With her arm still around Kayla's shoulders, she turned her attention to the raven-haired girl with the pixie haircut. 'Charlotte, I can't thank you enough for helping out here today. You're a real lifesaver.'

'No problem. When it was quiet, Celestine taught me a pretty awesome piping technique. I'm going to use it on my dad's birthday cake next month.'

'Celestine is a cake goddess, isn't she?' Tish acknowledged as she bent down to give Biscuit a pat on the head. Since she'd last seen the dog, his collar and kitchen twine had been replaced by a fluorescent yellow harness and a retractable leash, which was being controlled by Charlotte. 'Someone's moved up in the world.'

'Schuyler thought Biscuit needed to be wearing something more visible in case we need to walk him at night,' Kayla explained.

Tish stood up. 'And the leash?'

'It retracts so we won't trip over it.'

Schuyler Thompson had clearly thought of every eventuality. 'Ah, fancy.'

'You should see Biscuit's new bed,' Charlotte said. 'Kayla and I might not be able to find him to walk him in the morning.'

Kayla, prompted by Charlotte's comment about the morning, asked, 'Oh, yeah, is it OK if Charlotte stays over tonight?'

'As long as it's OK with your mom and Charlotte's dad, it's fine with me.'

'I called my dad. He's cool with it,' Charlotte confirmed.

'Mom is, too. Charlotte and I are sharing a giant sleeping bag in her room,' Kayla explained. 'By the way, Gregory's here. He brought his friend, Anthony.'

'That's great news,' Tish exclaimed. 'I'm so relieved your mother managed to get him to come.'

'More than that, he's staying the night. Anthony, too. They'll be on the pullout sofa in the living room, if that's OK.'

Tish was ecstatic to have Mary Jo and her children united under one roof, although the puzzle of how six people and one dog might comfortably share a two-bedroom apartment with one bathroom was a conundrum even the logistical masterminds at the CIA or MI5 would struggle to resolve. 'That's . . . wonderful. Absolutely wonderful. How is your mother?'

'Meh. She tried to call my dad and invite him to dinner tonight, but it turned into a shouting match. Gregory and I both tried texting him afterward to get him to come to dinner, but he never replied.'

'I'm sorry, honey. It's a tough time right now, for everyone, but your father loves you. He'll eventually come around.'

'Yeah, well, Gregory and I might have been a little bit . . . angry when we texted him. I think I used like a thousand exclamation marks. If I were him, I'm not sure I'd answer me either.' Kayla cast down her eyes and bit her lip.

'Hey, it's OK to feel angry right now. Give it a day and try contacting him tomorrow with a different tone. I'm sure he'll answer you.'

Charlotte folded her arms across her chest. 'That's what I told her.'

Charlotte, her mother having been sent to prison, had been working through her own anger issues of late. Tish draped an arm around each of the young women and pulled them close. 'The two of you possess such strength, brains, and beauty. You both make me very proud to know you. So, shall we go in and see what's for dinner?'

Kayla piped up. 'Schuyler ordered from Antonio's. We're getting pizzas, pastas, salad, and meatballs without sauce for Biscuit.'

'Your boyfriend is really great,' Charlotte praised.

'Pardon?' The term 'your boyfriend' caught Tish completely off guard.

'Schuyler,' Kayla clarified. 'He's totally sweet, and cool, and smart, and perfect.'

'Yeah, and he's kinda hot. You know, for an old guy,' Charlotte added.

Kayla nodded in complete accord.

Tish took umbrage at the girls' description of Schuyler as being an old guy, but she decided to laugh it off. 'I'll be sure to let him know his Geritol supplements are working.'

The girls probably hadn't a clue as to what Geritol might be, but it didn't matter. They were more concerned Tish might pass along their compliments. As they squealed and giggled and begged Tish not to tell Schuyler they said he was hot, Tish watched through the front windows of the café as the man himself, his sleeves rolled up to his elbows and a kitchen towel over one shoulder, conversed with Mary Jo and Celestine while he arranged the tables for dinner.

Kayla was right. He was perfect.

As if he could sense Tish watching him, Schuyler looked up and waved out the window before moving to the wooden screen door of the café.

'He's coming this way,' Kayla exclaimed.

The girls, tittering all the way, ran off with Biscuit.

'What's that all about?' Schuyler asked as he approached.

'They were just debriefing me on all your accomplishments this evening.'

Schuyler eyed the girls as they giggled at a distant corner of the parking lot. 'Uh-oh,' he stated in a tone of exaggerated concern. 'I hope I got a good report card.'

'It was quite exceptional, actually.'

Schuyler slid his hands around Tish's waist and pulled her closer. 'Good. Do I get an ice-cream cone?'

'Maybe. If you eat all your dinner. But for now . . .' She gave him a gentle kiss on the lips.

'Scratch the ice cream. I'll have more of that.' Spying Charlotte and Kayla watching and whispering, he changed the mood of the conversation. 'How was your visit with Zadie?'

'Good. She seemed to enjoy the scone and cream, even though she wasn't feeling well. Jules and I had to help her to bed, poor thing. I think this whole murder investigation is getting to her.'

'Understandable.' Schuyler removed his hands from Tish's waist and began leading her to the café.

'I'm going to check on her first thing in the morning.'

'Good idea. I promised Gregory a game of basketball early tomorrow morning, but I can swing by Coleton Creek afterward if you need my help.'

Tish was astounded by Schuyler's never-ending generosity. 'You have a basketball date with my best friend's son?'

'I know he's going through a tough time right now. If it helps to have another man around to talk to, I figured I might as well be that man.'

'If you don't stop, I'm going to be forced to kiss you again,' she teased.

'Then I'd better keep on going.'

Tish laughed. 'As for your offer to stop by Coleton Creek tomorrow, I should be fine. Celestine and Jules are with me all day. And it's a buffet, so it's far easier than a sit-down luncheon.'

'Well, if you change your mind . . .'

'Thanks. But I think you've done enough already. You helped me in the kitchen . . .'

'As I said, I like being near you.'

'You've taken care of dinner . . .'

'I placed a phone order.'

'And you took care of Biscuit.'

'It's been fun. I never had a dog growing up.'

'Was he good for you? He didn't make a mess, did he?'

'No. He went in the pet-store parking lot, just like he should, and he's been well behaved since we've gotten here. Still, I got some pads for tonight. Just in case he sneaks in to sleep with the girls.'

'You think of everything, don't you?'

'I try. Oh, I also stopped and got you a little treat. Remember that Chardonnay you liked during our wine-tasting trip to Charlottesville?'

'Not the one from Monticello?'

'The same. It's chilling in the refrigerator. I'll go pour you a glass,' he announced as they stepped over the threshold of Cookin' the Books.

As Schuyler traveled behind the counter to fetch the drink, Tish greeted Mary Jo and Celestine, who were busy setting the bank of café tables Schuyler had pushed together.

Celestine, wearing her typical workday garb of bright floral-printed sleeveless top, denim Capri pants, and orthopedic sandals, stood at the windowed side of the resulting banquet table, folding cloth napkins into triangles. As she placed each napkin on the table and gave it a sturdy crease, her oversized hot-pink earrings – orchestrated to match both her lipstick and pedicure – jingled like tiny wind chimes against her unnaturally crimson hair.

'Hey, Celestine,' Tish greeted.

'Hey, sugar. How was your day?'

'Busy. And yours?'

'Good. Great big lunch crowd, then everyone cleared out for the hot part of the day. Charlotte did good.'

In stark contrast to Celestine's bold style, Mary Jo stood on the opposite side of the table, nearest the counter. Devoid of all makeup and jewelry – including the yellow-gold and diamond wedding ring set she'd worn for nearly twenty years – Mary Jo had knotted her highlighted shoulder-length brunette locks into a messy bun at the nape of her neck and pulled on a pajama-like ensemble of black-and-white striped terrycloth tunic and white stretch-knit pants. She stood barefoot on the café tile as she meted out silverware and plates.

'How are you, honey?' Tish asked as she gave Mary Jo a hug.

She shrugged. 'I don't know anymore. I called Glen to invite him to dinner with the promise that if he came, I wouldn't argue with him, only to wind up in a huge argument over the phone.'

'Kayla told me. What happened?'

'Glen told me he couldn't make the dinner because he was spending the weekend with Lisa – that's his girlfriend's name – and felt he needed to put some distance between us in order to gain perspective on our life together and focus on what he wants from his future. Can you believe that? *Perspective.* If he'd had any sense of perspective to begin with, he wouldn't have tossed his family aside for some tart in her twenties!'

'Is that how young . . .?'

'Yes, *Lisa*' – Mary Jo hissed the name – 'is a first-grade teacher at our elementary school. One of Kayla's friends has a younger brother who's her student.'

Schuyler rescued Tish from having to provide further comment by depositing a chilled glass of Chardonnay in her hand.

'Anyhoo,' Mary Jo went on, 'I lost it. I shouldn't have, but I did. Not only was I angry that Glen, who rarely spent any time with us, was now spending the weekend with this trollop, but I was furious that he's so willing to push his children aside to start this wonderful new life. Our children – *his* children – are grappling with the fact that their father won't be living with them any longer, and all he can think about is *his* future?'

'It's as if he's lost his mind,' Tish remarked.

'Midlife crisis,' was Celestine's verdict. 'Mr Rufus went through one a few years back. Dyed his hair jet black and got *Carpe Diem* tattooed in big, red letters on his upper left arm. Only thing was, Troy, the tattoo artist, was a bit of a tippler in those days and forgot the first "e."'

Schuyler's eyes narrowed as he visualized the resulting artwork. 'Carp diem?'

'Yep. Mr Rufus didn't notice the mistake till he got back home. So he went back to Troy and asked him to fix it. Unfortunately, there wasn't enough space to add the "e," so Troy tattooed a giant fish underneath the letters, instead.'

Uncertain whether or not they should laugh, Tish, Schuyler, and Mary Jo fell into an awkward silence.

'So, um, yeah, he may not have gotten a fish tattoo, but Glen could totally be suffering a midlife crisis,' Tish submitted after several seconds had elapsed.

'I admit, I wondered that myself,' Mary Jo allowed. 'But it doesn't matter much now, does it? I know I'll survive this. And, someday, perhaps I'll forgive Glen for destroying our marriage the way he has, but if he continues to hurt our children by maintaining his "distance" – well, that's something I could never forgive.'

'I hear ya. If someone ever inflicted pain on my children, they'd be introduced the back of my cast-iron skillet,' Celestine agreed.

'I'm sure Glen will still be a father to Gregory and Kayla,' Tish maintained. 'He may not have spent much time at home, but he's always been there for the important moments. This is all new to everyone. Maybe a weekend without the kids will make him realize how much he misses them and needs them in his life.'

'I hope you're right. There was a time when I wouldn't have believed Glen could ever be unfaithful, let alone run off with some twenty-something schoolteacher, so I'm sorry if I'm not too optimistic about his parenting skills right now.'

'You've every right to be skeptical.' Schuyler placed a reassuring hand on Mary Jo's shoulder. 'Although we can't offer any guarantees regarding your husband's future conduct, we can promise that we'll be there for you and the kids every step of the way.'

'Amen,' Celestine seconded.

Mary Jo's eyes grew glassy. 'I can't thank you all enough. I don't know where we'd be without your help.'

Tish flashed a gentle smile. 'You'll never have to find out.'

'Unless, of course, the upstairs apartment floor gives way into the café,' Celestine joked. 'Four kids, two adults, and a dog in a tiny apartment. And I thought I was crazy.'

Mary Jo's face filled with sudden worry. 'Oh, you don't mind the kids having friends stay, do you, Tish?'

'Of course not. They need support just as you do, and it's good for them to have the distraction.'

'By the way, Tish, I dashed home and brought over some extra sheets and pillows, so y'all will be a bit more comfortable,' Celestine announced.

'Thanks, I'm afraid I have enough linens for the spare bedroom but hadn't actually thought of the sofa bed. I didn't anticipate needing it so quickly.'

'As a mother of four, grandmother of six, and wife of a man with a five-inch fish tattooed on his arm, I've learned to anticipate the unexpected.'

Tish laughed. 'Are you and Mr Rufus joining us for dinner tonight?'

'No, Schuyler invited us, but I have those cakes to frost for the luncheon. I did, however, take him up on his offer to order us a couple of pizzas to take home. Which was mighty generous.'

'Least I can do. I remember when you and my mom would work here all day and then have to figure out what to cook for dinner. I can't imagine having to do that after being on your feet for hours. And with cupcakes still to finish tonight,' he explained.

'And I can't imagine having to deal with some of the ying-yangs that parade in and out of your office,' Celestine chuckled.

'I guess we're square, then.'

At the mention of Celestine's pizzas, a young deliveryman appeared at the door of the café, bearing a corrugated cardboard box that once contained canned diced tomatoes. Atop the carton rested three square pizza boxes.

Schuyler paid the young man and returned with their feast. 'I believe these two are yours, Celestine.' He grabbed the top two boxes.

'Yep, one veggie delight with extra cheese for me and my daughter, and one pineapple and bacon for Mr Rufus. You know, I swear that man isn't human. Who, in heaven's name, puts pineapple on a pizza?' And with that pearl of wisdom, Celestine made her exit.

As Celestine made her way home, Schuyler unpacked the rest of the food from the box and distributed it accordingly. There was pasta primavera for vegetarian Charlotte, spaghetti and meatballs for Kayla, oozy, comforting lasagna for Mary Jo, chicken Parmigiana for Schuyler, lemony chicken Française on spinach for Tish, a large tossed salad to share, and, to satisfy the never-diminishing appetites of seventeen-year-old Gregory and Anthony, a large pepperoni pizza and two individual servings of baked ziti. Even Biscuit was given a plain meatball, cut into bite-sized pieces.

It was not the most cheerful of suppers, but it was light

years away from being the most miserable. Schuyler kept everyone's drinks refilled, while Tish and Mary Jo endeavored to keep the conversation light, focusing on such topics as favorite foods, school, movies, and Tish's plans for a Halloween-themed menu. It was, overall, what it was intended to be: a comfortable family-style gathering that provided not just proper nutrition to Mary Jo and her children but a sense of warmth, support, and stability.

When dinner was finished, Mary Jo ordered Tish and Schuyler to relax on the front porch while she and the kids cleared the table and did the dishes.

'But, Mom,' Gregory whined, 'Anthony and I were going to go to the skate park.'

'And you still can. It won't take long to put away leftovers and load up a dishwasher,' Mary Jo countered. 'Our family still has rules, number one of which is we clean up after ourselves.'

Leaving Mary Jo to supervise her clean-up crew, Schuyler and Tish, the bottle of Chardonnay in tow, retired to the porch swing. As the sun began to set, the heat of the day diminished, replaced by a slightly humid, but cooling breeze.

Tish leaned her head on Schuyler's shoulder and tucked her feet beneath her as Schuyler poured each of them a glass of wine and placed the bottle on a nearby coffee table.

'To you and your thoughtfulness.' Tish raised her glass. 'This dinner tonight was perfect.'

'And to you' – Schuyler touched his glass to hers – 'for making thoughtfulness easy.'

'Smooth.'

'Just wait until you hear my poetry,' he joked. 'Well, they're more like limericks really, but I guarantee you've never heard anything quite like them.'

'I'm sure I haven't,' Tish laughed and took a sip of wine. 'Seriously, though, you've been invaluable. You made what could have been a difficult day a pleasant one.'

'Thanks. I only hope to continue to be invaluable to you in the future.'

The setting sun reflected in Schuyler's eyes, transforming them from deep azure to a striking icy blue. Tish leaned her head toward his, her lips slightly parted, but before her mouth could land on

Schuyler's she was distracted by footsteps and kissing sounds coming from the café door.

Tish and Schuyler turned around to see Gregory and Anthony dashing out the screen door and down the front steps.

'See you later, Aunt Tish. Bye, Schuyler. Don't have *too* much fun. We have a date on the basketball court in the morning,' Gregory shouted, a devilish smile upon his face. 'Oh, and thanks again for dinner.'

'Yeah, thanks,' Anthony echoed.

The boys hopped on their skateboards and rode down the quiet, macadam-paved street toward Hobson Glen's new skate park.

When they were out of sight, Schuyler remarked to Tish, 'There have been several moments in my life when I've regretted not having children. That wasn't one of them.'

Tish laughed and leaned in again, only to be interrupted by Mary Jo screaming through the screen door.

'Gregory! Gregory! Gregory? Oh, that boy had better be home by ten thirty; otherwise, I'll . . .' Her eye landed on Tish and Schuyler snuggled tightly on the porch swing. 'Oh, I'm sorry. I thought Gregory was still out here. Um, just ignore me and go back to whatever you were, um, doing. I'll be upstairs with the girls watching *The Greatest Showman.* Hey, is it OK with you, Tish, if the girls and I shower tonight? This way we're ready to open the café and won't be in your way when you need to get out to Coleton Creek.'

'Yeah, that would be ideal, actually. As long as you're comfortable with that.'

'More than comfortable. We're gonna make some popcorn later and enjoy the movie in our pajamas. You're welcome to join us but . . . um, yeah, you two enjoy yourselves. Goodnight, Schuyler, and thanks again for everything, including taking Gregory to play basketball tomorrow. He's really looking forward to it.'

'Anytime, MJ. I gave you my number. If you ever need me, don't hesitate to give me a shout. Although I hope to be around here more often than I have been . . .' Schuyler gazed at Tish and pulled her closer.

'Ah, that would be nice. Well, I'll leave you to . . . I'll leave you alone.' Mary Jo gave the thumbs-up and OK sign to Tish before departing with a wink.

'The Okensholts aren't a subtle bunch, are they?' Schuyler observed.

Tish smiled. 'Well, they've been waiting quite a while for me to meet someone . . . worthwhile. Someone who knows I take my Italian food with spinach instead of pasta.'

'I might have been looking for brownie points there.'

'Well, you got them.' Tish tilted her head toward Schuyler's. This time their lips made contact in a slow, delicious kiss.

'Schuyler Thompson, y'old scallywag, I never thought I'd see you out here necking on your mama's front porch again!' came a shrill cackle from the road.

The sound shook Tish and Schuyler from the pleasant haze of their romantic interlude and sent them crashing back to reality. Wine splashed out of their glasses as they struggled to disentangle themselves from each other.

Standing at the entrance of the parking lot was an elderly woman. She was small, withered, and dressed in a purple-and-lilac housedress with a belted waist, a ragged beige cable-knit cardigan, and a pair of white lace-up wedge-heeled shoes. Her yellowish silver hair was piled high on to her head in an elaborate bun, the wayward tresses of which were being groomed by the small green parrot that sat upon her shoulder.

'That's the same reaction you had as a boy, too,' the woman continued to screech. 'Sitting up quick and pretending to be all proper.'

'Hello, Ms Kemper. Hello, Langhorne,' a blushing Schuyler greeted.

'Schuyler, you seem to have taken temporary leave of your manners. Show some respect,' she chastised.

The eccentric daughter of the inventor of lip balm, Enid Kemper was a spinster whose only family members had passed away long ago. Serving as friend, family, and sole companion, Enid's beloved green conure, Langhorne, was expected to receive the royal treatment wherever he traveled. Able to say 'hello' in ten languages, Langhorne was given frequent bubble baths, ate with Enid at the lunch counter at Tish's café, was permitted entry to the local movie theater, and even held his own bus pass.

'Good evening, Langhorne.' Tish made certain to give the conure top billing. 'Evening, Ms Kemper.'

'At least one of you has sense. Though sense don't help much if you don't have luck. I heard there was a murder where you were working today, Ms Tarragon.'

'Yes, it's quite unfortunate. It's definitely cast a pall over tomorrow's luncheon.'

'Hmm, sounds like I'd better eat at your café while it's still around. News like that can take a business down. You serving tomorrow?'

'We are, yes. Mary Jo, Kayla, and Charlotte will be covering for me and Celestine.'

'Tell them to reserve our spot. Langhorne and I will be in for sweet tea and that pimento cheese and fried chicken sandwich of yours after church.'

'The *Zelda Fitzgerald*. Sure, I'll let them know.'

'Only this time we'll have it without the biscuit. Langhorne and I are watching our carbs.'

'Oh, well, I hardly think you need to—'

Enid put a hand to the side of her mouth, separating her face from Langhorne's. 'It's for his sake, really. A bit too much millet lately.'

'Ah, I see. I'll tell them to put it on a bed of lettuce – extra lettuce.'

Enid nodded and winked.

'And maybe keep the biscuit to the side, just in case you change your mind. If you don't eat it, you can take it home for later. What time can I tell them to expect you?'

Enid tilted her head toward Langhorne as if to confer. After several seconds had elapsed, she announced, 'Around twelve thirty or so. Church lets out at noon, but Langhorne wants to stop home first to freshen up his feathers.'

'Of course,' Tish nodded.

Enid Kemper wandered away from the café, as was her wont, without a lick of a farewell on her lips.

'Night, Ms Kemper,' Tish called after her. 'Always a pleasure.'

Enid gave a slight wave of her hand and trudged off toward the Bypass Road, where the decaying Kemper House had stood for over a century.

'I have to hand it to you,' Schuyler praised. 'Enid Kemper might be the most ornery woman in Henrico County, but you handle her as if she were a newborn puppy.'

'I wouldn't go quite that far. I just try to put myself in her shoes. If I were living alone in a dilapidated house with nothing but a parrot to keep me company, I wouldn't be too jolly either.'

'Yeah, but she seems to take to you. You actually got a wave goodbye. I've lived here my entire life, and in those forty-one years she's never once lifted a finger at me in greeting.'

Tish broke into a broad grin. 'How can you be sure? Maybe she did wave to you and you were too busy here on the front porch kissing to see it.'

Schuyler blushed again. 'You're not upset by Enid Kemper's story, are you? That was a long time ago and I wasn't out here as much as she'd have you believe.'

'No, don't be silly. What happened in your past is your past. Besides, I'm the lucky beneficiary of all that practice.'

'Well, it wasn't that much practice,' Schuyler maintained and then, realizing he'd missed his cue, leaned forward and closed his eyes.

Again, before their lips could meet, they were disturbed by the sound of footsteps in the street and a man clearing his throat.

The pair looked up to find Daryl Dufour, the town librarian, pacing back and forth outside the parking lot, as if deciding whether he should stop and say hello or hasten along his journey.

Tish smiled and waved. 'Hello, Daryl.'

'Hey, Daryl,' Schuyler echoed.

Daryl Dufour stopped pacing and gave a tentative wave. 'I'm sorry to have disturbed y'all.'

'No, it's fine. We didn't anticipate there being so much traffic,' Schuyler explained.

Dufour looked puzzled. 'Traffic? I haven't seen a car on this road yet.'

'Foot traffic.'

'Ah.' Small in stature and bespectacled, Daryl Dufour had the kind of face that had looked middle-aged even in youth. His sandy, not-quite-brown, not-quite-blond hair was cropped close to the head and graying ever so slightly at the temples, and his weekend outfit of tucked-in polo shirt, baggy pleated khakis, and loafers would have looked more at home during the 1990s than it did in 2019, but he was a good man dedicated to returning the Hobson Glen Library to its days of glory.

'I was just on my way down to the Bar and Grill to watch the game with Edwin Wilson. The grill's serving up Nashville hot chicken and the Washington Nationals are playing against the Atlanta Braves. The Nats might make it all the way this year. Y'all are welcome to join us,' Daryl invited and then gestured to the wine bottle on the porch table. 'But it looks like you have your bases covered. See what I did there? Bases covered?'

'Clever,' Tish acknowledged.

'Thanks. Hey, did you have time to think about that children's storytelling and cooking program I'd like to do during the winter school break?'

'I did. I love your idea of getting the kids and their parents engaged in reading and proper nutrition. I already have a menu in mind for the program launch. I was thinking some *Cloudy with a Chance of Mini-Meatballs*, a sandwich platter featuring *Harriet the Spy*'s tomato and mayonnaise sandwiches, green egg sandwiches and ham sandwiches—'

Daryl narrowed his eyes. 'What makes the eggs green?'

'I'm sneaking some mashed avocado in there. I'm also subbing the mayonnaise in all three sandwiches with yogurt.'

'A Southern sandwich without mayonnaise? Heresy!'

'No one will miss it,' she winked. 'I'm also doing *The Very Hungry Caterpillar* fruit salad, miniature *Babar the Elephant* ears pastries, and *Paddington*'s marmalade tarts. The desserts will be sweetened with agave syrup instead of processed sugar.'

Daryl was incredulous. 'Ms Celestine agreed to making pastries with agave?'

Celestine had been Daryl Dufour's childhood sweetheart. A sweetheart for whom he still held a torch. 'Yes, she actually tested the healthier treats on her grandkids and marveled at how they didn't have that hyperactive reaction they usually got with sugar. She's a convert . . . for the grandkids, anyway.'

Schuyler chimed in, 'Yeah, just the other day she told me I could have her sweet tea when I pried it from her cold, dead hands.'

'Ha! That's the Celestine I know,' Daryl cried in admiration. 'Well, it sounds as if the winter break program is in very capable hands. I love your book selections and the foods you've chosen sound as though they'll go down well with both kids and parents.'

Tish nodded. 'Each day of the program I'll read one of the selected books and then have the children help me prepare the dish associated with the story. If the library wouldn't mind, I thought we'd print out the recipes so parents can recreate the dishes at home. I'll email you everything this week.'

'Perfect. I'd best be getting along before Edwin starts drinking without me. Have a good night and, by the way, y'all look good together.'

Tish and Schuyler thanked Daryl and wished him a pleasant evening. 'He's right, you know,' she stated. 'We do look good together.'

'We do, but you look a lot better than I do.'

'Not from where I'm sitting.'

'Oh, now look who's being smooth.'

The couple laughed, sipped their wine, and were cuddling some more when they were interrupted by an older woman on a bicycle, crying, 'Awww, how sweet!'

She was dressed in spandex yoga pants, a flowy floral-printed off-the-shoulder top, and a pair of Birkenstocks. She brought the bike to a halt in the parking lot, a cell phone poised in her hand as if preparing to snap a photo.

'Opal,' Schuyler shouted. 'If I've told you once, I've told you a thousand times, I can't be seen on one of your book covers. I'm an attorney. People don't want their wills drawn up by Fabio-wannabes.'

Opal Schaeffer, under the pseudonym of Marjorie Morningstar, was the seventy-year-old author of nearly twenty bestselling romance novels. 'I won't use your faces, darlings. But the pose is perfect. Such warmth and passion. It will look terrific on the cover of my latest work, which finds a young woman running away from a convent in Florence to find love with a pizza maker.'

'Dare we ask the title?'

'*Under the Tuscan Nun*.'

'Ah, a classic for the ages.'

Tish jabbed Schuyler with her elbow. She wasn't a fan of romance novels, but she quite admired the perseverance and creativity required to write not one but twenty of them. Nor was she in any position to criticize Opal's pun-laden titles. 'As flattered as I am at the possibility of being featured on the cover of one of your novels, I'd also prefer that you didn't use that photo. I'd rather customers came here for the food than to catch a glimpse of the model who posed as your Italian nun.'

'OK, OK. I'll delete it.' She pressed a finger against the screen of her phone twice in a row and then turned the display around in gallery view for Schuyler and Tish's approval. 'See? The latest shot is of my garden.'

Schuyler was appreciative. 'Thanks, Opal.'

'Yes, thank you,' Tish seconded. 'And what brings you out and about this evening?'

'This.' Opal reached into the basket of her bicycle and produced a canvas shopping bag. Handing it to Tish, she announced, 'My first butternut squashes of the season.'

Tish took the bag and peered inside to find two unblemished, ochre-skinned fruits of equal sizes and proportions. 'Oooh! They're beautiful. How much do I owe you?'

Opal was an avid gardener whose vegetable patch produced far more food than a single woman could consume, pickle, or can, so she sold the surplus to Tish and at local farmers' markets. 'Nothing. That's a sample. If you like them, you can purchase more. I have a bumper crop on the way. Oh, and I'll have more peppers for you too. Both sweet bell and chili.'

'Cool. I'll put some sage and butternut squash risotto on the menu this coming week. That will help me gauge how many I'll need.'

'Sounds delicious. I'll have to give it a try.'

'I'll save you a portion – on the house. I'll give you a call when it's ready.'

'Really? That would be amazing.'

'Of course. There wouldn't be risotto on the menu if you hadn't brought me the squash.'

'Thanks.' Opal hopped back on her bike. 'Now if only this heat would break so you can make some butternut squash soup. Ninety degrees in September when it's typically only eighty? Mother Nature must be off her meds.'

'I know, even the leaves on my plants are turning yellow.' Tish gestured to the robust pink-and-white blooms that grew in a round concrete planter just outside the door of the café.

'Funny you should mention that. I noticed them yesterday while chatting with Celestine over a chai soy latte, so I came out here and gave them a little check. I hope you don't mind.'

'Not at all. You have a far greener thumb than I do.'

'The soil felt adequately moist and they appear to be getting the proper amount of sunlight, so I was at something of a loss until it hit me. I think they're suffering from lime poisoning.'

'Lime poisoning?'

'Those are Mona Lisa lilies, cousins to the larger and more deeply colored Stargazers you find in wedding bouquets and flower arrangements. All lilies need acidic soil to thrive, but the concrete in that planter is highly alkaline. As the concrete is exposed to water and the elements, the calcium carbonate, or lime, in the concrete seeps into the roots of the plants. I had something similar happen to a rhododendron of mine after I replaced a brick walkway with concrete. I dug up the rhododendron, moved it to another spot in the garden and the yellow leaves disappeared.'

'Hmm, so if I transplant those lilies to a different container, they should improve?'

'They'll be right as rain.'

'I'll look for a new planter and move them over this week.'

'Let me know if you need a hand. Until then, I'll let you lovers get back to it. Have a good night and don't do anything I wouldn't do.' She punctuated the statement with a throaty laugh before disappearing into the enfolding darkness.

'Are we finally alone?' Schuyler half joked.

'I don't know. What's the population of Hobson Glen? Because I'm pretty sure there's still some folks out there we haven't seen.'

Schuyler took a sip of wine and placed his hand on Tish's knee. 'I hope you don't think this premature, or that I'm pressuring you in any way, but would you like to, um, maybe go to my place? It's quieter there.'

'It's not premature and you're not pressuring me at all.' Tish placed her hand on top of his. 'It's been wonderful, and if this were any other evening, I'd say yes. But, in addition to having to load my car for a bright and early start tomorrow, I'm not certain Mary Jo and her family are quite ready to be left alone just yet.'

'I can help you load your car, but you're probably right about Mary Jo and the kids. What with the Coleton Creek luncheon, you haven't been able to spend as much time with them as you should.

And I, following the same logic, should probably save my energy for basketball with Gregory in the morning. A forty-one-year-old challenging a seventeen-year-old to a game of one-on-one. What was I thinking?'

'You weren't. You were using your heart, not your brain.'

'Yeah, and now my body is about to pay the price.' Schuyler slumped back in his seat as if the game in question had already taken place. 'Agghhhhh.'

'On second thought, maybe I *should* stay at your place tonight. It might be our last chance for a while. You could be in traction until Christmas,' she teased.

'Thanks for the vote of confidence. Although you may have a point . . .' He snapped back to life and moved in for a kiss.

Tish happily obliged him with one and then put on the brakes. 'We'd better stop.'

Schuyler nodded. 'When the luncheon is over and Mary Jo and the kids are in a better place, we'll make a night of it. Dinner at the Roosevelt and maybe a cruise along the James?'

'It's a date.' She snuggled close to him and put her head on his shoulder, and the pair watched as the sun disappeared below the horizon before bidding each other farewell.

FIFTEEN

Tish waved and watched as Schuyler pulled his BMW out of the café parking lot and turned left on to the main road toward the center of town. When he was out of view, she turned on one heel and went back into the café kitchen where she collected the random pieces of equipment needed for the luncheon and then packed them in the trunk of her car.

With that task complete, she locked the car and went back inside. It was just going on ten o'clock.

Knowing that Gregory and Anthony would probably take full advantage of their final thirty minutes, Tish left the lights on in the café but latched the screen door and made her way upstairs to brush her teeth and change into her pajamas. If the boys did return early, Tish reasoned, they could either bang on the door or dial her cell phone.

On her way to the back staircase, Tish stopped at the thermostat and switched the café air conditioning to off and, figuring in the heat given off by six human bodies and one canine body in repose, lowered the apartment temperature to sixty-eight degrees Fahrenheit before continuing upstairs.

In the darkened living room, Tish could see that the sofa mattress had been pulled from its hiding place and made into a bed, replete with sheets, pillows, and blanket. She smiled as she recalled her college days with Mary Jo. How many times had MJ, already engaged to marry Glen, turned down Tish's bed and waited for her to arrive home safely after what was deemed to be a sketchy date?

No matter how disastrous the evening, Tish always knew MJ was waiting with a listening ear and either a pint of Häagen-Dazs chocolate ice cream or a bar of pepper jack cheese and crackers to hear her tale of woe. Very often Jules would hop into the game as well and the three of them would wind up laughing until dawn.

Funny how life works out, Tish reflected. Back then Glen was a catch – the guy who'd always be honest and true.

Today, he'd run off with his new girlfriend and refused to meet his children for dinner.

Tish breathed a heavy sigh and turned around to see a light glowing from beneath the door to the spare bedroom, accompanied by the sound of a man singing along with a full orchestra. She approached and gave the door a gentle tap, but there was no reply. Swinging the door slowly inward, she spied Mary Jo lying in the center of the bed, flanked on either side by Charlotte and Kayla. All three were dressed in their pajamas and fast asleep.

Biscuit, curled into a ball, rested atop the unused sleeping bag on the floor beside the bed. As Tish leaned down and stopped the movie playing on Mary Jo's laptop, the dog woke up and approached her, wagging his tail. Fearful that the sound of Biscuit's jingling tags might wake someone – and even more fearful that, if left in the room, Biscuit might have an accident on either the bed or the sleeping bag – Tish picked up the dog with one hand and the laptop with the other and deposited both in the living room before turning off the bedroom light and quietly shutting the door behind her.

Switching on the living-room lamp, she looked at Biscuit. 'Well, looks like it's just you and me.'

Biscuit looked up with a yawn.

'You might at least pretend to be excited,' she quipped before wandering off to the bedroom. Biscuit, tail still wagging, followed close behind. Under normal circumstances, Tish would have indulged in a long hot shower to wash away the grit of the day. However, as she'd already arranged to shower in the morning and she was uncertain when she might be called upon to unlock the front door, she stripped down to her underwear and threw on a pair of boxer shorts, a matching tank top, a pair of terry-cloth slippers, and covered up with a lightweight cotton pique robe.

From there, she moved into the bathroom where Biscuit stood guard from atop the laundry hamper and watched as Tish scrubbed her face clean and rinsed the back of her neck with cool water.

With her preliminary ablutions completed, Tish went downstairs and took Biscuit outside one last time before bed. As he had done previously, Biscuit led Tish to a corner of the gravel-lined parking lot and did his business. Not once did he attempt to relieve himself on the grassy outdoor eating area to the left of the café, nor was he even remotely interested in the contents of the café's planters or flowerbeds.

When Biscuit had finished, he wandered to the lawn, took several quick rolls on to his back, and led Tish back to the café door. Tish let Biscuit inside, where she removed his lead and patted him on the head. 'Good boy,' she praised, at which Biscuit licked her hand.

Perhaps, she pondered as she locked the front door, kindness was the answer to Biscuit's little problem. She had been with the dog for just eight hours, but in that time he seemed a far different creature than the one Orson Baggett described. If, as Baggett alleged, Shackleford had trained Biscuit to desecrate his neighbors' lawns and gardens, then why wasn't the dog doing it now? Indeed, rather than seeking to dig or defile Tish's garden area, Biscuit appeared to revel in its greenness, rolling around like a puppy on the cool, damp grass.

There was, of course, the possibility that Shackleford's 'training' was more akin to abuse. Given what Tish had learned about the man, it wasn't difficult to imagine him using violence to coerce Biscuit into doing his bidding.

The only problem with that theory was that Biscuit didn't exhibit any outward signs of having been mistreated. Not only was the dog well groomed, energetic, and seemingly healthy, but he had adjusted well to life at the café. Tish wasn't an animal psychologist but she could only imagine that had he met any harm at the hands of Sloane Shackleford, Biscuit might have either cowered in fear or lashed out aggressively whenever Schuyler, Jules, or any other man came near. Likewise, bathroom breaks might have proven a source of anxiety for Biscuit, but thus far he'd let his handlers know when nature called and quickly and happily carried out the task at hand.

Tish went to the kitchen to put the kettle on and give Biscuit a few of the organic chicken and salmon dog treats Schuyler had purchased. She watched as the dog chomped down on the crunchy cookies, feverishly licking up any crumbs that fell to the floor. If Biscuit possessed any information about his owner's death, he was reluctant to reveal it. Likewise, if he felt any grief over the sudden loss of his owner, he was keeping it well hidden.

The kettle came to a boil. Tish rushed to remove it from the burner before it could pierce the silence of the evening with a whistle. Pouring the water into a mug bearing a bag of chocolate Rooibos tea, she looked up at the clock. It was going on eleven.

Oh, Gregory, she thought to herself. *Where are you and what are you doing?*

Tish was concerned about her godson's welfare, but she felt slightly better knowing that at least he had a good friend with him – even if it was a good friend who should have had enough sense to call if they were going to be late.

Godson. The word triggered the memory of the photo on Zadie Morris's bedside table. The boy depicted in the photo had passed away when he was just one year younger than Gregory. How old would that boy be today? Fifty? Sixty? How did he die? A freak accident, prolonged illness, a genetic defect?

Most of all, Tish wondered why Zadie was still haunted by the boy in the photo all these years later. Tish knew of people who had photos of godchildren, nieces, and nephews on their refrigerators, desks, or sitting-room mantles. Indeed, prior to her move to

Hobson Glen, Tish's ancient Frigidaire boasted photo Christmas cards, school portraits, and random snapshots of both friends and their children. Keeping a photo by one's bed, however, suggested a relationship of great closeness and devotion between the owner of the bed and the subject of the photo.

In Zadie's case, that closeness and devotion had lasted some forty to fifty years. In all that time, had the cosmetics icon not encountered anyone else – lover, friend, mentor – who'd held a tremendous influence over her life? Someone whose photo better deserved a spot on her nightstand? Tish didn't wish to diminish Zadie's feelings for her godson, but why did she need to be reminded of this particular boy who had passed away so long ago? What was it about his life, and possibly his death, that still preoccupied her thoughts?

Tish's ruminations were cut short by the sound of two young men outside, talking and laughing. She placed her mug of tea on the counter, unlatched the café door, and ran out on to the porch. By the light of a streetlamp, she could spy Gregory, his arm draped over Anthony's shoulders, walking along the side of the road, ambling in the direction of the café.

Tish hurried off to meet them. 'Shh. Do you want to wake the entire house?'

'No, ma'am,' Anthony obediently answered.

'Everyone's asleep? But it's early,' Gregory slurred.

Tish placed her hands on her hips and growled, 'It's not early. It's eleven o'clock, meaning you're a full thirty minutes late. And if you hadn't been drinking, Gregory Thomas Okensholt, you'd know that.'

Tish's tone, combined with the use of all three of his names, gave Gregory pause. 'Whoa, you're not gonna tell Mom, are you?'

'I'm not telling her right this minute, no. But she will find out. Right now, I'm going to let her sleep. We're *all* going to let her sleep. So, you, sir, are going to tiptoe into that café, get yourself upstairs, and tuck your scrawny butt into bed without making so much as a peep. Do you hear?'

Gregory fell sullen. 'Yes, ma'am.'

'And I really wish the two of you had called me instead of walking home. Lord knows what might have happened to you.'

'Don't worry, ma'am, I had him,' Anthony assured.

'I know you think you had him, but what if, while carrying two skateboards' – Tish indicated the wheeled items tucked beneath Anthony's arm – 'and helping your drunk friend home, you staggered a little too far into the road and a car hit you because the driver didn't see you?'

Anthony shrugged.

'I know neither of you wanted to get into trouble by asking for a ride, but I'd rather be angry with you both than mourning you. And, Gregory, I know things are tough for you right now, but getting wasted on beer, or whatever you were drinking, isn't the answer. Use your heads.'

'Yes, ma'am,' they replied in unison.

'All right, now go on and get to bed,' she ordered.

Tish watched as the boys slunk off toward the café.

Schuyler was right. There were times when she too regretted she had never been a parent.

This, however, was not one of them.

The apartment above the café had been silent for hours, but still Tish couldn't sleep. Pulling up the covers, then throwing them off, turning on to her left side, her right side, and then on to her back, she could not seem to get comfortable. Her body felt tired and her eyes were heavy, but her brain simply wouldn't disengage.

Finally giving in to her insomnia, Tish shuffled downstairs to the kitchen to make herself some tea and an open-faced peanut butter sandwich. It was what her mother fixed when Tish experienced sleepless nights as a child, and even now the combination never failed to comfort, albeit not as quickly as it had in the past.

She walked to the cupboard to retrieve the bread and peanut butter, nearly tripping over the canine visitor who'd followed her downstairs. 'What are you doing here? You have a big beautiful Sherpa-lined dog bed with your name on it. Literally. Schuyler had it personalized.'

Suspecting the water Biscuit drank before bed might have traveled in a southerly direction, she walked to the door of the café. 'Outside?'

Rather than accepting the invitation with a wag of his tail, as was his wont, Biscuit's eyes grew large and he scurried to the rear of the café where he crouched beside the counter.

'What?' Tish asked the dog. Her question was answered by the sound of breaking glass emanating from the parking lot.

Tish looked out of the jalousied café windows and saw a figure, silhouetted by the moonlight, standing outside the Matrix. He or she held a long, thin striking object, which they proceeded to bring down on the car with great force.

Smash, came the sound of more glass shattering.

Tish's first instinct was to call the police, but by the time they arrived, her car might be trashed beyond repair. Running to the kitchen, she snatched a ten-inch cast-iron skillet from its spot on the stove, switched on the parking-lot light, and dashed out on to the porch.

The dark figure dropped the object in his or her hands and jumped slightly, as if startled by the light and her presence, before running away.

Without a word, Tish took off after them, brandishing the frying pan like a tennis racquet. Her eyes ill-adjusted to the darkness, she had difficulty seeing exactly where the individual went, but she was reasonably certain they were just a few paces ahead.

It therefore came as a tremendous shock when she felt a pair of hands at her back, pushing her to the ground. She fell, face forward, hitting her chin and right elbow on the gravel of the parking lot, sending the skillet sailing out of her hand. Her left hand reached out to soften the impact, only to land in a patch of glass.

Nearly a minute elapsed before Tish managed to catch her breath and pick herself up off the ground. Still trembling from shock, she stumbled back into the café to find only Biscuit awaiting her. The combination of closed windows, the hum of the air-conditioning system, and sheer exhaustion (and, in Gregory's case, alcohol) had rendered Tish's houseguests completely, and thankfully, oblivious to the melee just outside the café doors.

Tish collected her cell phone from the kitchen counter and dialed Sheriff Reade directly.

What seemed like a lifetime later, she saw the glow of headlights on the road and a familiar figure jogging across the parking lot and to the café door. She swung open the screen to greet him.

'I thought I told you stay inside with the door locked,' he scolded. His spiky hair was flat on one side, as if he'd been lying in bed, and he was dressed in a basic white tee, jogging pants, and a pair of beat-up running shoes. A holster encircled his waist and his right hand rested on the handle of his service revolver.

'I did. You're here now so I unlocked it.'

Reade frowned as he moved his hand from his gun to Tish's face. 'God, look at you. Are you OK? Are you in a lot of pain?'

Tish shook her head. 'Shock mostly.'

'What were you thinking?'

'I was thinking that I've sunk every dime into my café and can't afford to buy another car.'

'And did you happen to think about how we might replace *you*?' Reade challenged as he took her cut hand in his and examined it. 'There's a cast-iron skillet and a fireplace poker out there. What if the person who smashed your car windows had used one of those on you?'

'Um, actually, the skillet is mine.'

'You went out there with a frying pan? Were you trying to chase away the perpetrator or cook him?'

'Whatever it took to get him – or her – to stop trashing my car.'

Reade drew a deep breath. 'You were lucky. I do, however, think you should be seen by a doctor.'

The last place Tish wanted to be was a hospital. 'I'm fine. Just a few cuts and bruises, that's all.'

'You may have a concussion.'

'I didn't hit my head. And I really don't want to leave Mary Jo and the kids.'

Reade capitulated with a sigh. 'Do you have some bandages somewhere?'

'I have a first-aid kit in the kitchen.'

'Good. Let's get you cleaned up.'

'What about my car?'

'The car isn't going anywhere, but your wounds could get infected. Now, tell me where the first-aid kit is,' he insisted, his gray eyes full of concern.

Tish realized it was fruitless to argue. With a huff, she went into the kitchen and came back with the kit. A few minutes, several applications of antibacterial ointment, and one cup of chamomile tea later, her hand and chin were clean and bandaged, and Tish was feeling far calmer.

'Nice job,' she complimented as she surveyed Reade's handiwork. 'You ever thought about being a doctor?'

'Yes, but med school got too expensive, so I dropped out and joined the academy.'

Tish felt her jaw drop, much to Reade's amusement.

'Sousaphones. Med school. I'm full of surprises, aren't I? Now, let's go take a look at your car.'

She obediently followed him to the parking lot, where Reade shone a flashlight on the damaged Matrix. Both the front and rear passenger-side windows had been smashed into thousands of tiny pieces, and there was a large circular crack in the front windshield, but from a cursory inspection, everything inside the vehicle, despite being covered in glass, was still present and intact.

'Was there anything of particular value in the car?' he asked.

'No, but come on now, Clemson.'

At the sound of his Christian name, Reade looked up, slightly aghast.

'We both know this wasn't a case of attempted robbery,' she continued. 'Anyone looking to steal the contents of a car or the car itself would simply break a window, reach in, and open the door. They wouldn't break two windows and then move on to the windshield.'

'You're right,' Reade agreed, awkwardly adding, 'Tish, I admit this whole thing bothers me quite a bit. In my time as sheriff, I've seen some vandalism around here, but nothing on this scale. This is . . .'

'Malicious?'

'Yeah.'

Tish wasn't one for tears, but she felt like crying.

Reade, sensing the significance of her silence, wrapped a consoling arm around her shoulder. 'Don't worry. We'll find who did this. I'm going to put one of our officers on patrol here just to be safe. And as for the car, your insurance will cover it.'

She nodded.

'You, um, you mentioned you didn't want sirens and flashing lights and ambulances here tonight because Mary Jo Okensholt and her children are staying with you. You don't think her husband might have . . .'

'Come here and smashed up my car because he blames me for

keeping his wife and kids from him?' Tish filled in the blanks. 'No, I don't think so. He's the one who initiated the split. We also invited him for dinner tonight and he declined. Nor has he returned his children's text messages. No, he's focused on a new life with his girlfriend.'

'Sorry, but I had to ask. Domestic disputes can get nasty.'

'No, I understand. I'm glad you asked.'

'So, have you thought about how you're getting to Coleton Creek in the morning?'

'Huh?' It was an unexpected question.

'You can't drive this until the windows are replaced. I know you have a luncheon to cater, so how are you getting there?'

'Oh, I guess I'll borrow Mary Jo's car. Although she's covering for me here at the café and she needs to drop Gregory at the rec for a basketball game. I guess I'll call Celestine.'

'You can't call Ms Celly right now. It's too late. And you and Mary Jo don't need one more thing to do. I have to be at Coleton Creek first thing in the morning. I drive right past the café. Let me give you a lift.'

'Oh, no, I couldn't. I already dragged you out of bed tonight instead of just calling nine-one-one.'

'Don't be ridiculous. I'd have done the same thing as you if I had – how many people do you have staying here?'

'Five. And one dog. Speaking of which . . .' Tish went back into the café to check on Biscuit and ensure he hadn't followed her and Reade into the parking lot and wandered off into the dark.

After several seconds of searching, they found him curled into a ball beside the refrigerator, sound asleep. 'Some guard dog,' Tish quipped, although she was relieved to find the little dog safe.

'Yeah, I wouldn't expect a letter from the K-9 recruitment team anytime soon.'

Tish laughed. The movement caused her ribs to ache. 'Ow.'

'You'd best get some rest,' Reade instructed. 'Why don't you go up to bed? I'll wait until the patrol comes by and lock the door behind me.'

'Don't you need me for your report?'

'No, I've already got your story. I'll just take some photos of the damage and take the poker as evidence. You can sign the final report in the morning. I'll be here around seven fifteen tomorrow to pick you up.'

'OK,' Tish capitulated. She was far too exhausted and sore to argue. 'It's been a long day. For both of us.'

'Yeah, but I only had one job. You had two: the luncheon and listening to the residents of Coleton Creek spill the beans about Sloane Shackleford. By the way, I appreciate you telling me about that meeting between him and the Knoblochs. We searched Shackleford's house and found no fewer than a dozen bags of building materials like the one he brought to that meeting. Each of them was labeled with the name of a location within the Coleton Creek development.'

Tish's eyes narrowed, but she was incapable of conjuring a thought. 'How strange.'

'Yeah. We'll figure out what it means. In the meantime, thanks for being on the case, even if it's unofficially.'

'*On* the case? You saw my car. That's the work of someone desperately trying to scare someone off. No, I'm not just on the case, Clemson. I'm *in* it.'

SIXTEEN

Tish, wrapped in her robe, top sheet, blanket, and comforter, slept surprisingly well in the few short hours after Reade left the café. So well, in fact, that had the alarm on her cell phone not chimed at six, she would easily have slept several hours longer.

Tish switched off the alarm, stretched, gathered her clothes for the day, and tiptoed into the bathroom. There, beneath the steady stream of the showerhead, she let the hot water cascade over her body in an attempt to rinse away the fatigue and strain of last night's fall. It was not entirely successful.

After drying off and getting dressed, she applied some moisturizer to her face before returning to her bedroom to make the bed and put on her makeup. As Tish stepped through the bathroom door, she was met by a wild-eyed Mary Jo.

'I just looked out the window and your car—' Mary Jo stopped as she spied the bandages on Tish's chin and hand. 'Oh my God, what happened to your face? Your hand? What's going on?'

Tish put a finger to her lips and beckoned MJ to follow her downstairs. Over a pot of coffee, Tish detailed the night's events.

Mary Jo took a sip of the steaming hot beverage and then clucked her tongue. 'I've lived in this community since the kids were little and I've never heard of a car being damaged so badly during a break-in.'

'To say my car was broken into implies someone was trying to steal something, Mary Jo. That's not the case here.'

'You think someone intentionally trashed your car? But who would do such a thing and why?'

'I can think of just two possible reasons: to either scare me off the Shackleford case or to keep me away from the garden club luncheon.'

'Wait, I'm confused. Why would anyone resort to such measures to keep you away from the luncheon when they could just fire you?'

'Because the people who hate the luncheon, hate the garden club, and hate gardening in general aren't the people who hired me.'

'OK,' Mary Jo sang. It was clear she was still quite confused. 'And the Shackleford case? You told me you weren't on it. You told me you didn't want to get involved.'

'That was my original response to the whole thing, yes . . .'

'But?'

Tish placed her mug on the table and folded her arms across her chest. 'I can't help it if the residents talk to me.'

Mary Jo replied in typical motherly fashion. 'No, but you *can* help how you respond to them. Like by *not* asking questions that encourage them to talk even more.'

Tish pulled a face and drank her coffee in silence.

'You're right,' Mary Jo sighed. 'I forgot who I was talking to. You simply can't help yourself, can you?'

Tish shrugged. 'I like to know what makes things and people tick, that's all. It's like tasting a recipe and breaking it down into its individual ingredients.'

'Except that recipes don't send warning messages by damaging your private property. So what now?'

'What do you mean, "What now?"'

'What are you going to do?'

'I'm going to cater the luncheon and, at a more reasonable hour, make a call to my insurance company.'

'You're still going ahead with the luncheon?'

'Of course.'

'But what if the person who damaged your car tries something else?'

'Reade and his team have set up shop at Shackleford's house. They won't have far to travel if I need them. Oh, speaking of which, I'd better get ready. Reade will be here soon.'

'Sheriff Reade is coming here? Didn't he get everything he needed last night?'

'He did. I just need to sign the report. Oh, and he's giving me a ride to Coleton Creek.'

'Why? I'm here. I can easily drive you.'

'I appreciate your offer, MJ, but it's enough that you're helping with the café today. Also, you need to have a talk with Gregory this morning.' Tish described the young man's condition upon arriving home late the previous evening.

'I certainly will have a talk with him. I'm sorry you had to deal with that,' Mary Jo apologized.

'It's OK. I was stern with him and might have played the Southern mama for a bit, but my main objective was getting him and Anthony off to bed.'

'Whatever you did is fine. Thank you for waiting up and dealing with the situation, but you shouldn't have had to. It's not your job. I'm his mother.'

With Mary Jo's words, Tish's mind traveled, once again, to the photo on Zadie's nightstand. *It's not your job. I'm his mother.*

'Are you OK?' Mary Jo asked.

'Yeah, you just reminded me of something that's been nagging at me.'

'What is it?'

'I'm not entirely sure,' she frowned. 'Anyway, I hope that conversation with Gregory goes well. I'm sorry I won't be around to hear it. Actually, I'm sorry I haven't been around much at all this weekend.

Why don't we make a date for tomorrow? The kids will be in school, and you and I can sit down and talk about your next move. How does lunch sound?'

'Sounds like just what the doctor ordered. I'll call you later to find out what time you want to meet.'

'Meet? You and the kids won't be here?'

'No. I fell asleep before I could tell you, but Glen texted last night. He's moving in with Lisa and said we can stay at the house. He's willing to foot the bill for us right now, but eventually we'll have to negotiate who's responsible for what.'

'Sounds like we'd better get you an attorney and fast. Schuyler's giving me a list of divorce lawyers. We'll go over it tomorrow at lunch and then maybe we'll do a little retail therapy to settle the nerves?'

'I do need to pick up some odds and ends for the kids. Those back-to-school lists are endless.'

'I need to hit up the garden center for a new planter for out front. Preferably wood or terracotta.'

'What's wrong with the ones you have? I think they look nice.'

'Yeah, they do, but the concrete is turning—' Tish stopped talking and wandered toward the front door.

'What? What's out there? Is someone here?'

'No. No, it's the concrete. The concrete is turning my plants yellow. Yellow – just like the plants and lawns at Coleton Creek.'

'It has been an unseasonably warm September,' Mary Jo remarked.

'No, it's not the heat. Nor is it Biscuit. It's never been Biscuit.'

At the sound of his name, the little white dog came scampering down the stairs.

Tish leaned down and scratched Biscuit's ears. 'You tried to tell me it wasn't you, didn't you? What a good boy.'

'Um, Tish, are you OK? You didn't hit your head when you fell in the parking lot last night, did you?'

'No, I didn't hit my head,' Tish mimicked. 'The yellow spots at Coleton Creek are due to the cement. The cement, nails, and other building scraps Shackleford brought to his meeting with the Knoblochs.'

'Umm, OK. If you say so.'

'It's not because I say so. It's what happened. It's the only thing that makes sense.' Tish gave Biscuit one last pat on the head before chugging back the rest of her coffee and picking up her phone.

'Who are you calling?'

'Sheriff Reade. I have to tell him about the concrete.'

'Why are you calling him? He'll be here in just a few minutes.'

'Oh! That's right.' Tish shut the phone off and put it in her rear pants pocket. 'He's already on his way.'

Mary Jo frowned. 'Are you sure you didn't hit your head?'

Tish ignored the question entirely and sprinted toward the steps. 'I have to get ready. Check in with you later today?'

'Yes, please. And take it easy today, will you?'

'I'll try,' she promised and then sprinted up the steps two at a time, Biscuit close at her heels.

Mary Jo flopped back in her chair and hoped that her friend didn't trip. 'Yeah, see, Tish. That's not trying.'

It was fourteen minutes after seven when Clemson Reade's white sheriff's car pulled to a stop outside the front porch of the café. Tish, dressed in her typical catering day outfit of black tee, black crop pants, and leopard-print loafers, stood on the front stoop, a box of trays, serving pieces, and Cookin' the Books aprons in her hands. Alongside her stood Biscuit.

Reade exited the car and approached the front steps. 'Mornin'. That's a nice little Johnny Cash-inspired ensemble you're wearing there.'

Tish found it impossible to be her usual chatty, welcoming café-owner self; there was no time to waste. She looked down at her outfit and then thrust the box of supplies into Reade's arms. 'Thanks. I need to talk to you. It's important.'

'Yeah, sure.'

Tish watched as he loaded the box into the trunk of the patrol car and then waved him on to the front porch. 'Look,' she instructed.

Reade looked around in bewilderment before settling his eyes upon the white creature at Tish's feet. 'Um, it's a dog.'

'No, not Biscuit. But he's coming with us this morning. I hope you don't mind. Mary Jo is going back home today and she really doesn't need him under her feet.'

'Fine with me.' He gave Biscuit a vigorous head rub. 'So, what am I looking at that's so important?'

'Those lilies outside the door.'

'Ah . . . nice. My mother had those in our garden when I was growing up.'

'No, look at them. Really look at them. Does something seem wrong to you?'

Reade shrugged. 'The leaves look a little yellow.'

'Exactly!' The expression on Tish's face was intense and slightly deranged.

'Are you OK? You don't have a headache from last night's fall, do you?'

'Why does everyone keep asking me that? No. I'm trying to point out that the planter on my porch is made of poured cement.'

'Uh, yes. Yes, it is.'

'The same stuff found in bags all over Sloane Shackleford's house,' she prompted, hoping that Reade would fill in the blanks.

He remained obtuse. 'Yes . . . I don't see what you're getting at.'

Tish rolled her eyes. 'Get in the car. I'll explain it on the way to Coleton Creek.'

An obedient Reade did as he was told. As he started the engine, Tish picked up Biscuit and placed him on the backseat of the car before climbing into the passenger seat and buckling her seatbelt. 'Alkaline poisoning,' she announced.

'Huh? Poisoning? Who's been poisoned?'

'The lilies outside the café,' Tish explained.

'OK. By the way, I brought you a coffee.' He gestured to a pair of travel mugs in the center console. 'It's not as good as yours but I thought you might need the caffeine. I now see that was a ridiculous assumption on my part.'

'It's not ridiculous. I'm just running on adrenaline.' Tish picked up the mug in the passenger-side cup holder and took a sip. 'Mmm, that's very good. Thank you.'

'You're welcome. So you were talking about alkaline poisoning.'

'The lilies in my planter have yellow leaves because the concrete planter has been leeching calcium carbonate into the soil in which the lilies are planted. Which got me thinking about the building debris Shackleford has in his house. You said those bags are labeled by location, yes?'

'Yeah, and every location is a spot within the Coleton Creek community.' He pulled out of the parking lot and on to the main road.

'And does each bag contain concrete?'

'Yes, along with nails, screws, bolts – typical construction stuff.'

'Perfect. I think those bags contain building waste that Shackleford unearthed while trying to find the cause of the yellow spots and dying plants all around the neighborhood. The label on each bag denotes the location where that particular batch of waste was found.'

'Wait a minute. You said "unearthed." You think the builders' scraps were buried?'

'I do. I think the Knoblochs were looking to cut costs in any way possible, so instead of paying to have their trash disposed of properly, they buried it. That's why the Knoblochs banned the residents from having gardens. They were afraid that, with a bit of digging, someone would discover their dirty secret.'

'And that's why it was only when the homeowners' association reverted to the control of the residents that gardening was finally permitted,' Reade surmised.

'Precisely. It's also why the Knoblochs pressured me to cancel the garden contest luncheon. If they could link Shackleford's murder to the garden club and one of its members, they stood a better chance of changing Coleton Creek policy to once again prohibit gardening, thus preventing someone else digging up their dirty – quite literally – secret. What Mariette and Nathan didn't count on, however, was the very thing that prompted Shackleford to dig in the first place: that alkaline from the debris they were trying to hide would eventually leech into the soil and taint anything growing near it.'

'But what about Biscuit?' Reade asked, prompting a yip as the dog on the backseat recognized his name. 'Residents are willing to swear they saw him in their gardens.'

Tish reached into the backseat to give Biscuit a reassuring head rub. 'I'm sure residents did see Biscuit in their gardens, but what did they actually observe? A dog sniffing around their flowers and rolling on their lawns? I bet if you press those eyewitnesses, they didn't see much of anything apart from a dog whose owner was too busy with other nocturnal pursuits to walk him. You know how tightknit communities work. All you need is one person to say they saw Biscuit tinkling on their tomato plants and before you know it there are Biscuit sightings everywhere – digging up delphiniums, provoking pet cats, pooping on petunias.'

'So you don't think Biscuit is responsible for any of that damage?'

'I don't. He was with us all last night and he never once misbehaved. I know that's not a long period of time in which to cast a verdict, but it is long enough to spot something that's supposedly an established and recurring pattern of behavior.'

'I admit that your theory completely fits the situation. We found some landscaping receipts in Shackleford's house. Just this spring, he had to have all the birch trees in his backyard replaced.'

An excited Tish leaned forward in her seat. 'Birches like acidic soil. They'd be the first to show the effects of alkaline poisoning. Did the paperwork say why the original trees were replaced?'

The sheriff steered the car toward the entrance of Coleton Creek. 'No, but it's easy enough to call the landscaping company and find out.'

'Also, give a call to local labs and garden centers. Jim Ainsley told me Shackleford had some yellow patches dug up from his lawn this July. I have a hunch he might have sent that yellow grass and the soil surrounding the debris he found out for analysis.'

'You think he's been gathering evidence?'

'I do. Evidence that links the building practices at Coleton Creek with the dying plants.'

'Hmm,' Reade mused aloud. 'I'll contact Shackleford's attorneys and see if he had made mention of filing a lawsuit.'

'Good idea,' Tish praised. 'However, I wouldn't expect to find much. Had Shackleford spoken to an attorney, that attorney would have been present at the meeting Susannah Hilton overheard. No, it's more likely Shackleford went into that meeting to blackmail the Knoblochs.'

'Blackmail them for cash?'

'Cash. Property. Some other lurid yet lucrative agreement. Remember, this is a guy who got rich by defrauding sick people like Violet Abercrombie.'

'How could I forget?' Reade remarked.

'Speaking of getting rich,' Tish segued, 'have you checked out Callie Collingsworth's background?'

'I got a brief bio on her, but nothing in-depth. She struck me as one of the few people here who didn't mind Shackleford or his behavior.'

'Callie Collingsworth might not have minded Shackleford's behavior because she was getting something out of the relationship. She admitted yesterday that she's to inherit Shackleford's estate.'

'So, Shackleford left her some money? There's nothing illegal about that,' Reade shrugged as he pulled to a stop outside Coleton Creek's security gate and punched in a code.

'On the surface, no, but according to Pepper Aviero, this is the third time Callie's come into money. Both of her husbands died in unusual circumstances – the first while he was in bed with someone else, the second in a car crash.'

'Are you suggesting she killed them and Shackleford?'

'Not at all. What I *am* saying is that I can't envision Sloane Shackleford leaving his vast fortune – including apartments in Paris and New York and a vacation villa in the Bahamas – to Callie Collingsworth. He didn't even stand by Callie when she and Pepper Aviero confronted him in his kitchen the morning of the murder. No, Shackleford wouldn't have made Callie or any other of his playmates the beneficiary of his will. Those women served one purpose in his world and it wasn't to look after his properties and wealth.'

'Then how did Callie end up being named in his will?'

'Sounds as if you have yet another question for Shackleford's attorney,' Tish deferred.

'Goody. Nothing I like more than talking to lawyers,' Reade deadpanned as he pulled the car into the lifestyle-center parking lot. 'Especially the lawyer of a sleazy insurance guy.'

Tish smiled. 'Job highlight, huh?'

'One only rivaled by the time Enid Kemper called me to get Langhorne out of a tree.'

'But Langhorne can fly.'

'You know that. I know that. But try telling Enid Kemper that. She insisted I climb up a thirty-foot ladder to get the danged bird down from the top of the old magnolia in her front yard. No sooner had my foot reached the top rung than Langhorne flew down to Enid's shoulder. Enid was pleased as punch. Brought Langhorne in for a bath so he could recover from the experience. Meanwhile, I was left to climb down that thirty-foot ladder by myself.'

'Woof! That is a rough day. Still . . .'

'Still . . . falling thirty feet might be preferable to dealing with a crooked insurance company shill. Hey, while I'm on the phone with Dewey, Cheatem, and Howe, I don't mind looking after Biscuit for you.'

'Oh, no, I couldn't possibly. I said I'd care for him until other arrangements can be made and I intend to carry through on my promise.'

'Don't worry. You'll get him back. But I don't think he belongs in the kitchen when you're putting together a luncheon for a hundred people.'

'Well, I was going to set him up outside the kitchen, by the trash bins, like I did yesterday.'

'That's exactly why he should come with me. I've set up a marquee on the green across from Shackleford's house to serve as our mobile headquarters during the case. Biscuit would have shade, grass, and lots of people around to make sure he's fed, watered, and walked.'

Tish sighed as she gazed at the dog in the backseat. 'I feel as though I'm abandoning him.'

'You're not. Once the luncheon is over, he's all yours again. Until a foster home comes through, that is.'

As if to voice his opinion on the matter, Biscuit sat up and, leaning through the open plexi-glass partition between the front and back seats, licked the back of Reade's head.

'Can't argue with that, can I?' Tish laughed. 'By the way, thanks, Clemson. For the ride, for taking Biscuit, for everything.'

'Considering the progress you've made on this case, I'd say we're more than even. Do you need a hand with the box in the trunk? I'd be happy to carry it in for you.'

'Nope. I'm good, but thank you. Again.'

'No problem. I'll let you know what I find out about the Knoblochs and Collingsworth.'

'I'd appreciate that.' Tish exited the vehicle, and, with a wave to Biscuit, walked to the back of the car, opened the trunk, and removed the box of cooking paraphernalia before shutting the lid.

Just like the day before, music emanated from the pool area, but today the mood of said music was far more relaxed. As Reade pulled out of the parking lot and waved goodbye, Tish let herself into the outdoor pool area through the tall cast-iron gate.

She was surprised to discover Jules, dressed in a pair of turquoise shorts bearing embroidered palm trees and a white linen shirt unbuttoned to the waist, lying in one of the lifestyle center's many lounge chairs. Beside him rested a short, salt-and-pepper-haired elderly woman in a vivid, hibiscus-printed muumuu.

Both of them sported chilled eye masks on their faces and held a champagne flute of orange liquid in their hands.

'Jules? What are you doing here?' Tish asked.

Jules removed his eye mask and blinked against the strong rays of the sun. 'Tish? Is that you?'

'Yes, I'm here to prep for the luncheon. At seven thirty. Just as we arranged. What are you doing by the pool?'

'Trying to recover from Mrs Newman's lethal mojitos with some cool compresses and mimosas.'

'Wait a minute. You're hung-over?'

'Hung-over is such an ugly phrase. Mrs Wilkes and I prefer to say that we're sorely in need of a restorative,' Jules lilted.

'That's right, honey,' Mrs Wilkes seconded.

'Well, I'm afraid you're going to need to find another place to restore, Jules. With all the trouble I've had with the Knoblochs, I really can't afford to have you seen hanging out poolside while you're working for me, even if you are Mrs Wilkes's guest. It's unprofessional.'

'Oh, but Julian's more than a guest,' Mrs Wilkes argued.

'That's right,' Jules chimed in. 'Tomorrow, we're seeing Susannah Hilton about my resident permit.'

Tish couldn't believe her ears. 'Resident permit?'

'Yes, as soon as my lease is up at the end of the month, I'm moving in with Mrs Wilkes.'

Tish's eyes scanned back and forth between Jules and Mrs Wilkes to see if a trace of a smile crossed their lips, but the pair remained stony-faced. 'Jules, may I speak with you inside, please?'

'Of course.' Leaving his drink on the table between his lounge chair and Mrs Wilkes's, he followed Tish into the lifestyle center.

Finally able to see Tish and the bandage on her hand and the abrasions on her chin, Jules drew a hand to his mouth and let out a yelp. 'Oh my goodness. What happened to you?'

'Someone broke the windows on my car and I bumped my chin on the ground while chasing after them.'

'Oh, no,' Jules gasped. 'Are you OK? Should I try to call someone in to cover for you? Or contact Susannah to cancel?'

'I'm fine, Jules. I'll be OK once I start cooking. Today's luncheon needs to go ahead as planned.'

'I just can't believe someone would vandalize your car like that. Who would do such a thing?'

'I have no idea, but Reade is on the case.'

'Good. If I can do anything at all to make this day easier for you, you've got it.'

'You can, actually. For starters, how about you tell me about this whole residence thing?'

Jules was matter-of-fact. 'Simple. I'm moving in with Mrs Wilkes.'

'What? You're shacking up with some – some – how old is Mrs Wilkes, anyway?'

'Eighty-three next month.'

'You're shacking up with some octogenarian? How? Why? You haven't been kicked out of your place, have you?'

'No, I haven't been kicked out. It's just that Mrs Wilkes has a big house with two guest rooms and she loves to cook. All the ladies at Mahjong love to cook, actually. You should join us next time to swap recipes.' Jules took a deep breath. 'Anyway, Mrs Wilkes's children rarely come to visit. I think they've seen her twice in ten years. So, last night, after dinner, it was suggested that she rent out part of her house to some bachelor who enjoys home cooking and can help her with household repairs and give her a ride to doctor appointments. She was reluctant at first, but after a few more mojitos and a couple of rounds of Mahjong, she grew to love the idea and so . . . voilà! That lucky bachelor is me.'

'Jules, have you lost whatever sense you were born with? You just met this woman.'

'I know. That's why I'm putting off moving in until the end of the month. It gives us time to get to know each other better.'

Tish couldn't comprehend what she was hearing. 'But, Jules, this makes no sense at all. You're an attractive single guy. What if you meet someone? What if you think he's the one? You can't just bring Mr Right home to Mrs Wilkes's house. That would be like bringing him to meet your mother.'

'Tish, I'm forty-one years of age. I've spent the last twenty-five years hunting for Mr Right. I can't keep putting life on hold just in case he shows up. If I can't find myself a sugar daddy, then I'm quite content to settle down with a sugar mama.'

'A sugar mama? You've become a gigolo.'

'Not a gigolo,' Jules corrected. 'More like a rent-a-son.'

'Oh, that makes it so much better,' Tish mocked. 'You've done some weird things in your time, Julian Jefferson Davis, but this might just be the craziest.'

'Or the smartest,' he challenged. 'Think about it. Mrs Wilkes has someone to cook for and help her out with things. I get all that fine Southern cooking and we both get companionship.'

'Is that what this is all about? Loneliness?'

Jules shrugged and looked off into the distance. 'I just feel as though time is running out for me and I need to start making some decisions.'

'Well, moving to a retirement community isn't going to help with the feeling that time is getting short,' Tish reasoned.

'Just this Friday, you yourself pointed out that we're only a few years in age behind the residents here.'

'The sixty-year-old residents, not the eighty-three-year-old ones. Look, Jules, I need to get cooking if I'm going to be ready by noon, but I want to discuss this further with you.'

'There's nothing else to discuss. I've told you everything you need to know.'

'OK, then, can you at least promise me you won't make a final decision regarding Mrs Wilkes until after this weekend?'

He shrugged.

'Jules, you're being impossible. During an evening of heavy Southern food and mojitos, you and an elderly woman made the choice to cohabitate. That's not a valid life decision – it's an episode of *The Golden Girls*.'

'And here you criticized me for my *Cocoon* comment. Now look who's being ageist.'

'I'm not ageist. I'm exhausted,' she shouted. 'I spent last night in a two-bedroom apartment occupied by six people and a dog.

I had to reprimand my best friend's son for coming home late and drunk. The windows of my car have been smashed. I was pushed to the ground when I tried to pursue the perpetrator. I had to call Clemson Reade on the sly to report the incident so that I didn't wake the entire house. And this morning I had to hitch a ride with him to get here.'

'Sheriff Reade?' Jules's eyes grew wide. 'Reade was at your place all night? Hot!'

'Ugh, Jules. No. Reade was not one of the six people in the apartment.'

'Sorry, I just thought there might be a fun reason you were exhausted.'

'No, there isn't a fun reason. Jules, you know I love you and I'd do anything to help you, just as you'd do anything to help me. However, if you could kindly reschedule your existential crisis for a day when I've gotten more than four hours' sleep, haven't been assaulted, and don't have one hundred mouths to feed by noon, I'd greatly appreciate it.'

Jules nodded. 'I understand. I'll tell Mrs Wilkes I need more time to decide. I'm sorry if I've been selfish.'

Tish put the box down on the tiled floor and embraced her friend. 'You haven't been selfish. We all reach a point where we feel the need to step back and reassess our lives. As your friend, it's my job to make sure you think things through properly and don't make a terrible mistake.'

'I feel the same responsibility toward you.' Jules squeezed her tight. 'I'm so sorry I wasn't there for you last night. Although you did have Sheriff Reade. Smoldering, spiky-haired Sheriff Reade . . .'

'Jules,' Tish reprimanded as she pushed him away.

'Sorry, too many of those broody BBC romances.' He picked up the box of cooking supplies and walked in the direction of the kitchen. 'So, did I miss anything else last night?'

'Oh, a few things. Glen's moving in with his girlfriend, so Mary Jo and the kids are moving back to the house today. I think the soil here at Coleton Creek has been poisoned by building debris, which is the true cause of the yellowing problems – not Biscuit. Reade's checking out how Callie Collingsworth ended up inheriting Shackleford's estate. Schuyler Thompson is probably the single most patient, kind, and wonderful man in the world—'

Jules interrupted with a cheer. 'Oh, please tell me he was one of the six in the apartment!'

'No, I told you it wasn't a fun night,' Tish repeated as she unlocked the kitchen door with the key Susannah had provided.

'Drat.' Jules plonked the box on to the counter.

'And, finally, I think Zadie Morris is hiding something.'

'Something associated with Sloane Shackleford?'

'Maybe. Maybe not. I don't know, but I intend to find out.'

SEVENTEEN

After mixing the batter for miniature Yorkshire puddings and setting it aside to rest, Tish seasoned two top sirloin roasts and positioned them in a pan atop a pile of coarsely chopped onion, celery, carrot, and turnip. Upon placing the pan of veggies and beef in a 350-degree oven, she demonstrated to Jules the correct assembly technique for the prawn cocktails with Marie Rose sauce and set off for Zadie Morris's house.

Several oppressively humid minutes later, Tish arrived on Zadie's doorstep, her black T-shirt damp against her back and her brushed and blow-dried hair now distinctly wavy. Tish wiped the perspiration from her forehead with the back of her arm and pressed the doorbell. Thankfully, Zadie answered at the second ring.

She was dressed in a pair of pink satin pajamas, matching monogrammed slippers, and a white chenille bed jacket. Her face looked less tired and drawn than it had the previous evening, but there was still a lingering air of fatigue in her mannerisms.

'Good morning,' Tish greeted.

'Morning. Come on in out of that heat.' Zadie opened the door and ushered Tish inside.

'It's already hotter than it was yesterday afternoon. You'd better take it easy today, Ms Morris.'

'Looks like you oughta take it easy yourself,' Zadie replied, gesturing toward Tish's hand and chin. 'What happened to you?'

'Oh, I interrupted a saboteur last night.' Tish went on to describe the damage done to her car.

'This is the point where other women my age would shake their heads and remark how things aren't the same as they were. The problem with that statement is the world has always been a wicked place. People just find new ways to make each other miserable.'

Tish was taken aback by Zadie's jaded remark. She had always thought the cosmetics entrepreneur to be of such a positive mindset.

'You have some bruising coming up there on your left cheek.' The older woman, possibly sensing Tish's sense of shock, swiftly changed the subject. 'I have a foundation that will cover that.'

'Oh, no, thanks, I already put some on before I left the house. The rest of the bottle is in my bag back at the kitchen.'

'You can't count on average foundation to last in this weather. But I have a product I took on safari with me several years ago. Held up in even one-hundred-degree heat.' She wandered off toward the bedroom.

Tish began to follow, but Zadie stopped her with a smile. 'You wait here. I'll be right back.'

True to her word, Zadie returned less than a minute later, brandishing a small bottle of flesh-colored liquid. 'Sit on the sofa and I'll apply it for you.'

'Oh, I couldn't possibly,' Tish argued.

'Nonsense. It'll bring me back to younger days. I started out at a makeup counter in Richmond, you know.'

'I had no idea.' Tish sat on the spot on the sofa Zadie had occupied the previous evening.

'Well, I didn't say much about my personal life when I had the company. I let my cosmetics do the talking.' Zadie put a dab of concealer on her right middle finger and applied it to Tish's cheek, causing the younger woman to recoil slightly.

'Sorry, I didn't mean to hurt you.'

'You didn't. I'm just a bit tender.'

'You poor thing.' Zadie clicked her tongue. 'Still, they might have done worse. What possessed you to run after them?'

'Temporary insanity, I guess.'

'Although I'm glad you gave them what-for, the whole thing sounds terrifying.'

'Once the adrenaline wore off, I admit I was quite frightened that they'd return. I think the only reason I got any sleep is because the earlier part of the night had been a bit emotional as well. See, my seventeen-year-old godson came home past curfew and intoxicated.'

'Boys!' Zadie shook her head.

'Yeah, I was so worried when Gregory – my godson – didn't come home on time. I feared the worst. His poor mother has been through enough this weekend, what with the breakup of her marriage. I couldn't bear the thought of her losing him as well. Of course, Gregory came home in one piece, but the whole situation reminded me of you and your godson.'

'My godson?' Zadie repeated, as if unfamiliar with the term.

'Yes, the one whose photo is on your nightstand. The photo I saw yesterday.'

'Oh, y–yes. My godson, William.'

'I couldn't help but think of poor William's mother – what was her name?'

Zadie's fingers hovered over Tish's face and she appeared to enter a fugue state. 'Vera,' she whispered.

'I thought of Vera and how her son's death must have affected her. The poor woman must have suffered terribly.'

'She and I completely lost touch. She wasn't the same woman afterwards.'

'I can't even fathom how something like that might change someone.'

'When William died, Vera died with him.' Zadie lowered her head and fell silent.

Upon witnessing Zadie's grief and desolation, Tish felt like a voyeur. 'I'm so sorry. I didn't realize how painful the subject was for you.'

Zadie snapped from her reverie and went back to blending the concealer into Tish's foundation. 'It's all right. I'd just never really discussed it with anyone before, but it was . . . it was good to bring it out into the open.'

'Will you be attending the luncheon this afternoon?' Tish asked, eager to change the subject and feeling more than a bit embarrassed for having brought Zadie close to tears over a silly hunch.

'Yes, I'll be there cheering on Orson. I know he can be rough around the edges, but at heart he truly is a sweet man.'

'I'm sure he'll be thrilled to have you at his side.'

'If I'm ready in time,' she chuckled. 'I have a lot more wrinkles to cover than you do.'

'No, you have lovely skin.'

'You forgot to add "for a woman my age." That always seems to be the qualifying statement. It sets the bar rather low, doesn't it?' She smiled, yet there was a bitter worldliness in her words. 'There. Your bruise is concealed and should stay that way all day, as long as you don't smudge it with your hand.'

'Thank you.' Tish rose from the sofa.

'My pleasure, sweetie. I can't do anything about your chin, but at least folks will have one less thing to stare at.'

'True. And I'm sorry again about asking you so many questions.'

'Don't be. Old photographs draw us into their stories, don't they? It's tremendously difficult to look at them and not feel haunted by our own past.'

Tish nodded. That was precisely how she felt – haunted – yet she struggled to stay in the here and now. 'Well, I'll just grab the tray from the kitchen and let myself out. I'll see you later?'

'Yes, or at least some incarnation of me.' Zadie laughed a throaty laugh. 'I promise, beneath all the plaster, paint, and powder, I'll be there.'

'I'm sure you'll look fabulous,' Tish complimented before turning on one heel and setting off for the kitchen.

'Oh, Tish?'

Tish stopped in the doorway. 'Yes?'

'I hope you don't think me a sentimental old fool, but I wanted to tell you how much I admire you. Yesterday I said that you reminded me of myself and I meant it. Moving to a new town, reinventing yourself, starting a new business – I've done all three and it's not easy, but you seem to be handling it all with grace, integrity, and, most of all, kindness.'

Tish was flabbergasted. 'I don't know what to say.'

'Nothing to say. Just always stay true to who you are, Tish. That's my only advice.'

'I'll keep that in mind. Thank you.'

'Good. Now, you'd better get going. You have a luncheon to cater and the residents of Coleton Creek can be a handful. If they're not comparing your cooking to that of their great-aunt

Tilly, they're wrapping up whatever they can in napkins and squirreling it away in their handbags and pockets to eat later.'

Tish laughed. 'Don't worry, I have plenty of extra food and a thick skin regarding criticism.'

After collecting yesterday's tea tray from Zadie's kitchen, Tish said farewell and set out on the walk back to the lifestyle center. In the short time she had been at Zadie's, the sun had risen above the tops of the tallest trees, sending temperatures soaring well into the nineties and making the moisture-laden air feel like that of a greenhouse.

Even though the lifestyle center was air-conditioned, it was no day to be stuck inside a kitchen with oven and range blazing. However, far more worrying to Tish was the prospect of one hundred of Coleton Creek's aging residents sitting on the enclosed patio in the afternoon heat.

Fortunately, she didn't worry long, for within moments Tucker Abercrombie approached her. He was dressed in a casual ensemble of plaid shorts, polo shirt, flip-flops, and an Atlanta Braves baseball cap. 'Morning, Ms Tarragon. Mr Davis said I'd find you here.'

'Morning, Mr Abercrombie. How can I help you?'

'I have the fans for the patio, but I need you to unlock the door.'

'Fans?'

'Yeah, for the luncheon. It's what we do on hot days like this.'

'Perfect timing. I was just about to call Susannah Hilton about that.'

'She's actually the one who contacted me. You see, the company I retired from provides emergency generators, fans, transformers, and other electronic devices to businesses. I was an account manager there for over forty years, so they've agreed to provide the fans for Coleton Creek's events for free.'

'That's nice of them. So when you spoke with Susannah, did she mention when she might be coming in?'

'No, and it's darned odd of her, too. It's not like Susannah not to be here at a time like this. Sundays and Mondays are her days off, but when we have an event – especially an important event like the garden club luncheon – she's buzzing around here like a one-armed wallpaper hanger. She'll work on her days off, come in early, stay late. Sometimes I think she even camps overnight. So for Susannah not to be here now, just a few hours before the luncheon, is really quite unusual.' Tucker pulled a face. 'Then again, she didn't sound much like herself on the phone.'

'Oh? How did she sound?'

'Nervous. Jumpy. When I asked her if she was OK, she said she was fine, so I didn't push it, but there was definitely something wrong. No doubt something to do with her crazy bosses. They're always on her to do their dirty work.'

The comment got Tish's attention. 'What kind of dirty work?'

'Oh, things Nathan and Mariette had messed up and wanted her to fix. Things that might have gotten them in trouble, like firing the pool maintenance company who'd serviced the pools since the place was built. Not only did the Knoblochs still have over a year on their contract with the company, but by rights the homeowners' association should have had a vote on the matter. So instead of handling the issue themselves, they put Susannah on the firing line with both the company and the association. Things were eventually resolved, thanks to Susannah's brainpower and grace under fire, but it shows you how Nathan and Mariette operate.'

'Yes, it certainly does.' Tish wondered about the damage done to her car. How dedicated an employee was Susannah Hilton? Had the Knoblochs, worried about soil samples and further digging, entrusted Susannah Hilton to 'clean up the mess' of the garden club luncheon? Had Susannah been entrusted to scare Tish away from the luncheon by any means possible? Was she the person with the crowbar at the café last night? If so, that might explain why Susannah wasn't at the lifestyle center this morning. Susannah might have been under the impression that Tish wouldn't show up for the job and, therefore, the luncheon would be cancelled. Or Susannah was fearful that if they met again, Tish might be able to identify her as the culprit.

But if Susannah did believe the luncheon was cancelled, why call Tucker Abercrombie about fans? Was that simply to cover her tracks, so she could state, if questioned, that she believed the luncheon was going ahead as scheduled? Or had Susannah used Tucker as a means to determine whether Tish had actually shown up for work? After all, it was nearly nine in the morning and Susannah hadn't received a call from Tish cancelling the event.

'May I carry that tray for you?' Tucker Abercrombie offered, interrupting Tish's ruminations.

'No, thank you. I've got it. Let's get back to the lifestyle center so you can set up those fans.'

'Sure. Um, can I talk to you about something?'

'Of course. Let's talk as we walk.'

Tucker followed Tish's lead. 'Jim Ainsley tells me you're quite the detective.'

'Mr Ainsley overstates my abilities. I'm more of an amateur sleuth.'

'Nope, the Jim I know always sticks to the facts. Besides, I read the local papers. I know what you did in that murdered librarian case. My wife says you're working on Shackleford's murder, too.'

Tish was careful not to reveal that she had already spoken to Violet Abercrombie, yet she left the door open, just in case Tucker was aware of their conversation. 'I'm not working on the case, but a few individuals have disclosed certain details to me. If those details are important, I refer the individual to Sheriff Reade.'

'Has my wife been one of those individuals?' Tucker Abercrombie asked, his face pinched with concern.

At the word 'wife,' Tish stopped walking. Although she wasn't a police officer or attorney, she valued Violet Abercrombie's privacy. 'Don't you think that's a question you should ask her?'

'Probably. But if I ask her, she'll want to know why I'm asking.'

'Why *are* you asking?'

'I thought maybe she might know something. Something that she might have confided in you – you both being women and all.'

'Something?'

'OK, fine. I went to see Sloane Shackleford on Friday morning.'

'I thought you'd been slaving in the garden all morning.'

'I had been. Right after you, Mr Davis, and Jim Ainsley dropped by to view our garden, Violet went inside to make us lunch, and I went out to buy a copy of *The Virginian-Pilot*. I typically walk to the convenience store every morning for a paper, but because of the prep for the competition, I hadn't that morning. I thought it was a reasonable excuse to get out of the house.'

'So instead of picking up the paper, you went to Shackleford's,' Tish surmised.

'Yes, with the intention of picking up the paper after our meeting.'

'But we were on our way to Wren Harper's house at the time you left for Shackleford's – how come we didn't see you?'

'I watched to see which way you walked and went in the opposite direction. It was a longer walk, but it brought me straight to Shackleford's doorstep and I didn't have to pass Orson's or Wren's.'

'Clever.'

'Yeah, I thought so too, until I arrived at Shackleford's to find him dead.'

'Whoa, back up a minute. You found Sloane Shackleford dead and you didn't report it?'

'I panicked and ran back home as quick as I could. Not only was I afraid I'd be accused of the crime, but I didn't know how to explain to Vi what I was doing there.'

'What *were* you doing there?'

Tucker placed a bronzed arm behind his head and stared down at his toes. 'Oh, where do I even begin?'

He went on to tell Tish about Violet's cancer diagnosis and the insurance company's discontinuation of benefits. 'That was a difficult time for both of us, but mostly Vi. I mean, here she was, fighting for her life while knowing that the treatment saving her was ultimately bankrupting us.'

'So you went to Shackleford's seeking what? Compensation? Revenge?'

'Neither. I wanted him to drop out of the garden competition.'

'After everything he did to you, that's what you asked for?'

'I know it sounds weird, but it really isn't. Vi had always dreamed of having a big, beautiful garden. When we first got married, our backyard wasn't big enough. Then, when we got a bigger house and yard, she was too busy with the kids. When Vi fell ill, I promised her that no matter where we ended up, even if we had to sell the house, we would live in a place where she could have a garden. The days she'd go for her treatments, she was too weak to move, so I'd sit at her bedside and take notes of the plants she liked and the features that were important to her. Vi's been cancer-free three years now, and I swear it was the promise of that garden, and now the realization of that dream, that's made her recovery possible.'

'Like her own personal *Secret Garden*.' Tish drew a parallel between Violet Abercrombie's improving health and that of the story's Colin Craven.

'It's about more than just the garden. The whole time we've been married, Vi's looked after other people. Me, the kids, the grandkids, Jim Ainsley . . .'

At Ainsley's name, Tish felt a tickle in her throat.

'Even when Vi was ill, she worried about what would happen to me should she not recover.' Tucker drew a deep breath. 'I felt it was time Vi was recognized for an achievement apart from raising a family or caring for friends. Vi planned out that garden, drew out the designs, started the plants from seed, and made sure everything had what was needed to grow. Winning best garden in the competition would have been a celebration of her abilities and hard work. As her own person.'

'But even if Shackleford dropped out, you couldn't be certain your wife would win,' Tish was quick to indicate.

'I know, but Vi would have at least stood a better chance without him in the running. And he – well, that thieving, two-faced skunk had no place being awarded anything other than twenty years behind bars.'

'So you were going to "suggest" that Mr Shackleford drop out?'

'Oh, I already had. Last Monday. Friday was just to see if he'd changed his mind. Shackleford had those gardeners of his mowing the lawn and whatever else they did to help him win the competition every year. Bad back, my eye. Although I shouldn't have been surprised by anything the man did. Truth and he never were related.'

'So, you say you saw Shackleford last Monday,' Tish prompted, hoping to speed the man along. As fascinating as Tucker Abercrombie's story might be, she still needed to check on her roasts.

'Yes, I found him on the patio, sipping sweet tea and looking over some piles of broken cement. What he was up to, I haven't a clue, but I introduced myself – even though he already knew who I was – told him what he and his company had done to Vi and me years back, and told him that if he didn't drop out of the competition, I'd let everyone in Coleton Creek know just what a charlatan he was.'

'I can only imagine how well that went down.'

'About as well as a pork pie in a synagogue,' Tucker deadpanned. 'Shackleford started laughing like a madman. Then he went on to tell me that if I told folks about his insurance dealings, he'd tell them about my wife's affair with Jim Ainsley.'

Tish felt her face go red. 'Affair?'

'Precisely my reaction. There isn't an affair. Never has been. Vi has always been close with Jim. He's a man of integrity and the best friend a person could ever ask for. And Vi – well, everyone who knows her loves her. I can't blame Jim if he developed feelings for Vi at some point through the years. She's the most beautiful, kind, warm, and funny gal to ever grace this earth. But the two of them would never have an affair. Neither of them have it in their being. If anything, Jim has helped me to be a better husband. There was a time when I was working round the clock and traveling all the time. Jim sat me down and explained how he didn't mind keeping Vi and the kids company, but how it should be me watching a movie and eating popcorn with Vi and tucking the kids into bed at night. Right after that conversation, I asked my boss if I could be moved to telephone sales. I had to take a cut in pay at first, but it was worth it. Eventually, telephone sales became telephone and online sales and customer support, but the company gave us a good life and stuck with me when Vi was sick.

'You know who else stuck by me when Vi was sick?' Tucker continued. 'Jim Ainsley. There were moments – I'm not proud of them – but there were moments when I just felt like I couldn't go on another day if Vi didn't get better. Moments when I thought it might be better for me to go before she did. Jim was there during those dark times, walking me back to sanity. And I won't even go into how much he's helped us by letting us live here in Coleton Creek. I'm lucky to have both Vi and Jim in my life, and I'm doubly lucky to have the people I care most about also care about each other – not as lovers, but as the bestest of friends.'

All these years, Tish thought to herself. *All these years Tucker Abercrombie understood there was a special bond between his wife and Jim Ainsley. And all these years, Violet Abercrombie had been trying to hide it.*

'Have you ever told your wife what you told me just now?' she asked.

'No, she knows how I feel about Jim.'

'Yes, but she doesn't know that you know how *she* feels about Jim. That's led to a fair amount of guilt and secrecy over the years.'

Tucker's jaw dropped open. 'So Vi has spoken with you.'

Tish nodded. 'She told me about your history with Shackleford and then told me that neither you, she, nor Mr Ainsley had killed him.'

Tucker closed his mouth and tried on a puzzled expression. 'All three of us?'

'Well, when she saw you return home for lunch Friday without a newspaper and looking frazzled, she probably thought the worst. However, coming to me to say her husband was innocent would have put me, and subsequently the police, right on your scent,' Tish explained.

'So she diverted the focus from me by putting it on all of us,' Tucker surmised. 'She never ceases to amaze me.'

'Your wife is a very intelligent woman.'

'Again, I'm a very lucky man.'

'Yes, let's just hope that luck holds when you speak with Sheriff Reade.'

'Sheriff Reade? I told you, Shackleford was dead when I got there. Why do I have to talk to the police? I'm telling you the truth.'

'Given that you were in the clear until you spoke to me, I tend to believe you. However, your story presents us with a clearer timeline of the murder. Did you pass anyone on the way to or from Shackleford's?'

'No. Not a soul.'

'Are you certain? Not even a car or bike or dog walker?'

'I'm positive. It was a typical hot day here at Coleton Creek. Most folks walk their dogs or tend their gardens early in the morning or in the cool of the evening. From noon onward to about five, you'd be hard-pressed to find anyone out in the sun.'

'Which route did you take back home? Did you go back the same way?'

'No, I wanted to get away from Shackleford and back home as quickly as possible, so I went the shorter way. Past Wren's and Orson's. You, Jim, and Mr Davis were on Wren's front porch when I went by, but you didn't see me. Glad of the fact too, since I couldn't rightly explain why I was walking so fast.'

Tucker's description of their visit to Wren Harper's was correct, thus only further substantiating his story, which in itself caused another conundrum. At the thought of it, Tish heaved a heavy sigh.

'What's wrong, Ms Tarragon? I'm telling you the truth. Apart from the three of you on Wren Harper's porch, not a single person crossed my path.'

'I believe you, Mr Abercrombie. That's the whole problem, isn't it? If the people who visited Shackleford prior to you are also telling the truth, then the murderer had just fifteen to twenty minutes to enter Shackleford's garden, strike him dead with a garden spade, and make his or her getaway.'

'Sounds plausible to me,' Tucker Abercrombie shrugged.

'To me as well. But if I'm not mistaken, there are only two approaches to Mr Shackleford's house – the one you took and the one we took. Correct?'

'Yes, that's right.'

'And none of us passed another person along the way – except for, eventually, each other.'

'Right.'

'So where did the murderer go, Mr Abercrombie? Where did he or she go?'

EIGHTEEN

After allowing Tucker Abercrombie admittance to the patio, Tish reported to Sheriff Reade via telephone, only for her call to be forwarded directly to voicemail. Upon leaving a message about Tucker's visit to Shackleford on Friday morning, Tish returned to the lifestyle-center kitchen, where Celestine, Jules, and two medium-rare roasts awaited.

'Hey, honey. I took the liberty of removing your roasts from the oven,' Celestine greeted.

'Thanks, Celestine.'

'You're welcome. Now let's take a look at you.' The woman gave Tish a hug and inspected her wounds. 'Jules told me what happened. You were very lucky.'

'I know,' Tish moaned. She was tired of discussing her good fortune. 'Where are the cakes?'

'In the fridge,' Jules replied. 'Ms Celly wouldn't let me see them until you got here.'

'You're darn right I wouldn't. These beauties deserve a proper introduction.' She extracted three boxes from the refrigerator and lined them up on the counter. 'Rose cakes with raspberry frosting,' Celestine announced as she removed the lid from the first box to reveal row after row of pristinely pink cakes topped with fresh raspberries and crystallized rose petals.

'Ooooh,' Tish and Jules cried in unison.

Celestine lifted the lid off the second box. Inside stood dozens of miniature loaf cakes with a light, whitish glaze and purple flowers. 'Lavender and lemon cakes with lemon glaze and whole sugared violets.'

Tish and Jules's second response echoed their first.

'And, finally, something for the gluten-free folks.' She opened the third box, which was filled with tiny golden Bundt cakes filled with billowy soft peaks of cream and garnished with tiny yellow flowers. 'Corn flour and orange blossom chiffon cakes with crème-fraiche frosting and candied honeysuckle blossoms straight from my backyard.'

'These might be the most beautiful cakes I've ever seen,' Tish gushed. 'As well as the most fragrant.'

'I know they ate fairy cakes in the book, but I thought using the garden as inspiration might be fun,' Celestine chuckled.

'These are absolutely brilliant, Celestine. And they'll look terrific on our vintage cake stands.'

'I got some lemon leaves to decorate with too. Just for a little extra pop of green.'

'The heck with lemon leaves. I can't believe I'm drooling over something gluten-free,' Jules declared. 'When do we get to taste them?'

Celestine happily cut up one of each cake for a quick – and ultimately divine – taste test before settling into the day's work.

Even with a late start, the day's tasks were accomplished smoothly and on schedule. At precisely five minutes to twelve, the buffet table was practically groaning under the weight of a luncheon fit for royalty.

There were silver platters piled high with crustless tea sandwiches on country white or artisan wheat bread: salmon and cream cheese, egg mayonnaise, cucumber, and spicy Coronation chicken. Martini glasses were filled with prawns, greens, tomatoes, and creamy Marie Rose sauce. A sectioned chafing dish presented both golden miniature Yorkshire puddings packed with sliced roast beef and horseradish cream and buttery sage-and-onion-infused sausage rolls. And, on an antique platter in the center of the table, stood a pyramid of plain and savory cheese scones accompanied by bowls of clotted cream and homemade strawberry preserves.

Indeed, the morning workload was completed so efficiently that Jules even had time to devise a new cocktail.

Determining that a second specialty cold-beverage option might prove more popular in the ninety-five-degree heat than a warm pot of tea, Jules brewed half of his Earl Grey tea supply, chilled it, added homemade lavender lemonade (made from the lavender Celestine had left over from her cakes), a splash of gin, and a cucumber slice for a drink he dubbed the *Arnold Palmerston*.

'You know, the former British Prime Minister?' Jules explained to bewildered guests. Despite their puzzled reactions, the drink was an unmitigated success.

Tish and Celestine waited behind the buffet table and watched as the luncheon food rapidly disappeared into the mouths of hungry guests and Jules served up drinks with his usual élan.

'Everything surrounding this event may have been chaotic, but I'd say this was a triumph,' Celestine whispered to Tish.

'Pardon me if I refrain from celebrating until the last of our guests is home safe and sound and is still breathing in the morning.'

As if on cue, Sheriff Clemson Reade appeared in the glass door of the lifestyle center. 'See?' Tish gestured in his direction.

'What's that boy doing here? Doesn't he realize he's about as welcome as a porcupine in a nudist colony?'

Tish rushed to the door before Reade's presence was noticed. 'Hey,' she greeted as she stepped into the lifestyle center.

'Hey. Sorry for interrupting you. You got a minute?'

'A brief one.'

'I wanted to tell you your hunches paid off. It being Sunday, I couldn't get in touch with any labs in the area, but some nosing into Shackleford's financial records showed that he made payments to both Virginia Tech Soil Testing Lab in Blacksburg and a private environmental engineering firm in Roanoke as recently as last month. I couldn't find the results of their work, but our team did a cursory pH test of the soil included in those bags and they were highly alkaline. But that's not all. Guess who showed up at headquarters first thing this morning?'

Tish shrugged. 'No idea.'

'Susannah Hilton. It appears Mariette Knobloch called Susannah at her home last night demanding that something be done to stop today's luncheon and, in Mariette's words, "scare the garden club into disbanding for once and for all."'

'So Susannah was the one who vandalized my car?'

'Nope. When Susannah refused, the Knoblochs fired her.'

'That would explain why she wasn't here this morning,' Tish mused aloud.

'Yep. Based on Susannah's complaint, we took the liberty of visiting the Knoblochs in their home. When we arrived, Nathan was putting some trash in the bins by their garage. In that trash was a hooded sweatshirt, the sleeves of which were covered in what appeared to be glass particles. Before I could even call for a warrant, Mariette came out of the house and confessed to the whole thing. Nathan vandalized your car. She was the one who pushed you to the ground. We have them both in custody.'

'Did they say anything about the building debris?'

'They admitted they cut corners and that Shackleford was on to them, but they both denied being involved in his murder.'

'Wow, that's some fast work,' Tish commended.

'Thanks. But wait, there's more,' Reade added in a voice similar to that of a television spokesperson. 'I did some checking into Callie Collingsworth and it appears there's no record of her anywhere prior to 2015.'

'But how? She only bought her house here at Coleton Creek a few years back. They must have checked her background for a mortgage.'

'She paid cash for her home. Meaning all she would have needed to provide were a couple forms of identification, like a driver's license and social security card. Easy to get decent forgeries of those these days.'

'What did she say when you confronted her?'

'I didn't. I stopped by Ms Collingsworth's house to chat at our predetermined time, but she wasn't there.'

'Yes, she said she had an appointment to meet with you today.'

'Well, either she forgot it or she had no intention whatsoever of speaking with me.'

'Hard to believe she'd pull up stakes before receiving her share of Shackleford's will,' Tish opined.

'Unless she thinks someone's on to her.'

'Callie, or whatever her name is, said she was meeting a friend in Richmond for dinner yesterday evening. Perhaps she's staying there.'

'I tracked down Ms Collingsworth's car – a 2018 Jaguar XE R-Sport in cobalt blue – as well as the license plate number from the Virginia DMV. They match what Susannah had on file here. I'll put a call out to the Richmond police.'

Tish frowned. 'Do you think Callie killed Shackleford?'

'My guess is she's more a grifter than a murderer, but I could be wrong. By the way, I got your message about Tucker Abercrombie. What's going on?'

Tish summarized Tucker's story.

'Do you believe he's telling the truth?'

'I do. He saw us standing on Wren Harper's front porch. That's a detail that's hard to fake.'

'Unless he ran past you on his way home from murdering Shackleford.'

'If he committed the murder, why talk to me at all?' Tish argued. 'He'd be safer sitting tight and waiting.'

Reade scratched his chin. 'If Tucker Abercrombie's account is true, it changes a lot of things. Callie Collingsworth would be in the clear. She was seen at the pool at twenty-five minutes after eleven and didn't leave until you bumped into her in the lifestyle center.'

'It rules out Jim Ainsley too, since he was with me and Jules the entire time the murder took place.'

'What about Violet Abercrombie?'

'Tucker said she was at home making lunch.'

'Exactly. "Tucker said." What if he invented this whole story to cover up for his wife? That would be a good reason for speaking with you – to provide her with an alibi. He nearly lost Violet once to cancer. He wouldn't want to risk losing her again – this time to prison.'

'And Violet Abercrombie came to me in order to shift suspicion from herself and on to her husband or Jim Ainsley?' Tish challenged. 'That doesn't sound quite right either.'

'Maybe they're in it together,' Reade suggested.

'Again, Tucker wouldn't put his wife at risk.'

'Hmm. Well, I'll pay him a visit after the luncheon and hopefully I'll gain a new perspective on things.'

Tish nodded. 'I'd better get back in there and clear dishes before the awards ceremony.'

Tish and Reade bade farewell and went back to their respective posts, Reade to the makeshift headquarters on the green outside Shackleford's house and Tish back to the patio where she and Celestine loaded the leftover food and used dishes on to a pair of tiered carts and wheeled everything back to the kitchen.

After loading the dishwasher and setting it to run, they stacked a cart with piles of dessert plates, serving pieces, and cakes, and wheeled it back to the patio, where they waited near the door and quietly watched the ceremony unfold.

'And the award for most improved garden,' Jim Ainsley announced into an ancient microphone as he stood before the buffet table and opened a sealed envelope, 'goes to Emily O'Malley.'

An auburn-haired woman in a green dress rose from the audience and, with a brief curtsey to the cheering crowd, stepped forward to accept her prize.

'Congratulations, Emily,' Ainsley praised and handed the woman a small loving cup trophy. 'And now for the moment you've all been waiting for. The prizes for garden of the year.'

The lady Jules had seen walking her little white dog the morning of their arrival at Coleton Creek presented Ainsley with a sealed envelope on a silver salver. Ainsley took it and began tearing at the flap. 'Our third-place prize goes to . . . Violet Abercrombie and her cottage garden.'

Tucker and Violet Abercrombie embraced and shared a kiss before Violet rose from her seat and approached the front of the room. There, she gave Jim a hug and held her wall-plaque trophy aloft for all to see. 'Thank you,' she mouthed as the sound of her words was drowned out by the audience's applause.

Ainsley waited until Violet was back at her seat before announcing the next winner. 'Our second-place winner for best garden goes to Orson Baggett and his colonial garden.'

Unlike Violet, Orson appeared disappointed by his win until a grinning Zadie Morris, seated on his left side, threw her arms around his neck and planted a kiss upon his cheek. Blushing a bright scarlet, he leaned in and reciprocated with a kiss on the lips that Zadie appeared to greatly enjoy.

'Come get your trophy, Orson,' Ainsley prodded. 'You can finish collecting your other prize later.'

At Ainsley's comment, the luncheon guests broke into raucous laughter and even more thunderous applause. Still red-faced, Orson jogged up to the front of the room, shook Ainsley's hand, and held his wall plaque high above his head before returning to Zadie's side.

'And, finally, Coleton Creek's garden of the year is' – Ainsley drew out the pause for maximum effect – 'Wren Harper's wildflower garden.'

While Violet and Orson's reactions to victory were ultimately joyous, Wren's was that of complete shock. Her mouth agape, she drew her hands to her face and broke into sobs, prompting her tablemates, including Violet Abercrombie, to flock to her side in tender support.

Their presence didn't fully calm the first-prize winner, but it settled her sufficiently enough for her to collect her trophy – a bronze statue of a hand holding a garden trowel – and issue forth an emotionally wrought, 'You have no idea how much this means to me right now. Thank you.'

As the residents of Coleton Creek gave Wren Harper a standing ovation, she returned to her seat, drew a handkerchief to her face, and stared down at the table.

Taking Wren's silence as his cue, Ainsley stepped to the microphone and called everyone to order. 'Ladies and gentlemen, although I'm sure she appreciates your accolades, let's give Ms Harper some space in which to absorb the news of her victory. It's been a trying weekend for all of us, what with the sudden loss of Mr Sloane Shackleford. Although he was not the most popular member of our garden club, his horticultural work raised the bar on this little competition of ours and it's my sincerest hope that

Mr Shackleford – our neighbor, friend, and fellow gardener – is in a better place.'

Ainsley's makeshift eulogy elicited a few murmurs of 'Hear, hear' from the crowd. Apart from that, the room was perfectly silent.

'Before we break for dessert, I'd like to thank the judges, gardeners, and everyone else who made this year's event a tremendous success. And to the staff of Cookin' the Books – Tish, Celestine, and Julian – thank you for a magnificent luncheon and' – Ainsley raised his *Arnold Palmerston* glass in Jules's direction – 'a most delicious lesson in British history.'

The room erupted in a round of cheers and applause, spurring Jules to take several deep bows interspersed with a few blown kisses. Tish and Celestine, meanwhile, curtsied, waved, smiled, and then wheeled their cart to the buffet table to start the dessert service.

Several minutes later, the patio was filled with the sounds of clanking forks, satisfied 'yums,' and quiet conversations.

Tish used the break in her serving duties to congratulate Wren Harper. 'Ms Harper,' she addressed, 'I won't keep you from your dessert. I just wanted to pass along my congratulations. I'm glad you won. Your garden is simply divine.'

'Thank you, Ms Tarragon. That garden's kept me alive these past few months.' She frowned. 'It's almost been like having a child again. Planting the seeds, anticipating them coming to life, providing them with nutrients and care. Getting this award is validation that all my nurturing paid off.'

'Well, I'm very happy for you.'

'Thank you. And thank you for doing the catering. This is the best food we've ever had at one of our luncheons. Y'all should come back next year.'

'We'd love to. Maybe put in a good word with Mr Ainsley for me,' Tish requested.

'I don't have to.' Wren pointed over Tish's left shoulder.

She whirled around to find Jim Ainsley standing behind her, his dessert plate laden with the remnants of all three of Celestine's cakes. 'No one needs to put a word in my ear. If you'd told me last week that I'd be standing here enjoying cakes with flowers baked into them, I'd call you crazy, but here I am. These might be some of the best cakes I've ever tasted.'

'Thank you, but the glory belongs to Celestine. She's the one who dreamed them up and baked them.'

'Ah, I'll go over and pay my compliments. But please do keep us on the calendar for next year,' he urged before heading off to the buffet table.

As Celestine and Ainsley chatted, Tish set about clearing additional glasses and used plates and utensils from the guests' tables and placing them on to the tiered cart. It was an exceptionally hot day and it wasn't long before every tier of the cart was stacked with glassware. Not wishing to disturb Celestine's conversation, yet not wanting to leave her alone on the patio without notifying her first, Tish gave a quick wave and pointed a finger toward the door.

Celestine gave a knowing nod and then went on to describe to Ainsley her recipe development process.

Tish pushed the cart toward the lifestyle-center door where a kind male guest held it ajar for her. 'Thank you,' she smiled as she wheeled past the guest and into the corridor.

As she steered the collection of glassware over the tiled floors and toward the kitchen, she noticed a deep-blue sedan idling just outside the lifestyle-center front door. Drawing closer, she watched as a familiar blond, dressed in oversized sunglasses, skintight white capris, and a flowy turquoise tunic, opened the rear driver's side door and tossed a black bag inside.

Whipping her phone from her back pocket, Tish redialed the number she'd called just hours earlier. This time he answered. 'Reade.'

'Callie's here. The lifestyle center.'

Tish disconnected and, leaving the cart in the hallway, dashed out the front door. 'Ms Collingsworth. Ms Collingsworth!'

'Can't talk. I'm in a hurry, Ms Tarragon.'

'Just a minute of your time. Please.'

'Sorry, but I'm running late.'

'Ms Collingsworth, please.'

The woman didn't answer, but instead opened the front passenger door of the Jaguar and placed her oversized handbag on the seat.

'If that's even your real name,' Tish ventured.

The comment had the desired effect. Callie Collingsworth

stopped in her tracks and gazed back at Tish, her face a blend of surprise and horror. 'I–I don't know what you're talking about.'

'Callie Collingsworth doesn't exist, so who are you?'

It was just the delay Tish needed. Before Callie could open her mouth to answer, Reade's car came barreling into the parking lot. At the sight of the police, Callie ran to open the driver's side door, but Tish rushed forward to block her entry.

Callie yanked at Tish's arms and shoulders in an attempt to pry her away from the automobile, but Tish, her rear end pushed as close to the door handle as possible, could not be moved. 'Get off of my car,' Callie screamed.

'You get off *me*,' Tish shouted in reply.

Reade bolted out of the sheriff's car, leaving the driver's side door open. 'Ms Collingsworth,' he addressed as he placed a commanding hand on her shoulder.

Callie tried to shrug off the sheriff's grasp. 'Get your hands off me. Anything you need to say to me can be done through my attorney.'

Reade only tightened his grip. 'And what name should we give to this attorney? Because it's clearly not the one you gave us.'

Tish pointed to the duffel bag in the backseat of the Jaguar. 'She was trying to smuggle something out of the lifestyle center.'

With his right hand still holding on to Callie's arm, Reade used his left to open a rear door of the Jaguar. Reaching down, he unzipped the bag. It was filled with financial documents.

'You can't do that. You don't have a warrant.'

'Probable cause, ma'am,' Reade answered flatly. 'Between avoiding our interview this morning and living under an assumed name, you're the walking definition of it.'

Reade took a few sheets of paper out of the bag. 'These belong to Sloane Shackleford.'

'You're quite perceptive, Sheriff,' Callie taunted.

'Where did you get these?'

'From Sloane's gym locker. He never trusted banks. Said people all over try to rob banks, but a gym locker's different. No one breaks into a gym locker expecting to find anything other than a pair of smelly running shoes.'

'So you broke into his locker?'

'No, he gave me the combination. Said if something were to

ever happen to him, I'd find all his banking and other important information in there. I just waited until today to retrieve it. Figured, with the luncheon going on, I could sneak into the men's locker room with minimal risk of walking in on someone.'

'Why would Sloane Shackleford trust you to take care of his estate?' Reade quizzed. 'And why did he make you the beneficiary of his will? Who are you? A forger? A confidence trickster?'

'Oh, Sheriff, what a vivid imagination you have,' Callie laughed. 'No, I'm Caroline Shackleford. Sloane's wife. Well, ex-wife, really.'

'Can you prove that?' Tish challenged.

'Of course. I have our old marriage certificate and the divorce papers back at my house.'

'Why the assumed name?' Reade questioned.

'Oh,' Caroline sighed. 'It's a complicated story.'

'Go ahead. I'm a complicated guy.'

'It was 1968 when we got married. I was eighteen, Sloane was ten years older. I'd always known Sloane was a flirt. He'd chat up waitresses, the girl at the bakery counter, flight attendants, but it wasn't until we'd been married half a year that I realized he was doing far more than just flirting. It was a blustery, rainy Sunday in early February when *she* showed up on our doorstep.'

'She?' Tish prompted.

'A woman. I only saw her through the window. I couldn't tell you how old she was or how pretty. She had a young child with her and she was under the impression that she could move in with Sloane. She was under the impression that he wasn't married. Sloane blew up at her, called her crazy, and sent her away, but it was clear what had happened. If the woman had the impression that Sloane wasn't married, it was because that was the impression he had given her. Our marriage didn't end then and there. Sloane engaged in multiple affairs before I finally got wise to the fact that I would never be the only woman in his life.

'Sloane and I divorced,' she continued, 'and I went on to marry twice more. Neither marriage was particularly good or happy, as I mentioned outside the kitchen yesterday, Ms Tarragon.'

Tish nodded.

'I did inherit a bit of money along the way – as Pepper Aviero was quick to point out during our scuffle – but nothing earth-shattering.

Through it all – the marriages, the deaths, the break-ups – Sloane and I remained friends. I had fun with him, you know? When the whole marriage and fidelity thing was out of the equation, we got along amazingly well. So well, in fact, that when my third husband died, Sloane suggested I move closer to him.'

'Is that when you moved here?' Reade asked.

'Yes, Sloane gave me the cash outright to purchase my home.'

'But you didn't move in with him?'

'No, that would have caused problems. I'd lived apart from both my previous husbands and had developed a taste for doing whatever I want whenever I want. I'm also more of a traditionalist style-wise – chintz, florals, animal prints – whereas Sloane was all about sleek and modern. Most of all, though, my living with Sloane would have cramped his style.'

'The women?' Tish clarified.

'Yes. That's why I'm Callie Collingsworth. I'd been Caroline Shackleford since our marriage. I never changed it with my subsequent marriages. I always remained a Shackleford. I liked the name, and I think Sloane liked that a little part of me still belonged to him. But when I moved here, it wouldn't do for him to explain to his latest conquest that his ex-wife lived in the neighborhood and that we were "friends with benefits," so we changed my name and got fake IDs made up. Sloane had always called me Callie – an amalgam of Caroline and my favorite flowers, Calla lilies.'

Tish felt her jaw tighten. It was just like Shackleford, a man who so obviously enjoyed wielding power over others, to retain 'possession' of his ex-wife and then, when it no longer suited his purposes, request that she hide any such relationship. 'And Collingsworth? Where did that come from?'

'Oh, that was the name of a character on some night-time soap opera I was watching at the time.'

Tish recalled Jules's comment about Callie Collingsworth's name being like that of a soap opera star. 'It's like he has a pop culture sixth sense,' she marveled beneath her breath.

'Everything OK, Tish?' Reade inquired.

'Yes. Sorry. Don't mind me.' She waved to Reade to continue the interrogation.

With a raised eyebrow, he complied. 'If you and your ex-husband were on such good terms, Ms Shackleford, then why were you in competition with Pepper Aviero?'

'That was . . . oh, that was me just being insecure and foolish. Sloane didn't love Pepper and I knew that.'

'But?'

'But she was different from all the others. She wasn't looking for Sloane to wine and dine her and lavish her with gifts. She wasn't looking just for fun and sex. She was cooking him dinner and baking him treats and planning weekends away to visit her family. Pepper Aviero was playing for keeps.'

'And so you competed with her, cooking chicken and dumplings and trying to win your ex-husband back,' Tish presumed. 'And you believed you had the upper hand until the two of you confronted him and he cast you both aside.'

'Is that why you murdered him?' Sheriff Reade presented. 'Because he dumped you?'

'He did not dump me,' Caroline shrieked. 'He was angry because I had been jealous and acting ridiculously. I knew the rules when we made our arrangement. I knew I wasn't to interfere with his dalliances, just as he wasn't to interfere with mine. Sloane had every right to be angry with me, but I know we would have made up later. We always did. And as for killing him, I wouldn't have harmed a hair on that man's head. Despite everything we'd been through, all our ups and downs, I never once wished him ill. I couldn't.'

'Oh? Is that why you went out of town and didn't show up for our meeting this morning? Because you didn't hurt him? Or were you afraid I'd find out you murdered your ex-husband because you were so angry you couldn't see straight?'

'I needed space in which to grieve,' she shouted before breaking into sobs. 'I know it might seem odd to you, but I loved Sloane. I truly loved him. And for the first time in over fifty years, I have to learn to live without him.'

'Where did you go for this grieving?'

'A friend of mine has a loft in Richmond. She plays the golf circuit and is rarely home. I stayed there.'

'Alone?'

'Yes, of course alone,' Caroline was indignant. 'I have the key on me. I'll give you the address. You can go check if you like.'

'I would love the address, when we're done. And why did you come back here today?'

'I already told you, to collect Sloane's papers. His bank and most of his other business dealings were in Richmond. Tomorrow being Monday and me being his next of kin, I thought I should start notifying credit card companies and such about his death. Sloane's lawyer is also in Richmond; I thought I'd stop by and pay a visit.'

'You'll have to settle for a phone call,' Reade instructed. 'This is a murder investigation. No one is to leave town.'

'Technically, I didn't leave town. I just relocated.'

'Uh-huh. You can un-relocate as soon as I take your statement.' Reade escorted Caroline to the squad car and placed her and the bag of paperwork in the backseat. 'Thanks for your help, Tish. I'll see you later.'

Tish gave Reade a brief wave and then went back into the lifestyle center to tend to the dirty luncheon dishes, but something in Caroline Shackleford's account of her marriage to Sloane raised a question in Tish's mind.

NINETEEN

It was quarter past five when Tish, Jules, and Celestine finished the last of the dishes, stacked them back in the lifestyle-center kitchen cabinets, and gave the countertops one last wipe down with disinfectant cleaner before inspecting their work.

'I think it's even cleaner than when we first got here,' Jules stated, his hands on his hips. 'Good job, team.'

Celestine gave him a fist bump. 'Tish, honey, can I give you a ride home?'

'Under normal circumstances, I'd say yes, but I need to pick up Biscuit.'

'I'll drive you,' Jules offered. 'I have no one waiting for me at home.'

'Are you sure? I also want to stop in on Ms Morris. She didn't seem herself this afternoon.'

'Yeah, I cleared her plate away.' Celestine frowned. 'She hadn't eaten much at all.'

'It's this godawful heat,' Jules complained. 'On days like this, all I want is a liquid diet.'

'Isn't that every day?' Tish teased, knowing Jules's penchant for white wine.

'Funny. Well, since I have a reputation to uphold, do me a favor and don't let me forget the jug of leftover *Arnold Palmerstons* in the refrigerator.'

Tish laughed. 'Don't worry. There's a bunch of stuff in there that I need to bring back to the café. We'll make sure the *Arnolds* are included. Celestine, you have your leftovers?'

'Yep, dinner for Mr Rufus and me.' She removed a reusable shopping bag of foil containers from the refrigerator. 'Two nights off from cooking in a row. I can't remember when I last had it this good.'

Jules and Tish escorted Celestine to her minivan and wished her a good night. As the baker drove off for home, Jules and Tish continued across the parking lot. 'While you're checking in on Zadie Morris, do you mind if I pop in on Mrs Wilkes? When I left her, she still had a headache. I want to make sure she's properly hydrated.'

'Of course,' Tish allowed. 'It's been ridiculously hot.'

'And Mrs Wilkes is a bit frailer than Zadie. Hard to believe they're only a few years apart in age. Are you sure Zadie's as old as you say she is? She looks so much younger than Mrs Wilkes.'

'Better not let Mrs Wilkes hear you say that,' Tish teased. 'Zadie's made a lot of money out of looking good, so I'm sure she's tried every skin serum out there. But, yes, I'm certain she's around eighty years of age. She has to be. You remember those big loud commercials for her Grunge line back when we were teens, don't you? She had a few streaks of silver in her hair even then.'

'She might have been going prematurely gray,' Jules suggested as he typed something into his phone.

'Not too premature. That was nearly thirty years ago, so she would have been about fifty.'

'Thirty years? Please. No numbers. It's far too depressing. Let's see . . . Zadie Morris.'

'Are you Googling to see how old she is? You honestly don't believe me?'

'I do believe you. However, as a journalist, it's my duty to fact-check. Ah, here we go. Wikipedia.'

'Wikipedia is hardly what I'd call fact-checking.'

Jules ignored her and read aloud, '*Zadie Morris. Born Vera Ruby Waterston, November 6, 1940, is an American businessperson and philanthropist*. You're right, she is nearly eighty.'

Tish felt a sharp pain deep in her gut, as if someone had leveled a blow directly to her stomach. 'What did you say her birth name was?'

'Vera Ruby Waterston. She was born in Richmond, too. Huh. I always thought she was a native New Yorker.'

The photo of the young boy, the image of a young woman and a child standing on Shackleford's doorstep, the Richmond makeup counter, the quick getaway by Shackleford's murderer. They all started coming together in Tish's mind, but the story they told still wasn't entirely clear.

'Hey, you OK? You look like you've seen a ghost.'

'I think I have. I, um, I need to get to Zadie's. I'll meet you at the lifestyle center later?'

'Yeah, I'll be hanging with Mrs Wilkes. Just text me when you're done. Unless you want me to come with you.'

'Thanks, Jules, but this is something I need to do on my own.' Tish gave his hand a squeeze and jogged off. Shortly thereafter, she arrived at Zadie's front door. Determined to find answers. She pressed hard upon the front doorbell.

Zadie answered within a matter of seconds. 'Tish, come on in.'

Tish entered the hallway and watched as Zadie, her face scrubbed clean and dressed in a pink floral housecoat and slippers, shut the door behind them. 'What brings you here?'

Tish was pulling no punches. 'William. The boy whose photo is beside your bed. He was your son, wasn't he?'

The glow that had graced Zadie's face – that last rosy vestige of youth that gave the businesswoman a livelier appearance than her contemporaries – vaporized into the ether. 'Yes,' she nodded. She wandered into the living room and sat on the sofa. 'I knew I'd told you too much this morning. What gave it away?'

Tish stood in the living-room doorway, her arms folded across her chest. 'Vera. Vera is your real name. Jules found it on Wikipedia.'

'That's what I get for not being part of the digital age,' she chortled, but she was not smiling.

'Was Sloane Shackleford William's father?' Tish demanded.

'No. I met Sloane Shackleford when William was five years old. The age he was when I snapped that photograph. William's father, Calvin – my husband at the time – was abusive, both emotionally and physically. I wanted desperately to take William, leave town, and divorce him, but I had nowhere to go and no money with which to start a new life. We barely earned enough to feed and clothe ourselves. There was no way I could save anything out of the household budget.

'When William started preschool, Calvin allowed me to keep a part-time job to help pay the bills,' Zadie continued. 'But there were strict guidelines. The job couldn't interfere with my housework, my getting supper on the table at six, or taking care of William, and it couldn't put me in touch with male co-workers or customers. It took some time, but I finally found a job at the cosmetics counter at Miller and Rhoads department store in downtown Richmond. Needless to say, I loved it. It got me out of our tiny rented house and gave me an opportunity to interact with other women and experiment with cosmetics. Naturally, I had to wipe off any makeup I put on during the day before I went home since Calvin viewed the stuff as "prostitute paint."'

With a grimace, Zadie repositioned herself on the sofa cushion.

'Are you OK?' Tish asked.

'Just arthritis,' she dismissed and went back to her story. 'You're probably too young to remember, but department stores back then, particularly in the South, had tearooms. Miller and Rhoads was no exception. One day, during the pre-Christmas rush, a waitress called in sick. Our cosmetics counter was well staffed, so I was called upon to go up to the fifth floor where the tearoom was and replace her. That was where I met Sloane Shackleford. It was a Friday and Sloane was there for his weekly Missouri club sandwich and chocolate silk pie. I was his waitress.

'I could tell you that Sloane Shackleford was handsome or dashing or exceedingly well dressed, but he was none of those things. What he was was talkative, flattering, and charming. And

I – well, I was lonely. He complimented me on my looks and my figure. Told me some jokes to make me smile. And I, starved for attention and affection, devoured every word. At the end of that lunch, he left me a generous tip and asked if he could see me again. I said yes. The following week, I coordinated my break so that I was available after he ate his lunch. I ate my lunch in his car and we talked. However, it wasn't long before we were meeting at least twice a week, sometimes in his house, and neither of us was doing much in the way of talking.'

'Were you in love with him?' Tish inquired.

'Passionately. I thought, for once, I had found someone who truly cherished me. I was wrong. It was a Sunday in February, two months into our affair, when Calvin, after drinking beer and watching boxing all afternoon, spotted William playing with a doll our neighbor's daughter had left behind. Calvin,' Zadie sobbed, 'took it from William's hands and began beating him with it while calling him a "sissy boy" and "faggot." I begged Calvin to stop, but it only incensed him further. I threw myself in front of William so that Calvin would beat me instead of him, but he picked me up and tossed me into the television stand. He then began beating William with his fists. The more William screamed and cried, the angrier Calvin became. He was so angry that he picked William up and threatened to hurl him through our front picture window. I couldn't let that happen, so I went into the kitchen and grabbed a metal stepladder from beside the refrigerator and smashed it over Calvin's head. I'm not sure if he blacked out or not, but he let William drop to the floor. I scooped him up, grabbed our coats and my handbag, and ran out of the house for the bus. I didn't know what to do or where to go. I should have called the police. I know I should have, but I wanted to find a safe place away from Calvin. I wanted my little boy to be somewhere safe where I could clean him up and hold him and he'd never be afraid again. I was also afraid I might have killed Calvin. I didn't know what to do, so I went to see Sloane. I figured he'd know what to do.'

'You didn't realize he was married,' Tish guessed.

'It was more than the fact he was married. He shouted at us. He called me crazy. He pretended not to know me and told me to take "that brat" and get lost. That brat who was visibly bruised and his mother who was so obviously desperate that she showed up on his doorstep with not even a suitcase. I understand that he was surprised and upset to see his mistress at his front door, but he could have handled it differently, humanely. I wasn't looking for him to throw his arms around me and tell me he loved me. I was looking for sanctuary. Instead, he sent both of us back into the sleet with not even a second thought as to what would happen to either of us.'

'What did happen to you?'

'I took William to the emergency room to be examined. The staff there called the police. Calvin, however, had already called them and told them I had gone on a rampage, beaten William, hit him with the stepladder, and then kidnapped our child. William was taken from me and I was thrown into jail. Fortunately, the public defender got the charges dropped. However, I never regained custody of William or even visitation. Calvin found out about my affair with Sloane Shackleford from one of my co-workers. He used that and my stepladder attack on him to have me declared an unfit mother.'

'I'm sorry,' Tish whispered.

'Thank you, although some might say I had it coming, given what I'd done,' Zadie lamented. 'Richmond wasn't quite the cosmopolitan city it is now. It was more like any other Southern town in the 1960s. When news of my affair and divorce broke, I lost my job at Miller and Rhoads and no other shop downtown would hire me. Thankfully, my supervisor at Miller and Rhoads cosmetics counter was sympathetic to my situation. She was older, single – a spinster, some might say – but she was kind. She let me stay at her apartment after Calvin kicked me out. And when I lost my job, she called a friend of hers in New York who ran a cosmetics shop. I didn't want to move that far away from William, but I also couldn't afford to stay where I was. So I accepted the offer and took a tiny studio apartment in the East Village. That was before the Village became trendy. The rents were low back then, so my neighbors were artists, students, and hippies. All I did, however, was work. Whatever money I could tuck away, I did, so that I could mount a legal war against Calvin.'

'Did you eventually regain custody?'

'No. My living in New York was another strike against me. Calvin's lawyer depicted me as a shrewd, calculating career woman with no interest at all in children. The fact I hadn't remarried didn't work in my favor either, if you can believe it. The judge cited it as evidence that I wasn't looking to provide a stable environment by settling into a "woman's natural role as wife and mother." Oh, and being in the cosmetics field did no favors, either. It proved that I was in the business of deception.

'I went on fighting and appealing, but soon William was old enough to weigh in on the case. Calvin clearly told him that I'd abandoned him. I also have no doubt he probably threatened to hurt William if he sided with me. I'll never forget seeing William in the courtroom that day. I hadn't seen him in six years. The baby face was gone, and so was the innocence. He had a haunted look to him, a deeply rooted unhappiness. The judge asked him if he wanted to see his mother and he said "no," but as the officer led him past me out of the courthouse, William looked at me and I could see he was torn.'

Zadie pulled a lace handkerchief from the pocket of her housecoat and blew her nose. 'I spent the next five years trying to file appeals and have the court's decision overruled. The last hope was William's sixteenth birthday. In Virginia, sixteen is the age of emancipation, meaning that William could decide for himself whether he wanted to see me or not, and there was nothing the court could do about it. So I drafted a letter and sent it, via my attorney, to William as I wasn't allowed to contact him personally. Several weeks later, my attorney called. The letter had been returned to him unopened. When he investigated the matter, he discovered that William was dead. He had died, by hanging, on his birthday. The verdict was suicide as there was a note found by his body. What was contained in that note, I don't know. I was never permitted to read it, nor were the police able or willing to share it.'

'You said that Vera died that day,' Tish mentioned.

'She did. Both literally and figuratively. I was not the same woman. Everything I'd lived for those sixteen years – everything I'd planned, dreamed, and hoped for – died along with my son. In the months that followed, I seriously contemplated suicide. However, Camille – my boss, my gracious friend, and mentor – had recently retired and had left the cosmetics boutique to me.'

'You worked at the same boutique all that time?'

'More than worked. Camille put me in charge of creating new products and scents. She taught me about marketing and packaging and everything one needs to know about the industry. After all Camille had done for me, how could I throw away everything she'd built? So I cast aside my old life and threw myself into my work. As a symbol of that rebirth, I changed my name. Zadie in honor of my paternal grandmother and Morris for my maternal grandmother. I launched a new line of cosmetics under that name as a sign that Camille's was entering a new phase with a new woman at the helm. That line sold out in days and then the next and the next. The rest, as they say, is history.'

'And now? Did you come back to Virginia to look for Sloane Shackleford?' Tish questioned.

'No. I'd thought of him, of course, and wondered what happened to him. I wondered if he was even still alive. And, yes, I secretly hoped he'd met some sad, tragic fate. However, my motive for moving back here was more mundane. Simply put, I'd retired and was growing tired of New York City winters. I also suppose it's true what they say, that we all long to return to our roots as we age. I looked at some condos and older homes in the downtown area, but city life no longer held the allure for me that it once did. I wanted quiet and green spaces for my walks, so I began looking outside the metropolitan area to the suburbs. That's when my real estate broker showed me this place.

'To say that I was shocked to find Sloane Shackleford that day would be the understatement of the century,' Zadie described. 'At the sight of him, all the anger, all the pain, all my disgust and regret and shame came surging back. And yet, deep down, somehow I had expected to see him again. Deep down, I knew there was unfinished business between us. I went back to my hotel that evening – I was staying in a suite at the Jefferson while house-hunting – and thought about what to do. I liked this house, of course, but there was something karmic in finding Sloane again after all these years. It was as if the universe was sending me a message.

'When I moved in, I received my second shock. Sloane Shackleford didn't remember or recognize me at all. Indeed, he came over to welcome me to the neighborhood and proceeded to hit on me by inviting me back to his house for a drink.'

'A long time had passed since he'd last seen you,' Tish reasoned.

'I acknowledge that I've aged and that my appearance has changed with time. I'm also far more worldly, confident, and mature than I was back then. However, I also dropped the occasional hint along the way: that I used to live in Richmond, how much I loved the old department stores downtown, that I left town in 1969. Nothing.'

'Some memory loss can be expected with age,' Tish continued to allow. 'How old was Mr Shackleford? Seventy-nine? Eighty?'

Zadie shook her head. 'No, that man was sharp as a tack. He recalled his house on Church Hill – the house he was living in when William and I made our unexpected visit – and Miller and Rhoads, and Thalhimers and their Santa displays, but I could see in his eyes that he didn't remember me. It wasn't forgetfulness either. I'd accepted years ago that Sloane Shackleford was never in love with me, but seeing him that day and observing his behavior with other women here at the Creek made me realize that I was absolutely nothing to him. Not a name or a face, but just another body for him to use for his own amusement.

'It got to me,' Zadie admitted, a tremor in her voice. 'Seeing him harass that poor Ms Hilton up at the lifestyle center. Listening to him berate his gardeners for trimming his lawn too short. Spotting Pepper Aviero and Callie Collingsworth sneaking in and out of there at all hours. Watching him inappropriately touch, flirt, and fondle nearly every woman in our community. Sloane Shackleford was an abuser and bully. He ruined lives – lives like mine – and he needed to be stopped. So I hatched a plan to kill him. I devised a plan to murder Sloane Shackleford.'

Zadie's words hit Tish like a thunderbolt. She had suspected Zadie had known Shackleford and had possibly been intimate with him, but she couldn't bring herself to believe that Zadie Morris – this icon from her youth – could commit so violent a deed. 'No! No, that's not possible. You're too smart. Too self-possessed. You wouldn't have simply smashed his head in with a shovel. That . . . that's not a plan.'

'That's because it wasn't the plan. Just when I'd come up with the best way to do away with Shackleford and just when I'd resigned myself to actually doing it, my life suddenly found meaning again.'

'Orson Baggett,' Tish guessed.

'Yes. You may find it difficult to believe, but I'd sworn off men and relationships after my split with Calvin. All I wanted was my son, and then after he passed away, all I wanted was for Camille's business to be a success. I'd gone all that time thinking there were no good men left on the planet, at least not for me, and then I come here to find him. I know Orson's gruff and a bit rough around the edges, but he's decent and kind and loving. He's made me very happy.'

Tish heaved a sigh of relief. 'Then you didn't do it.'

'Oh, no, Tish' – Zadie looked Tish straight in the eye – 'I did.'

'But why? You just said Orson made life worth living again. Why jeopardize that?'

'Because, try as we might to run from it, bury it, or ignore it, the past still finds a way to come crashing down upon us,' she explained as a single tear trickled down her cheek. 'I'd gone for my usual walk Friday morning, and had been out maybe fifteen or twenty minutes when I realized I'd forgotten to bring along a birthday card that needed to be mailed. So I returned home to retrieve it. As I entered my back kitchen door – I use that when I walk so I don't track dirt through the house – I caught a glimpse of Sloane Shackleford sunning himself in his lounge chair. The sight of him made me ill. And then he actually had the audacity to speak to me. He made some snide remark about Orson's garden and how he should probably throw in the towel, and then invited me, again, to have a drink with him. This time I agreed and walked over to his yard. There he was, basking in the sun like some bloated, bronzed, blood-sucking lizard. After all he'd done, after all he continued to do, there he was, grinning ear to ear, drinking a mimosa, and working on his tan, while my son – my beautiful, sweet boy – was dead.'

Zadie licked her lips and swallowed. 'I suddenly felt the same way I did when Calvin was attacking William on that February afternoon. On my way into the yard, I'd noticed a garden spade standing against the wall of the garage. As Shackleford suggested I get a glass from his kitchen, I walked over to the garage, grabbed the spade, lifted it in the air, and let it come down on Sloane Shackleford's head. I don't recall how many times I hit him. I just know that I did it until the grin disappeared from his face. I then wiped the handle clean of fingerprints, went into my house to wash up, grabbed the envelope from the kitchen table, and went back out to post my mail as if nothing happened. I'd only just gotten back when you, Jim Ainsley, and your friend Mr Davis discovered Shackleford's body.'

Several seconds elapsed before Tish could even respond. 'This can't be true. You couldn't have done it,' she argued.

'But I did do it, Tish. Now, if you would, please tell Sheriff Reade that I would like to confess.'

'No,' Tish refused. 'I can't. I won't.'

'Tish, if you don't go out there and tell him, I'll just lean out the living-room window and scream. So, please, just go out and bring him in here. Let's not drag this out any longer.'

Tish, blinking back her tears, nodded and turned toward the front door. Zadie stopped her. 'Before I forget . . .' She stretched out an elegant French-manicured hand. In it were two tiny drawstring velvet bags.

Tish stepped forward and collected them. As she did so, Zadie grasped Tish's wrist. 'I'm so sorry, Tish, but I needed to make things right.'

Without a word, Tish removed her hand from Zadie's and walked through the foyer and out the front door.

TWENTY

As twilight began to descend upon the lifestyle-center parking lot, Tish and Jules rested upon the front bumper of Jules's Mini Cooper. 'Do you want to go back to Zadie's house and see what's going on?' Jules asked as Tish blew her nose into a wad of tissue.

'Why, so we can watch Reade take her away in handcuffs? I don't think either of us could bear to watch that.'

'I know, but I just feel badly for the woman.'

'I do as well, but there's not much we can do. You heard Sheriff Reade; we can't be in the same room with Zadie while she's giving her statement, and unless we're her legal representation, we can't talk to her during the booking process. Besides, what Zadie really needs right now isn't moral support – it's a good lawyer.'

'Think Schuyler could help?'

'He could and would,' Tish asserted, 'but I'm certain Zadie has attorneys in New York City who'd run circles around our Richmond lawyers.'

'True,' Jules frowned. 'I don't think they'll keep Zadie in jail for long, do you? I mean, given her age.'

'I should hope not, especially as she's not a threat to anyone else. Of course, she can also probably afford to pay whatever bail they set.'

'Then we'll pay her a visit when she's back home,' Jules declared.

'Absolutely,' Tish agreed. 'The time she spends awaiting trial and enduring judgment in the court of public opinion is going to be extremely rough. She's going to need all the friends and allies she can get.'

'And you?' Jules prompted.

'What about me?'

'How are you doing? I know you kinda idolized her.'

Tish shrugged. 'I'm shocked and still in disbelief. I just can't picture her leveling a shovel at someone's head the way she did Shackleford.'

'But Zadie told you she'd done it once before to her ex-husband.'

'Yes, but that was different.'

'Was it?' Jules challenged. 'Everyone has a trigger, Tish. Clearly, William was Zadie's. And who could blame her? He was her son.'

'You're right,' Tish agreed. 'Here I am saying I *can't* believe Zadie is a murderer when the truth really is I don't *want* to believe it.'

'What's the old saying? Never meet your heroes?'

'Yes, but I still rather like mine.' Tish drew a deep breath and rose to her feet. 'Look, I know it may sound selfish, but right now all I want is to load up the car, pick up Biscuit, go home, and forget this place for a few hours.'

'I hear ya,' Jules commiserated. 'And I don't think it's selfish at all. This weekend's been a serious trip for you – and not in a good way. You want to wait here and rest while I get Biscuit and the leftovers?'

'No, I just want to get going. How about I get the leftovers from the kitchen and you walk over and get Biscuit?'

'Deal,' Jules agreed, but before either of them could act upon their plan, the heavy evening air was shattered by the sound of sirens. 'Oh! They must be taking Zadie to headquarters.'

'Clemson Reade wouldn't parade an elderly woman through the neighborhood with the lights and sirens blaring. He'd leave her some sense of dignity.'

Jules pulled a face. 'It's getting closer.'

'And it seems to be coming from the road.' As if summoned by Tish's words, an ambulance appeared at the security gate and sped past the lifestyle center toward the center of the development.

Tish had no reason to suspect that one specific resident of Coleton Creek might require urgent medical care more than another – indeed, in a senior living community, anyone could have been in need of emergency services – but at the sight of the ambulance, she gasped, 'Zadie.'

With Jules close at her heels, she followed the lights and the sound of the siren through the tangle of streets to the vehicle's final destination. Tish's intuition was correct, for the ambulance had come to a stop directly in front of Zadie's sprawling ranch home. The driver and passengers of the van were already inside the house.

Pushing past the fresh-faced police officer cordoning off the house with yellow tape, Tish and Jules jogged across the lawn and to the front door, where they were halted by Sheriff Reade himself. 'Sorry, guys. The paramedics need space to work.'

'What happened?' Tish demanded.

'Ms Morris collapsed after giving us her statement.'

'Probably all the stress,' Jules judged.

'She was quite tired last night, too,' Tish added. 'I doubt she's been sleeping well.'

Clemson Reade gave Tish a look that suggested Zadie's health issues were far more serious than simple exhaustion.

'What? What's wrong, Clemson?' Tish questioned.

'The paramedics are with her now; that's all I can tell you. When I know more, I'll let you know.' With that, Reade went back inside.

'Come on,' Jules waved her to the front path. 'Let's get out of their way.'

An obedient Tish followed Jules to the street, where a group of curious Coleton Creek residents had gathered. Among the crowd, Tish spotted the anxious face of Orson Baggett.

'What the hell is going on?' he asked as she approached, his tone frantic. 'That young buck of a police officer told me to wait out here but wouldn't tell me anything else. What's going on? Where's Zadie? She hasn't been murdered too, has she? Because if she has—'

'Zadie hasn't been murdered, Mr Baggett.' Tish placed a quieting hand on his arm. 'She was speaking with the police and collapsed. The paramedics are treating her now.'

'What were the cops doing talking to Zadie? Don't they realize she doesn't know anything about Sloane Shackleford? She only just moved in a few months back.'

Tish refrained from comment. It wasn't her place to tell Orson about Zadie's past or the fact that she had murdered Sloane Shackleford. Even if it had been her place, Tish possessed neither the strength nor the words to convey the news in a manner that wouldn't leave the man utterly devastated.

The crowd outside Zadie's house had grown exponentially in the short time since Tish and Jules's arrival. Residents still dressed in their garden luncheon finery mingled with those who'd changed into T-shirts, shorts, or casual dresses, and still others who'd already given in to the comfortable allure of their pajamas and nightwear. All spoke in hushed tones as they speculated about what might be going on with their new neighbor, while others optimistically planned for her return from the hospital.

'I can bring her dinner on the first night,' one woman could be heard saying.

'I'll do the second,' another volunteered.

'I can't cook worth a damn, but I'd be willing to send my housekeeper over a couple of hours a week to help Ms Morris with whatever needs doin'.'

'What if she hires a nurse?'

'Doesn't matter. There's not a nurse in town who can make a broccoli and rice casserole as good as mine. It's my mama's recipe.'

Fifteen long minutes and a month's worth of convalescent meal delivery planning later, Sheriff Reade stepped from behind the front screen door and down the steps. The grim expression on his face said it all.

'Mr Baggett, Tish, Jules, I'm afraid we lost her. I'm so very sorry.'

Orson buckled at the knees and for a moment it appeared he might faint. 'I knew it would end like this. I just didn't expect it to be so soon. She told me she still had months to go.'

Tish, Reade, and Jules exchanged puzzled glances. 'What do you mean she still had months to go? I don't understand,' Tish sought clarification.

'Zadie had terminal bone cancer. It was one of the reasons she moved south. She wanted a milder climate and for her life to end where it began – near Richmond. I just thought we had more time together.'

'She never said anything to me about being ill.'

'She didn't want anyone to know because she didn't want anyone's pity. That was Zadie. Always smiling on the outside, even when she must have been in a good deal of pain on the inside. "Everyone's fighting their own battles," she'd say to me if I'd been short-tempered with someone.' Orson's voice cracked and he brought his left hand up to the bridge of his nose. 'Oh, Zadie.'

Tish placed a comforting hand on Orson's back.

'Again, I'm so very sorry for your loss, Mr Baggett,' Reade extended his condolences. 'Do you know if Ms Morris had any family?'

'Don't think so. She said I was the only person she had left in the world. She had a son once. William. She never told me what happened to him, except that he was dead. I don't think she ever got over losing him. Though I expect you never do get over losing folks; you just get used to them not being around. I used to bring her a bouquet of Sweet Williams from my garden each week. Zadie would keep them in a vase on the kitchen table. She really liked that. Said it was a living memorial.'

The screen door to the house swung open again as a uniformed paramedic stepped out on to the front stoop.

'The paramedics will be bringing her out just now, Mr Baggett. If it's too upsetting, I'll tell them to wait until you're gone,' Reade offered.

'No, I want to say a quick goodbye, if I may.'

'You may step forward for a few moments.' Sheriff Reade led Orson up the path that led to Zadie Morris's front door.

The first paramedic stepped inside and, with the help of a second, wheeled a gurney bearing a vinyl-covered body down the steps and on to the path. They paused before Orson Baggett, who immediately removed his fedora and got down on one knee. 'Oh, Zadie. If you'd only told me how sick you were, I'd have married you before you left this world. You made me a better man, and although I feel like kicking and screaming and swearing at God for taking you away from me, I'll remember the lessons you taught me. Wait for me, Zadie. Wait for me, please.'

Sheriff Reade helped Orson up from his kneeling position and gestured to the paramedics to proceed.

As the body of Zadie Morris was loaded into the ambulance, the crowd fell silent. Tish watched as an uncharacteristically sympathetic Callie Collingsworth, perhaps softened by her own grief, consoled a distraught Wren Harper. Just behind them, Tucker Abercrombie embraced his wife tightly and bestowed her forehead with a kiss that conveyed a renewed sense of commitment and appreciation. A few feet to their right stood a grim Jim Ainsley, his arms folded across his chest and his head bowed as if lost in either prayer or thought.

Ainsley was awakened from his fugue state by the appearance of a teary-eyed Pepper Aviero at his side. The couple gazed at each other for several seconds and then, without a word, Ainsley pulled Pepper to him and wrapped his arms around her. Pepper, amid a bevy of sobs, reciprocated, and the couple, arm in arm, moved on to console Orson Baggett.

It was, Tish noted as the ambulance drove off and tears streamed down her face, a sad irony that the woman for whom happiness had, until now, remained elusive should have inspired so much love and reconciliation upon her death. And yet, for a woman who encouraged three generations of women to be as strong and beautiful as they could be, there could not have been a more fitting tribute.

'Rest in peace, Vera,' Tish whispered beneath her breath. 'Rest in peace.'

TWENTY-ONE

'Are you sure you want to do this?' Jules stood on the front porch of Cookin' the Books Café with Biscuit's lead in one hand and a bag containing his bed, food, and dishes in the other.

Tish had changed out of her cropped trousers and T-shirt and into a pair of baggy shorts and a tank top. 'Positive. It's a perfect fit. Given he was left to roam Coleton Creek on his own each evening, I suspect Biscuit's led a rather lonely existence. Although Kayla and Gregory would love to keep him, Mary Jo doesn't feel that she can care for a dog at this time, and as for me – well, aside from being busy with the café and catering jobs, having a dog here would make health inspections that much more complicated. That leaves you to give this sweet little guy a home.'

Jules gazed down at Biscuit with a broad smile. 'Don't worry. I'll spoil him rotten.'

'That was the expectation.' Tish bent over and scratched Biscuit between the ears.

'And I'll be sure to bring him around for visits.'

'That was also the expectation.'

'It's funny. I always wanted a dog when I was a kid, but Mama didn't want to have to vacuum up the extra hair. And lately I've been kinda envious of other people at the station bringing their dogs to work with them. But I'd never given a thought to getting one of my own.'

'Strange how fate works, isn't it? I'm sure Biscuit will be an extremely popular member of the newsroom. I also have a hunch that he'll be an excellent roommate, a great companion, and a slightly better fit for your lifestyle than an eighty-three-year-old woman.'

'Well, I still plan on visiting Mrs Wilkes, Mrs Newman, and the other pool aerobics ladies.'

'And you should, but just remember you can be a positive component in their lives without giving up yours.'

'How is it you always know what to do?' Jules asked as he hugged his friend.

'Oh, if only that were the case,' she laughed.

'It's true, honey. I'm not sure where any of us would be without you.' He let go of Tish and snatched up Biscuit. 'Are you sure you'll be OK tonight? We don't mind staying.'

Tish smiled. Jules and Biscuit were already a 'we.' 'I'll be fine, Jules. I just want to have a bath and go to bed. But I appreciate you staying and heating up those leftovers. I was hungrier than I thought.'

'Well, you know me. If stress-eating were an Olympic event, I'd take gold. Now, you're positive you don't want me to call Schuyler and get him over here to stay with you?'

'Positive. I already told him what happened today and we're touching base tomorrow. Also' – she modeled her outfit – 'we've yet to reach the point in our relationship where I'd let him see me like this.'

'Probably a smart move,' he teased and gave her a kiss on the cheek. 'Bye, darlin''. I'll give you a shout after work tomorrow. Come on, Biscuit. Let's go home and watch some TV. BBC America is airing *Sense and Sensibility* tonight.'

Tish watched Jules and Biscuit drive off in the Mini Cooper before locking up for the night. With everyone gone, the café was oddly quiet. For a fleeting second, Tish wondered if she should have kept Biscuit for just one more night as a way to ease herself back into the silence, but she quickly dispelled the thought. She was so bone-achingly weary that even walking upstairs to her apartment felt like an arduous task, let alone taking Biscuit on his brief pre-bedtime outing.

After a lengthy soak in lavender-scented bathwater, Tish toweled off, slipped into a cotton nightgown, tucked herself into bed, and fell asleep within the hour in spite of the lingering thoughts of Zadie Morris echoing through her brain. She slept soundly until seven thirty in the morning, when she was awakened by the sound of someone knocking on the front screen door of the café.

Sliding her cotton pique robe over her nightgown, Tish padded downstairs to find Clemson Reade waiting on the front porch.

She unlatched the main door and then the screen. 'Hello,' she welcomed with a question in her voice.

Reade was sporting his usual stubble, but instead of a T-shirt and jeans, he was dressed in a button-down shirt and dark trousers. 'Morning. Sorry for bothering you so early, but I'm on my way to town hall and I wanted to deliver something.'

Parked behind Reade was his standard sheriff's car as well as a dark-red four-door sedan from which a man in a mechanic's jumpsuit alighted. He approached the porch with a set of keys. 'She's all yours,' he announced as he handed them to Tish.

'Mine?'

'Albert here runs the garage on the edge of town. We use him to tow wrecks and to service all our vehicles. I asked him to get you set up with a car rental while yours is being repaired.'

'Thank you, but I haven't called my insurance company yet.'

'No worries. When you do, just call Albert with the claim number, the name of the insurance company, and your driver's license information, and he'll put his paperwork through. Until then, he's letting you borrow this as a favor to me.'

'Even though I'm pretty sure you owe me one, Clem,' Albert quipped before hopping into the passenger seat of the sheriff's car.

'This is amazing. Thank you.'

'You can't very well be a caterer without a vehicle,' Clemson explained.

'True. And I do have to pick up a couple of serving pieces I accidentally left at Coleton Creek yesterday.'

'Yeah, about that. I got an unofficial preliminary report from the coroner and Ms Morris's cancer had metastasized throughout her entire body. She also said there was a tumor pressing on Ms Morris's heart that might have caused her cardiac arrest. As I said, nothing is official, so don't go telling anyone, but I thought you'd want to know just in case . . . well, just in case you were afraid you may have precipitated something. I know I wondered about it myself.'

Tish nodded. 'Thank you. That puts my mind somewhat at ease. Not much, but somewhat. The person I really feel bad for is Orson Baggett. He truly was in love with Zadie.'

Sheriff Reade cleared his throat and awkwardly shifted his feet. 'Shame. Well, I'd better get going. I have reports to prepare and file.'

'Yeah, thanks again, Clemson. For everything.'

'No problem. See ya in the morning for my usual.'

'Sure I can't interest you in the special? I was going to test-run *Children of the Corned Beef Hash*, but since Opal said there's a bunch more peppers coming my way, I've opted for *The Grits of Wrath* instead.'

'Silly question, but why are your grits angry?'

Tish laughed. 'They're not really. They're just topped by a pair of eggs poached in a fiery tomato-and-pepper sauce.'

'Ah. Sounds delicious but—'

'But you'll stick with *Portrait of the Artist as a Young Ham*. I get it. You're a man of routine.'

'Not necessarily. I'm a musician. I can improvise. Someday I might just surprise you.'

'Uh-huh,' Tish replied as she waved farewell and went back inside to put on a pot of coffee.

The night's sleep, combined with the prospect of a relaxing lunch and shopping trip with Mary Jo, had done wonders for Tish's mindset and energy levels. Although still saddened by Zadie Morris's confession and death, and dreading the visit to Coleton Creek to collect the remainder of her kitchen stock, she was determined to make the best of the day.

As the coffee brewed, she went back outside and, in anticipation of transplanting them, dug up the lilies from their concrete planter and placed them in a set of plastic pots she had saved from her last garden center visit.

With that task complete, she settled in at a café table with her laptop to catch up on the news of the day while drinking coffee and consuming a leisurely breakfast of seeded wholewheat toast topped with mashed avocado.

Her stomach pleasantly full, Tish yawned and stretched and then went upstairs to get dressed. Having thrown on her favorite red polka-dot dress and a pair of canvas espadrilles, she smeared daily moisturizer on to her face and set about applying some makeup, only to find her cosmetics bag missing from its usual spot in the drawer of the bathroom vanity.

Recalling that she had taken the bag with her to Coleton Creek for touch-ups on her cuts and bruises, she traveled to the bedroom and reached into the red handbag she carried everywhere. As she did so, her fingertips came in contact with the two velvet drawstring bags from Zadie.

Tish opened one bag, only to find the *Pink Organza* lipstick favored by Jules's mother. Putting that aside, she opened the second bag and extracted the intricately carved golden tube to reveal a deep red named *Joie de Vivre.* With everything that had transpired, she lost track of the fact that Zadie had promised her a tube of the limited-edition product.

Fighting back tears, Tish took the tube of lipstick and her cosmetic bag into the bathroom and focused, instead, on getting ready. Opening the gorgeously retro tube of *Joie de Vivre*, she gave the swivel mechanism a few turns and then guided the lipstick across her bottom lip. She had forgotten just how supremely smooth and how vibrantly pigmented Zadie lipstick was. The creamy unctuousness of the product filled all lines and crevices in its path, yet wasn't waxy like most drugstore brands. And the color was sublime – a dark brick-red with blue tones.

Tish gave her top lip a thin coat and then blotted by kissing a sheet of facial tissue. She smiled in the mirror to survey her handiwork. The shade was a perfect complement to Tish's fair skin, boosting the rosiness of her complexion while amplifying its creamy whiteness. Zadie was right. It was truly incredible what just a simple smear of lipstick could do for a face.

Lipstick.

Zadie claimed that she never stepped out of her front door without a full face of makeup or a swipe of lipstick, even if it was just to take a walk or pick up her mail. Yet the day Tish, Jules, and Jim Ainsley discovered Sloane Shackleford's body, Zadie's face was scrubbed clean.

Scrubbed clean even though Zadie claimed to have been out taking a walk.

It was possible that Zadie might have overstated her reliance upon cosmetics, but Tish didn't think so. Every other time she'd seen Zadie, she was impeccably made up.

Which begged the question: why was Zadie not wearing makeup the day Shackleford died? Zadie stated that she had been on a walk, returned home, killed Shackleford, and then resumed her walk as if nothing had happened. She also claimed that she had only just finished that walk when she saw Tish, Jules, and Ainsley in Shackleford's garden.

However, Zadie's complete lack of makeup suggested that she was at home. So why would Zadie have lied? She'd already confessed to the murder; why lie about where she was prior to the discovery of the body?

Also, Tucker Abercrombie claimed not to have passed anyone along his journey to and from Shackleford's house. Tish had assumed Tucker's timeline was slightly off and that he had arrived at Shackleford's a bit later than eleven thirty, meaning that he and Zadie had, quite literally, just missed each other. But what if Tucker's time estimates were correct? Where was Zadie? Why didn't Tucker see her walking about the neighborhood?

Simple. Because she wasn't there.

Zadie's lack of makeup – including lipstick, the anchor of any makeup-wearer's arsenal – suggested she wasn't out and about, but indoors, at home. But why lie about it?

Tish felt her skin go clammy and her heart begin to race. There was only one possible reason Zadie would have lied: to protect someone else.

If Zadie had been at home, she could have seen the murder transpire. Both Zadie's kitchen window and her expansive bedroom windows afforded a perfect view of the patio next door. Zadie could easily have been in either room when Shackleford was murdered. But then, why not tell the police that? Why confess to a murder she didn't commit?

Terminally ill, Zadie had nothing to lose by confessing to the crime, but for whom would she be willing to go so far to protect? Orson Baggett?

No, Orson was a man in love. He wouldn't have allowed Zadie to take the blame for a crime he had committed. No, there was only one other person in Coleton Creek for whom Zadie would have been willing to make such a sacrifice. A person who could have left the scene of the crime and not have been seen by Tucker Abercrombie.

A person who had also lost a son.

Tish called Mary Jo to cancel their lunch plans and drove to Coleton Creek, reaching the gates at approximately twelve o'clock.

She was surprised to see Susannah Hilton driving through the gates in the opposite direction.

'Going to grab lunch,' Susannah shouted through her open driver's side window.

'I thought you were fired,' Tish replied.

'I was, but the president of the homeowners' association called me back to work last night. The board had a meeting this morning and I'm interim manager. A formal vote will be held among all residents at the end of the month, but it looks like I'm a shoe-in for the permanent position.'

'That's wonderful news. Congratulations! I know how much this place means to you.'

'Yeah, I look forward to staying on. Oh, if you're here for your serveware, I stacked it and put it behind my desk.'

Tish thanked Susannah and the two parted ways. Thinking it best to collect her serveware before any emotional distractions caused her to forget it, she stopped off at the lifestyle center before moving on to Wren Harper's house. There, she found Ms Harper, in a white sundress, sitting by the pond in her prize-winning garden.

'Ms Tarragon,' Wren greeted, her face registering both surprise and alarm. 'What brings you here?'

'Ms Harper. I think we should go inside to talk. It's more private.'

Wren agreed and led Tish through the garden and into the back kitchen door. 'Would you like some sweet tea?' she offered as she waved Tish to sit at the kitchen table.

Tish refused both the seat and the tea. 'Shame about Zadie Morris, isn't it?'

Wren's eyes welled with tears. 'Yes. She was a good woman.'

'I can't believe she murdered Sloane Shackleford, can you?'

'No,' Wren answered as her body convulsed into sobs.

'It was you, wasn't it?' Tish challenged. 'The story Zadie told me about Shackleford making degrading remarks that morning – you were the recipient of those remarks, not her. Is that why you murdered him?'

'I don't know what came over me. I was in my garden pulling weeds, trying to ignore him out there sunning himself while I was breaking my back, but he called out to me. He called to me and told me I was wasting my time, seeing as he was going to win the competition. I tried, again, to ignore him, but then he . . . he mentioned my boy, Benjamin. He said, "Sorry, I forgot that's all you have left, isn't it? There's really nothing else left for you to fuss over since your boy got killed." Then he made some comment about how had my son been smarter and taught how to fight better, he might not be gone. I–I couldn't see straight I was so angry. I'd only just gotten Benjamin's dog tags in the mail that morning. My daughter-in-law sent them so that part of Benjamin could be with me at the competition. I guess I was in a state after receiving them and maybe down with the heat or . . . I don't know. I just don't know what came over me, but I went around the fence and saw the spade lying against Shackleford's garage, grabbed it, and brought it down on his head. I don't remember how many times I hit him. I just remember I wanted him to stop sneering at me. I think I must have blacked out because the next thing I remember after hitting him was Ms Morris standing beside me. That's when I realized what I'd done. Oh, the blood! I thought I'd be going to jail, but Ms Morris told me not to worry. She took the spade, wiped my fingerprints from the handle, put it down on the patio, and told me to go home and say I'd been inside to escape the heat.'

'That's why you'd been crying that day,' Tish presumed.

'Yes, I was terrified someone would find out what I'd done.'

'But Zadie handled it. Did you know she was going to confess?'

'No. The day after, when she came with me to talk to the police, she said, if needed, she'd do something that would take all suspicion away from me. But if she did it, I needed to promise I'd leave Coleton Creek and move in with my daughter-in-law and grandbabies. I argued with her and told her I didn't want her doing anything that might get her into trouble, but she insisted. She said she'd had a boy once, but she did him wrong. Helping me, she said, was her penance. A way to set things right before she met her maker. I had no idea that she . . .' Wren's voice trailed off into sobs.

Penance. Tish turned the word over and over in her mind. After all these years, Zadie still felt guilty about what happened to William. 'Did you make the promise? To move away?'

Wren nodded. 'I called my daughter-in-law yesterday. A real estate agent is coming to appraise the house later this afternoon. Unless you're . . .'

'I don't know what to do, Ms Harper. I don't want to send you to prison. You're obviously in an extremely fragile emotional state, which would reduce your sentence, but I don't want you to be separated from the only family you have left. Yet an innocent woman's reputation has been tarnished forever. And although Zadie might have been fine with people thinking she was a murderer, I'm not sure I can live with that on my conscience.'

Wren Harper sat down at the table, desolated. 'I wish it were different, too, Ms Tarragon. I wish I hadn't done what I did. I wish I was brave enough to step forward, but I'm not. I keep thinking of my grandchildren and what they've been through, losing their grandfather and then their father and now . . .'

Tish drew a deep breath. She wished *she* was brave enough to follow through with Zadie's wish without trepidation. 'I need some time to think, Ms Harper. If you don't mind, I'm going to pay Orson Baggett a visit. May I leave my car here?'

Wren nodded. 'I'm not going anywhere. And I mean that. Whatever you decide, Ms Tarragon. I need to pay my penance at some point too, be it in this life or the next.'

Tish acknowledged Wren's statement with a nod of the head before exiting the kitchen and walking to her car. From the trunk, she pulled out the pots of lilies and carried them to Orson Baggett's house. Approaching the backyard gate, she could see Orson in his garden, harvesting vegetables. His clothes were uncharacteristically sloppy and wrinkled, and his face looked haggard and worn.

'Mr Baggett?' she called.

He looked up with a wan smile. 'Ms Tarragon, I thought you'd seen the back of this place.'

'Soon. Just tying up some loose ends. May I come in?'

Orson rushed to open the gate and then took the lilies from her hands.

'I wanted to check in on you.'

'To see if a man can still live after having his heart plucked out of his chest?' he half joked. 'I'm all right. Been better, but trying to remember the things Zadie said to me during the time we were together.'

'I'm sorry. It can't be easy for you.'

Orson shrugged. 'What did you bring? Lilies? You're not going into the traveling nursery business now, are you?'

'No, I thought you might like these for your garden. They'd look good amid the Sweet William.'

He smiled. 'Indeed they would. Mona Lisa lilies. A fitting tribute. Smiling on the outside, never revealing what was going on inside.'

'She was a good woman,' Tish assured.

'Yes, she was. I'm glad you saw it, too. Sure, there are hundreds of other people in these parts who'll say otherwise now, but the person who murdered Shackleford wasn't my Zadie. She wasn't the woman who lived here at Coleton Creek. I just wish I could have given her more comfort.'

'Oh, but you did,' Tish gushed. 'She told me that you made her very happy, that just when she'd given up, you made life worth living again. She thought the world of you, Mr Baggett. Never doubt that.'

Orson raised a finger to the corner of one eye to dab a tear. 'Allergies.'

'Yes, it's that time of year,' she allowed. 'Ragweed.'

'Thank you for coming here, Ms Tarragon. I needed to hear from someone who can look past the front page and see Zadie for how she really was.'

'I'm sure there are plenty of people out there who can attest to her character. Why, her death has had a positive impact on some. Jim Ainsley and Pepper Aviero are back together—'

Orson chuckled. 'I'm happy for him, but I'm looking forward to teasing him just as bad as he teased me over Zadie.'

'And it seems the Abercrombies are closer—'

'Yes, they've invited me for dinner tonight. Tucker's grilling so Vi has the night off. Never thought I'd hear that!'

'And I – well, I just feel better for having known Zadie.'

'That was Zadie's way. She couldn't help but make things better. "Look to the living" was her motto. Leave the past behind and enjoy life and take care of those around you.'

Look to the living . . . enjoy life. The words struck Tish like a lightning bolt. *Joie de Vivre.* Joy of living. The name of the lipstick Zadie had left for Tish. 'Wise words.' She looked over the fence to see Wren Harper back in her garden, watching the pond meditatively. 'I hope this isn't the last I'll see of you Mr Baggett. You're welcome at my café anytime. How does breakfast on the house sound once you're feeling better?'

He smiled. 'Depends. Do you do biscuits and gravy?'

'How could a café in Virginia not?'

'You might just see me there. Oh, now that the competition is over, I'm doing some harvesting. You need any lettuce or tomatoes or eggplant?'

'I'll take whatever you have, unless you have a need for it.'

'Nah. Cooking for one these days. I'm donating most of this to the local soup kitchen. Zadie suggested it a few days ago.'

'Then donate mine, too. But if you don't mind, I would like some flowers for my tables.'

'Sure thing. Sweet William?'

'Sweet William.'

Tish collected her flowers from Orson Baggett and, after giving him a hug and getting him to swear to visit the café, returned to Wren Harper's house. Wren was still in the garden, seated on a wooden bench.

Tish approached, a large bunch of Sweet William in her hand. 'Zadie Morris was an idol to me, but more than that, she had become a friend. A few days ago, Ms Morris advised me to stay true to who I am. In order to do that, I simply can't let you go scot-free.'

Wren looked up, tears in her eyes. 'Oh, I agree. I can't keep it secret anymore. I don't know if I can even look my grandchildren in the eye, knowing what I've done. I told you: like Zadie, I want to do my penance.'

'But I also don't want to deny Zadie her penance. When she left Richmond all those years ago, it was as a "fallen woman." She left her home under a hail of accusations and insults. She wouldn't want the same thing to happen to you.'

'This neighborhood has already dragged Ms Morris's name through the mud,' Wren acknowledged.

'I'm suggesting that we call Sheriff Reade to explain the situation and see what he recommends so that you can confess to the crime, quietly, with dignity. And also so that you can deal with your grief, privately and with dignity.'

Wren grasped Tish's hands. 'Do you think he can help?'

'I know he'd do everything in his power to do so.'

'Then let's call,' Wren agreed.

Minutes later, Reade appeared at the rear garden gate.

'Ms Harper,' he greeted in a gentle tone. 'I'm going to take your statement, and then, when you're ready, a plain-clothes officer in an unmarked car will take you to headquarters to booking. There will be no handcuffs. No fanfare. And I will make no public announcement about your arrest. As far as the news outlets are concerned, Mr Shackleford's murderer died yesterday. That won't change.'

'Then I won't have to give up my garden trophy?' she cried.

'No one in the garden club would have reason to ask you to do so,' Tish confirmed.

Wren appeared momentarily elated. 'But how will I tell my daughter-in-law?'

'I'll be with you when you make the call. I'll be at your side through all of it. Just like Zadie would have been.'

Reade gazed down at Tish as she nestled beside Wren on the garden bench, his face a blend of surprise and admiration.

'How will we explain my absence? I mean, that I'm no longer here?'

'I'll explain to everyone that you've gone for treatment for your grief and your nerves.'

Reade cleared his throat. 'If you don't currently have an attorney, Ms Harper, we can have one appointed to you. However, as the mother of an officer killed in the line of duty, you may be able to call on the military for legal aid.'

Tish looked up at Reade and mouthed a silent 'thank you.'

'Thank you,' echoed Wren Harper. 'Thank you for helping me through this. For promising to keep this private.'

'I promise not to tell another soul. Just promise me that when this is all over and when you get to your new home and new garden, that you plant these.' She handed Wren a few stems of Sweet William.

'I will,' a tearful Wren swore. 'Thank you.'

'Don't thank us. Thank her.'

TWENTY-TWO

Tish spent the remainder of the day distracting herself the best way she could – by cooking. After mixing up biscuit dough, bread dough, scone dough, and muffin batter for the next morning's bake and cooking up spicy tomato-and-pepper sauce for the egg-and-grits special, she turned her attention to the beautiful butternut squash Opal had provided.

But not before making an important phone call.

'Hey,' Schuyler's rich voice came lilting over the phone line. 'How are you?'

'I'm OK. I was thinking, how would you like to have dinner tonight? I mean, if you're not busy.'

'I'm never too busy for you. Where do you want to go? What are you in the mood for?'

'Oh, I thought I'd cook here. I want to test my butternut squash and sage risotto recipe.'

'Are you sure? You've been working all weekend. I can pick something up or I can even try cooking.'

'I'm positive,' Tish confirmed. 'Cooking is my therapy. Just as long as you don't mind being my guinea pig.'

'Are you kidding? Test away. How about I pick us up a nice bottle of wine?'

'Perfect.'

'Is there anything else you need? Dessert? Bread? Salad?'

'No, I've got everything here. All I need is you.'

'Likewise.' Tish could hear the smile on Schuyler's face. 'I have a few things to finish up before I leave the office, but after that I'm on my way. I should be there no later than six thirty.'

'Sounds great. Um, Schuyler?'

'Yes?'

'Maybe you could stay tonight?'

'Yeah. Yeah, if that's what you'd like. I hope you know I wasn't pressuring you Saturday night.'

'No, I know you weren't.' Tish had spent much of the afternoon reflecting upon Zadie's sage words: *Look to the living*. 'I just want to be close to you, that's all.'

'After I pick up the wine, I'll stop by my place for a change of clothes for tomorrow. Then I'm all yours.'

'I'd like that.'

'I'm looking forward to it, too.'

A man of his word, Schuyler Thompson, bottle of wine and duffle bag in tow, arrived at Cookin' the Books at approximately twenty-five minutes past six. Tish was on the swing waiting for him.

As he stepped on to the front porch, she rose to her feet and threw her arms around his neck.

'Hey,' he greeted as he returned the embrace with his free arm and clutched the wine with the other. 'How was your day?'

She looked at him, her eyes glassy with tears.

'Want to talk about it?'

'No. Just hold me.'

'You've got it.'

The couple embraced on the front porch for several seconds before Tish led Schuyler inside.

Meanwhile, just a hundred yards away, Sheriff Reade's car stood idling in the road. Having witnessed Tish and Schuyler's affectionate display, Reade berated himself with a few choice words and, turning the car around, drove instead to meet his band mates at the Hobson Glen Bar and Grille.

Beside him, on the passenger seat, rested a bouquet of stargazer lilies.